playdate

playdate

thelma adams

Thomas Dunne Books

St. Martin's Press

New York

This is a work of fiction. All of the characters, organizations, and events portrayed in this novel are either products of the author's imagination or are used fictitiously.

THOMAS DUNNE BOOKS.
An imprint of St. Martin's Press.

PLAYDATE. Copyright © 2010 by Thelma Adams. All rights reserved. Printed in the United States of America. For information, address St. Martin's Press, 175 Fifth Avenue, New York, N.Y. 10010.

www.thomasdunnebooks.com
www.stmartins.com

Library of Congress Cataloging-in-Publication Data

Adams, Thelma.
    Playdate / Thelma Adams. — 1st ed.
        p. cm.
    ISBN 978-0-312-65666-9
    1. Married people—Fiction.   2. Couples—Fiction.   3. Cuckolds—Fiction.   4. California—Fiction.   5. Domestic fiction.   I. Title.
    PS3601.D3975P57 2010
    813'.6—dc22

                                                              2010037733

First Edition: January 2011

10   9   8   7   6   5   4   3   2   1

To Ranald, without whom this book
would never have been possible

acknowledgments

To my friends and writing circle—Amy J. Moore, Caryn James, Hilton Caston, Dennis Dermody, Galen Kirkland, Natalie Chapman, Lynne Ryan, Anna Esaki-Smith, Andrea Chapin, Lynn Schneider, and Bari Nan Cohen—who know how to make me laugh and when to take me seriously. I'm eternally grateful to my agent, Rebecca Oliver at William Morris Endeavor, and my editor, Kathleen Gilligan at Thomas Dunne Books, and art director, David Rotstein at St. Martin's Press. Cheers to my mother and fellow writer, Rosalie Schwartz, and my father-in-law, Lt. Gen. Ranald T. Adams, Jr. And, finally, to my children, Trevor and Elizabeth, who taught me how (and how not) to parent.

Those hot dry winds that come down through the mountain passes and curl your hair and make your nerves jump and your skin itch. On nights like that every booze party ends in a fight. Meek little wives feel the edge of the carving knife and study their husbands' necks. Anything can happen.

—Raymond Chandler, *Red Wind*

The township itself was twenty miles (32 km) west of the Santa Ana Mountains, where the infamous winds came from. Time to time they blew in, dry, warm, steady . . . He had seen minor barroom brawls end up as first-degree homicides. He had seen burnt toast end up in wife-beating and prison and divorce. He had seen a guy get bludgeoned to the ground for walking too slow on the sidewalk.

—Lee Child, *Bad Luck and Trouble*

"It's hotter than we expected, eh?"

—Anonymous Canadian tourist,
San Diego Wild Animal Park

part I

tuesday

chapter 1

Vermonters ignore nor'easters. Tornadoes in Tulsa are local news. Santa Ana conditions come with Southern California real estate. So, that first October morning when hot winds swooped in from the high deserts across the drought-stricken county, most San Diegans didn't cancel plans or playdates. And then the chaparral began to burn like flammable pajamas.

At dawn, an eighty-five-mile-per-hour gust snapped a power line east of rural Ramona. Sparks ignited the eucalyptus below. Fragrant flaming leaves littered the patched roof of a Witch Creek Canyon ranch house, which appeared deserted even in use—as a meth lab. The ensuing chemical explosion dispatched an armada of flames that, once airborne, replicated the process. The Witch Creek Fire was born.

High winds carried bright-eyed embers west, burning

buildings and brush in Rancho Bernardo and Poway. The walls of fire would later accelerate with a rapidity that stunned the laid-back locals. Still, that first morning, it had yet to jump Interstate 15 to threaten the coast. There, fifty miles to the west, it was a chill fifty-five degrees at six-thirty A.M. Free of cinders and ash, the sky hung banner-blue above the quaint ENCINITAS sign that arched over the main drag in the sleepy seaside San Diego suburb (population 59,620, median household income $76,500).

A few blocks uphill, morning dew soaked the lawn surrounding Rancho Amigo Elementary School. A half mile farther, the school day yawned open at 1212 Pacific Breeze, where stalks of orange-streaked birds-of-paradise and fuchsia bougainvillea fringed the relatively modest two-story stucco Spanish Revival. Inside, morning light eased rather than burned through the French doors in the downstairs bedroom, adjacent to the empty nursery. It stretched across the carpet and onto the icing-pink floor of a pristine Barbie Dream House. Inside, ten-year-old Belle's box turtle thrust his bucket-shaped head against the faux-kitchen window, orange eyes aglow.

Above Boxy's head, in the dollhouse's lilac and lavender second-floor bedroom, Prince Charming Ken reclined on the white canopy bed stripped naked, crown intact. Little Red Riding Hood Kelly lay on her side facing him; she was fully dressed, yes, but the wolf, inevitably, was poised at their feet. Nearby, Businesswoman Barbie's legs protruded from a plastic crib like the stiff limbs of a corpse in a Dumpster.

Upstairs, in the big house, the king-sized bed shuddered

from the quiet ministrations of Darlene, thirty-four, who had given her husband, Lance, a quick blow and then mounted him. She was working slowly and quietly back and forth, trying to find the right spot, the right speed. She had promised Lance that they would try to make another baby, and though she hated approaching sex like just another box on her checklist, here she was, at six-thirty A.M., with her hands planted on Lance's shoulders as her back arched and then flexed.

Lance's eyes remained closed. The thirty-five-year-old had been dreaming of awakening in his mother's cottage with the smell of fish cooking and the sounds of a distant struggle, and he couldn't quite climb back there to determine what was coming next, so he submitted to his supple wife in a not-unpleasant dreamy way.

Darlene had her hand cupped over his mouth so he stayed silent and was building up speed, panting quietly, when the bedroom door opened. Belle stood inside the doorway. Their only child wore faded, green-striped Ariel the Mermaid pajamas and clutched a droopy Mrs. Bunny by the waist. She dropped the weary, wash-worn stuffed animal she had had since birth (and which had recently reappeared nightly in her bed, after being relegated to a distant shelf for nearly three years). Belle stood rooted to the carpet and stared uncomprehendingly, until her mother sensed her presence.

Darlene gazed abstractedly over her shoulder, her blond stringy hair matted to her flushed forehead, rubbery in her tan nakedness. For a beat, she stared at Belle, not seeming to recognize her. Then Darlene's eyes cleared. "Belle," she called, reaching an arm back toward her daughter, "Belle." That was when the girl found her slipper-clad feet and flew out the bedroom door.

"We're only making love," Darlene called after Belle.

"Only?" Lance said, opening his dark eyes for the first time, and rising out of himself like a diver surfacing.

"I was talking to Belle," Darlene said, prematurely pulling off Lance. His dick thwacked his own belly as it landed. "Didn't you see her?"

"See her? She was in here? Shit, Darlene, didn't you lock the door?"

"We never lock the door," Darlene said.

"I do."

"Well, you didn't this time."

"You jumped me," Lance said, rubbing the sleep from his eyes and pulling the clock closer to see the time. "That was a sleep fuck."

"Sometimes a girl has to take fate into her own hands."

"Or mouth."

"Is that a complaint?"

"No, Darlene." Lance swung his legs out of the bed and grabbed two baby wipes from the bedside table, swabbing his penis with one, then his armpits and chest with the other. "If Belle hears us arguing, she'll think she's done something wrong."

"Well, *we* weren't doing anything wrong," Darlene said. She grabbed a blue chenille bathrobe and shrugged it on.

"I know, baby, I know," Lance said, approaching Darlene

and tying the self-belt around her waist. He kissed her gently on the center part of her hair. "I salute your initiative."

"You certainly did," Darlene said, laughing.

"I'll start the coffee and talk to Belle while you take your shower and get ready for work. Do you want Cracklin' Oat Bran for breakfast?"

"Can you manage eggs?"

"Sure," said Lance.

"Pepper jack omelet?" she asked.

"Deal," he said while rummaging in the hamper for yesterday's board shorts and the T-shirt that had become his uniform. When they left Barstow (the isolated desert city 160 miles northeast that ranked as one of California's ten poorest), Lance went from professional weatherman at a local news station to stay-at-home parent. He missed the external reinforcement of regular employment, but he embraced the satisfactions of full-time parenting in a way that Darlene didn't. He had become Rancho Amigo Elementary School's most active male volunteer and the sole father to have appeared regularly at the weekly Girl Scout meetings. He put on the dirty clothes, then stuffed the rest of the laundry in a pillowcase and tossed it over his shoulder. "Hi ho, hi ho," he muttered, as he headed out the bedroom door and down the stairs to find his daughter.

Belle was hiding out in the laundry room beyond the kitchen and adjacent to the doors to the garage and the backyard. She would have gone outside if she could have figured out the locks and the security code. Perched on the dryer, pointy chin on knees, she stared out the window at the gently steaming swimming pool, her face taut. Rashy patches were rising on her cheeks. Belle mostly resembled her father, olive-skinned, long-legged, and dark-eyed. Her high arched brows were her best feature, opening up her face with an intelligence she hadn't yet grown into. She was handsome rather than pretty, her features softened by the feminine mouth she'd inherited from Darlene along with her mother's appeasing smile, nowhere in evidence at that moment.

Since the Ramsays left their Barstow backwater on Route 66 in January, Belle had become graver, and the adjustment period showed no signs of lifting. Her face had grown thinner and longer, losing the rounded girlish cheeks; it was finding its way toward the woman she would ultimately become, the face she would shape through her own experience.

And this morning had only complicated the situation. It was as if her mother had become a total stranger, to be avoided like an unfamiliar person in a car offering candy; this frightened Belle, almost more than the fact that the naked woman she'd walked in on only moments earlier had shown no glimmer of recognition, no acknowledgment of a connection between the two of them. That woman glaring at her upstairs hadn't been Belle's mom but some vampire sucking the lifeblood out of her father.

At the time, Belle's first instinct had been to rescue her father, but she had feared getting in trouble; yet for what? What had she seen: her mother atop her apparently dozing (if not dead) father? Oh, tartar sauce, Belle thought, what crime had she committed? What rule had she broken? So she had crossed the threshold into her parents' room. Since when had that been forbidden? The door wasn't locked. But there was her mother, or an unreasonable facsimile, shooting daggers.

Belle feared her parents' anger, not because it occurred frequently, but because she was a good girl. Her self-esteem hinged on this, as it did on an A average in school (not counting gym and music), and the atypical ability to speak only when spoken to in the company of most adults. It certainly didn't hang on her dramatic ability or natural beauty. Belle's exaggerated fear of parental reprisal was just on the cusp of adolescent revolt.

On that early October morning when the haze still clumped like dust bunnies to the western horizon, Belle was desperate not to slip from her parents' good graces. Like most middle-class, college-educated parents of their generation, Lance and Darlene had never hit her, although the occasional quick shake, hard squeeze of an arm, or twist of a collar was allowed. The primary disciplinary threat was exile, being sent outside the circle of their love.

Belle had stumbled into a clearing in her own house where she was unwelcome. She didn't like this new house anyway, with her parents' bedroom upstairs and hers down below and miles away. Darlene had tricked her into moving with promises of goodies and a private swimming pool. Darlene had assured Belle she would make new friends in Encinitas—things parents said to get their way. Belle had traded the friends who understood her jokes for a canopy bed, a Barbie Dream House, and a turtle. She hadn't even held out for a puppy.

"Hey, doll face," Lance said softly as he entered the laundry room, as if trying not to frighten away a dove.

"Are you okay?" she sputtered from her dryer perch.

"Of course I'm okay, baby," he said reassuringly.

"I saw Mommy sitting on top of you, choking you," Belle whispered, "and when she turned around, she had her demon face on."

"Mommy's sorry," Lance said. "She didn't mean to scare you. She was surprised to see you. You scared her as much as she scared you."

"I don't think so, Dad," Belle said, wiping her drippy nose with the back of her hand.

"I think so. She was right: we were just—" He stopped, thinking of tantric terms, and then used the limp, "making love."

"If that's making love, I'm going to be a nun."

"You can't," Lance said. "We're not Catholic."

"We could convert," Belle said. "Or maybe I'll just try screwing."

"Where did you learn that word?"

"Mom," she said.

"Great child-rearing technique," he said to himself.

"You married her."

"Her who?"

"Mom," Belle said. "Do you like her?"

"Of course I do. I love her," Lance said quickly. But realistically he knew it was the reflexive "love" of married couples treading choppy water.

"I don't like her," Belle said defiantly. She looked into Lance's eyes to register his reaction, and saw the pinprick of hurt; she'd scored a direct hit.

"Sure you do," Lance said. "You just may not like her today."

"Why do parents want to know what you feel, and then tell you that you don't feel it?" Belle asked. Right then, Belle really did dislike Darlene. But this was the first time she'd said it aloud. Even Belle knew that pushing her father away wouldn't work. She understood that while parents agonized over preferring one child over the other, kids didn't. If they preferred one parent over the other, so be it. Belle favored Lance; she always had. She looked up to him literally and figuratively. He was the Zeus of her world, loved and feared. She wanted to tell him everything. And he wanted to hear it—but that didn't mean she'd make it easy on him. Especially after whatever weird thing he was doing with Mom.

"I do want to know what you feel, Belle."

"I don't belong here," Belle said. "I want to go back to Barstow."

"We can't," Lance said. "Mom's got a job here."

"You don't, Dad. Why not leave her here?"

"We're a family."

"She could visit us on weekends," Belle said. She resented

that her mother kept saying the move to Encinitas was good for all of them, but it had mainly been good for her. She was so consumed with being busy and driving a new car and buying shoes at Nordstrom's that she didn't seem to realize that she had dragged them all out of Barstow and away from their friends and stranded Belle in the dreaded Rancho Amigo Elementary School. And Mom expected her thanks, as if it were an improvement to fall to the dregs of the school food chain. "Or we could come here on weekends. I could handle this place on weekends."

"Is school that bad?" Lance asked, as he reached into the full laundry basket beside the dryer where Belle was sitting and pulled out a fitted sheet.

"Worse." Belle's mouth was squeezed into a knot.

"Here," Lance said, "help me fold the sheets. I never get the fitted ones right by myself."

Belle slipped off the dryer. She faced her father with her palms up. He flicked the far end at her and she caught a length of elastic. They were silent as they sorted out the corners, retreated a few steps away from each other to stretch the sheet straight, and gave it a shake to flatten it between them.

"I miss my friends," Belle said.

"You have friends here," Lance said, tucking one corner into its mate. "What about Sam?"

"He's a boy."

"I'm a boy."

"You're a dad," Belle said dismissively, walking toward Lance to relinquish her corners and taking up the fold they'd made below. "I miss my real friends. I miss me with my friends. No one gets me here. They're too stupid."

"No, they're not," Lance said.

"See? I tell you how I feel, and then you tell me I'm wrong."

"You can make friends here. It just takes time," Lance said, and then he turned his attention to finishing the sheet to stem the flow of stock parent statements from flying out of his mouth.

Sensing she'd pushed too far, Belle said, "You're my best friend."

"Me, too," he said, carefully placing the folded sheet in an empty basket beside the full one. "C'mon. Help me crack eggs."

"Hug first?"

"Big hug."

"You smell funny."

"Funny how?"

"Like baby powder," Belle said.

Lance led Belle into the adjacent kitchen; she choo-chooed behind, her hands on his hips. He opened the stainless steel refrigerator and gathered the eggs, milk, and grated cheese, then transferred the armful to the granite kitchen isle. He reached for a Pyrex bowl from a cupboard, bent for a whisk from a drawer, and placed both on the counter. Then he began to crack eggs with Belle beside him. He handed her the whisk so she could scramble, then asked, "Eggs for you, too?"

"No," Belle said. "I want Cinnamon Toast Crunch."

"Deal," he said. "But you have to have O.J."

"Gag me. It tastes yucky with cereal."

"Apple juice?"

Belle shrugged and said, "Let me see your neck."

"Why?"

"To check for strangle marks."

"Why would Mom strangle me?"

"I don't know," Belle said. "You tell me."

"You missed that yolk," Lance said, ashamed. As they stood side by side in the kitchen, with Belle's wild head of black curls at Lance's hip, he experienced such a feeling of oneness that it scared him. How would he pull himself back together if something happened to her? He relished these moments of gooey eggs on their hands; the brush of his arm hair against Belle's; and the simple knowledge that Cinnamon Toast Crunch was his daughter's favorite cereal, having vanquished Lucky Charms and an austere period of plain organic yogurt.

This quiet harmony Lance and Belle shared was what he had imagined he would experience with Darlene as their marriage ripened. Instead, as the newness of their passion waned, a gulf had appeared between them, competitiveness entered the void, and, it seemed to him, a desire on Darlene's part to assign blame. He still wanted to bridge that gulf, but wasn't sure how.

Lance was a go-with-the-flow guy in the choppy waters of a marriage in flux; his instincts were to dive under the wave and catch the next one. He fought that gut feeling, and tried to hang on to how it used to be. In the beginning, he had welcomed Darlene's vitality: she glowed in a way he didn't. It was as if the sun were a desk lamp aimed at her. Sure, she had a vulnerable side that he connected to, a flurry of self-doubts that she wasn't afraid to share with Lance. In the early days, he had been her father confessor. But it was her passion that attracted him; other women had seemed as dull as faded denim in comparison. She dreamed big and included him in those dreams. And yet Lance hadn't anticipated Darlene's restlessness, how she courted drama and then retreated to Lance to smooth her ruffled feathers. Lance gazed down at Belle and the bowl's frothy eggs: was he selfish for still wanting someone who laughed at all of his jokes? Shit, yes, but that didn't change a thing.

Lance and Belle looked up as Darlene click-clacked down the tile stairs from the bedroom to the great room, which was open to the kitchen where they stood scrambling. Darlene clattered across the Spanish tile floor in a khaki suit with a pencil-shaped skirt slit high on one thigh; her orange silk blouse was open deep at the neck, and long orange cuffs drifted out in casual irregularity from her blazer's tailored sleeves. She wore high orange Coach sling-backs and gold chandelier earrings to sex up the suit even more than her body naturally did.

Lance didn't let himself acknowledge that Darlene was dressing for someone else. He preferred his wife in floating India cotton dresses that were sheer when she stood against the sun, revealing legs that might have been shaved a few days before, or not. He missed the days when her toenails were half-ass painted, done while they sat together on the couch and watched sitcoms, laughing more at them than with them, their ratty sofa bed mirrored in the TV set. Often she would straddle his lap during the commercials and they would have mad make-out sessions. ("Giddy-up, horsey," she would joke.) The next day he might find small patches of hot orange or inky blue-black on his knees or thighs, smudged toe-prints. He never scrubbed them off.

Now Darlene got professional manicures. She waxed her legs. Having crossed the tiled great room, she swooped down on Belle, kissed her lavishly, and said, her eyes wet with tears, "I'm so sorry, honey. I love you. I feel so bad."

Belle, dry-eyed, received the flood of kisses. "Drama queen," Belle said.

"Drama princess," Darlene responded. She slipped her heavy gold chain over her head and put it around Belle's slim neck, before boosting herself up on a barstool. She pulled the *San Diego Union-Tribune* closer to her and skimmed the newspaper while awaiting her eggs. "Since when did the high become eighty-five?" she asked.

"Since today," Lance said.

"What happened to high of sixty-eight?" Darlene asked.

"That's yesterday's news, Darlene. Today's high is eighty-five, low fifty-five," Lance said, switching on his objective weatherman voice.

"Do you need a green screen with that weather report?" Darlene joked.

Lance raised his right arm robotically, finger pointing

authoritatively, and continued, "Offshore winds, morning gusts to fifty miles per hour. . . ."

"Cold today," Belle said, mimicking his monotone, "hot tamale."

"Maybe I shouldn't have worn silk," said Darlene.

"Keep your shirt on," Lance said. Belle stifled a laugh.

"I so totally don't need a Santa Ana this week," Darlene moaned, as Lance served her breakfast. She was already a bundle of nerves wrapped in barbed wire, even before that morning's mishap. She wished she were at her best in these situations but, swamped by work pressure, she was watching herself behave like her own evil twin. Next Saturday—only four days away— was the grand opening of Darlene's Diner, the corporate out-growth of the kooky little café Darlene had opened eight years ago in Barstow. The new restaurant on Balboa Avenue in a Pacific Beach strip mall was the prototype of a franchise that was supposed to ultimately go nationwide.

Darlene had had the idea of scheduling the restaurant's open-ing on Belle's eleventh birthday, and had invited 250 adults and kids to the birthday bash. Projecting from her own desires, she had assumed her daughter would love a huge party. Belle, to her credit, was not quite buying the commercialization of her own personal holiday. She had no desire to stand in the shadow of a life-sized Barbie cake. She shunned crowds in general and couldn't be less impressed by the area's premiere kiddy band, Barry Beige and His Scary Monsters.

The nascent Darlene's Diner franchise had started modestly enough in a battered Barstow trailer. After eight years of hard work, Darlene had shuttered her funky but successful café the previous January. The Ramsays had moved to Encinitas, persuaded by Darlene's new business partner, Alexander Graham Marker, that she would make a mint if she went national. It was her ticket out of that desert backwater, and she had bet the farm on the future business with a down payment on their Pacific Breeze villa.

Darlene carried the dual worry of future success and present mortgage payments as she stepped away from the countertop, her breakfast half eaten, and left the house to drive south toward Pacific Beach, returning once for her car keys and a second time for her new sunglasses. She raised her cheek for Lance to kiss. (She smelled like a department store.) "I fucked up. Sorry," she whispered, and then turned her face to return his kiss even though it meant smearing him with newly refreshed lipstick. She tried to hold still in the moment, but she was moving too fast on the highway of her to-do list. She pulled away, then paused to look into his eyes and asked, "Is everything okay?"

"Sure thing, babe," Lance said. That was not entirely true. But given the pressure Darlene was now under, Lance knew his wife couldn't handle any added stress or uncertainty, so he sucked it up. She would have exploded if she knew he was holding anything back; that wasn't the type of relationship she believed they had. One thing was for sure, Lance and Darlene hadn't made a baby that morning. Pass interference.

From there the morning sped up. Lance bused the breakfast dishes and loaded the dishwasher. The countertop crumbs dust-busted; the granite sprayed with Fantastik and wiped clean. Lance did a quick inventory of the Girl Scout cookies (he had volunteered to be in charge of distribution for Belle's troop), and noted on a handwritten list taped inside the pantry door how many mothers he had to call to remind them to pay up. He dreaded those collection calls.

Meanwhile, Belle dawdled putting on her Girl Scout uniform in front of an episode of *SpongeBob SquarePants* that she claimed she'd never seen before, but even Lance had seen it twice. He began to get frustrated that she wouldn't put on her socks and shoes, so he entered her room to get her backpack and discovered from a flyer on Belle's desk that today was the deadline for the Reuben H. Fleet Science Center field trip money. He lacked exact change, which sent him upstairs. He riffled through his pockets, then Darlene's, until he found $10 in singles and change. It was only then that Lance realized he was really looking for something else (a pack of matches, a pink crumpled phone memo), some transparent evidence of suspected misdeeds. He found nothing.

When Lance and Belle climbed into the van, he slid his coffee mug into one cup holder; she slotted her chocolate-milk box in the other. He fumbled for his Wayfarers; she pulled them off his head and handed them over. "Buffalo Springfield or Hannah Montana?" she asked, fingering the CDs.

"How about a compromise: Judy Collins?"

"Too depressing," Belle said.

"Dusty Springfield?"

"Cool."

Lance pulled out of the driveway, passing their neighbors the Montoyas' Mediterranean Revival mini-mansion, and the scarred earth of the building sites to the right, the new homes with their glowing white driveways, the industrial greenhouses that emitted a pasty sweet jonquil smell.

"So, if Mom wasn't choking you, what exactly were you doing this morning?" Belle asked, although she had her theories.

"Some stuff kids don't need to see," Lance said, and paused, searching for the right phrase. "Like their parents having sex."

"So, that's what making love is?"

"Yep," Lance said.

"I still don't get it," said Belle. "I used to think parents made babies if they shared the same bed, but that's not right. I've laid in bed with you and nothing happened."

"Don't go there," Lance said. They passed Encinitas Park, where a lone Mexican nanny rocked a carriage in stoic boredom. Farther down the road in front of a sun-bleached and seemingly vacant Italian villa, a gardener pruned poinsettias.

"Also," Belle continued, "a man and a woman don't have to be married to have babies."

Lance nodded. "True."

"And I think I get the penis and vagina thing."

"You do?" Lance said with a strained chuckle. He wanted to be truthful about sex but he didn't know the appropriate way to string the words together. "Maybe you can explain it to me."

"Julia told me."

"Julia?"

"Sam's babysitter."

"The girl with the tattoos?"

"And the pierced tongue," Belle said, nodding.

"Charming," Lance said.

"Julia lisped when she first got it done, but now she can talk normally. Discussing sex didn't freak her out like you guys. She said it's like a plug and an outlet. The man's the plug and the woman's the outlet."

"When did Julia start working at Home Depot?"

"She said when you add mouths and butts, everyone has outlets."

Their next-door neighbor, Coco Montoya, passed them in her gold Lexus with daughter Jade strapped in the backseat. Mrs. Montoya braked and flashed Lance a smile, teeth sharply white against fuchsia lipstick. She raised her fist to her ear and mouthed, *Call me; cookies.* Lance rallied a noncommittal finger-point and nodded.

"What else did Julia say?" Lance asked, parking in front of the school.

"It's not just about babies." Belle looked down and pulled up her green knee-highs. "Julia said sex is fun. And sometimes boys do it with boys, and girls do it with girls, but Sam and I agree that's way gross."

"If you knew all this, why did this morning freak you out?"

"I wasn't freaked out, Dad."

"You were, too, Miss Blotchy Face sulking on the dryer."

"Maybe a little."

"Okay, I was, too." Lance wanted to confess how useless he was explaining sex to her, but that wasn't particularly parental. He was supposed to know how to do these things.

"Hey, Dad, if making love is so fun, why did Mommy look pissed off?"

"Don't say pissed off, honey. You sound like a trucker."

"And saying penis doesn't?"

"A trucker would say something else."

"Penis, penis, penis," Belle chanted until the school bell rang. She opened her door and hopped out of the van. Her Girl Scout skirt wafted up like a *Fantasia* blossom.

"That went well," Lance said to himself as Belle crossed the lunch court and swished behind a pillar. She was brighter than Lance ever was. Gifted, according to the Barstow teachers; reading seventh-grade level in second grade, but still with the sticky emotional life of any other little kid. He knew Belle saw things in him that he was unaware of himself. Fatherhood was such a huge responsibility to be better than you really were—more vital, fearless, and decisive—but the truth was kids saw you at your worst, too. They could sense every change in routine, every hiccup in tone of voice. They could sense every whiff of sex or attempts to cloak it, even if they couldn't deduce what those clues meant.

If Lance had more kids, he reflected, at least he could benefit from his mistakes with Belle. The instinct was to protect your kids; still, you could take that too far and have children that clung to your pant leg whenever they encountered a carpenter ant. But it was impossible to protect them from yourself, from that part of you that was so ingrained you stopped seeing it, like a mole on your cheek that you didn't recall having until your kid asked with a poke, What's this, Daddy, this brown thing?

Lance realized that this day was already going askew, although he couldn't entirely blame the Santa Ana winds, rumored to make you crazy. (In junior college, he'd studied that increased positive ions irritated serotonin levels, inspiring hyperactivity, nervous imbalance, and road rage, among other unpleasantness.) He was going to have to steer in the direction of this emotional skid. He had largely lived in female-dominated households since he was Belle's age, and was prepared for swift changes in emotional direction.

It had been different when he was a little kid, before his parents separated and he'd become the man of the house by default. Until he was ten, he lived in a five-bedroom New Jersey Tudor on a rolling lawn that swooped down to its French Colonial neighbor; a house built for a level of entertaining and child-rearing his parents never achieved. Lance had run with a pack in that upscale suburb. There were no playdates, no plans, no organized sports; just his best friend Carl, whom he'd known since before they both could walk, and all the brothers and sisters and cousins and neighbors who swirled around like lightning bugs in their mass games of hide-and-seek that spread from lawn to lawn and backyard to backyard and into the bramble beyond. All fences could be climbed. Lance had been so certain of his place that he'd been unaware he had one until he moved with his mother to California when he was ten. That was a shock.

Lance drove slowly across the tracks for the Coaster commuter train and then braked at the light before turning left onto Coast Highway 101. He wondered whether it was possible that he craved another child so that he could finally have another male in the house. That was too Freudian an explanation. What he wanted right now was a Starbucks; that was far less complicated.

chapter 2

Lance had wanted to delegate the sex chat to Darlene. She was terrific at setting goals and marching them forward, but she could no more talk about sex than she could rebuild a car engine.

Lately, since Lance and Darlene had started trying to get pregnant again, sex had been a drag. And not just because Darlene was on the fence about expanding the family to begin with, which just added to the tension. Ask anyone, make-baby sex loses its charm. Two people who had come together over lightning-strike sex inevitably started to unravel over damp preplanned rendezvous. Sex with a purpose was about as titillating as a joint tax return.

Lance remembered Darlene posed on the new sofa last month, prim and stiff dressed in some kind of thirties movie ideal of sexy. She wore a cream satin negligee and marabou slippers, her lips (and her two front teeth) a coral shade she'd never worn before. The fancy-lingerie fuck element did nothing for him. So rather than sliding up to her, he had joked, "Dude, what the fuck's happening?" Darlene had scurried upstairs with a cry of, "Juvenile!" and slammed the bedroom door. He had coaxed her back into some sort of mood, but their lips had a blubbery Novocain disconnection. He was always either behind or in front of the wave, heading toward wipeout. And Darlene didn't want to discuss it—or couldn't. The problem, and its resolution, was his.

So it was inevitable that Lance was the one who had discussed lovemaking with Belle even though Darlene had left the bedroom door open. Thanks a lot. What was he going to do when she hit menstruation? He'd better reference Barnes and Noble for that one, Lance thought while driving to Starbucks after he dropped Belle off at Rancho Amigo. He made a left into the parking lot for his ritual morning latte. He entered and waited patiently in line to have his order taken by a fierce-eyed, tattooed surfer who wore gauge earplugs in his lobes. Lance imagined the dude as an old man with lobes that swayed like infant swings in the breeze. Grossed out by that image, he sprang for a dark chocolate bar. Maybe the self-mutilation thing worked as a marketing ploy: gross customers out and they spent more money. It seemed dubious; caffeine addiction was the more likely culprit.

Lance doctored his latte—three sugars, two shakes of chocolate powder, a splash of half-and-half, and then he climbed back into his van and drove south to the surfer beach. He parked by the side of the road, then sat on the cliff by the steep wooden stairs and watched a steady stream of surfers carrying their boards under their arms or atop their heads. They passed each other leaving or coming to the big waves like ants on a work detail, with the occasional grunt of, "Dude."

Far below Lance's perch, the surfers rode the waves. They dipped and weaved, purposeful and laid-back, a tricky balance between opposites. The waves were strong today; the wind had shifted, coming in warm from the northeast, but the weather at the beach remained pleasant. No worries, Lance told himself.

Okay, Lance worried. Everything he had learned about parenting he got from his mother, Ethel, but he had been shrewd enough not to quiz her about sex. Certainly his dad had told him squat. When Mr. Ramsay had left Lance and his mother for the neighbor's wife, Lance had briefly pressed his father for what the attraction was, then let it go in the face of his father's rueful smile, awkward ruffle of his child's buzz cut, and the statement, "Someday you'll get it, son, but not today."

So now Lance got it. But what was he supposed to do with the knowledge? He could hardly explain it any better than the old man. And his mother never got it. Ethel died married to his father in her mind, till death do us part, even though his father had gone and had another family. Ethel had been a tiny, chipped teacup of a woman, Japanese-American with a dark pixie haircut sugared with gray and a single phantom dimple that rarely appeared once they left his father behind in Princeton

Junction. People discounted her because she was small, but she wasn't slight, not to Lance. She had turtle energy, slow to anger, slow to change. She didn't sweat the small stuff, but she was immovable once she had made a major decision of any kind.

Ethel had been born in Fresno, California, in 1935. And, having been given a good American name (unlike her sisters Jasmine and Hiromi), she was a child who never caused trouble. She never asked for more than being surrounded by her family, a robust seed nestled in a sweet orange. The youngest of her generation in a large farm family, she had grown up strong and healthy, surrounded by grandparents, maternal and fraternal, aunts and uncles, siblings and cousins.

And then it was over. Ethel was six when the Japanese bombed Pearl Harbor. She was eight when FDR's government relocated her entire family to the racetrack at the Big Fresno Fairgrounds, and then she and her sisters accompanied her mother and aunts to the Manzanar War Relocation Center. Summers scorched; winters froze. Her mother couldn't console herself, much less her daughters. And, although Ethel had survived the years in the internment camps, she had seen her family's orange grove disappear along with their spirit to replant. Ethel never ate another orange and it was as hard for her to appreciate sweetness as it was for her to get rid of the bitter taste in her mouth. After Manzanar, it was tough for Ethel to have faith. It became impossible once Lance's father ditched them.

Lance rarely discussed his mother, but he missed her. She could change a flat tire; she knew the rules to every card game, and the name of every native California plant. She was the most patient of listeners; people tended to underestimate her strength and her powers of observation, but she rarely exploited the advantage this gave her. She knew how to deal with a child as an individual, without treating him as an adult. Okay, so that wasn't always possible when there was just the two of them and her personal sorrows bled out in long quiet stretches, but she always treated Lance with respect. He was never invisible to her. And their connection seemed to come in the rest between beats, waiting for Ethel to decide whether to discard a seven in gin rummy, her delight in beating Lance only slightly greater than her satisfaction when he played a difficult hand well.

His father was another story. Lance's parents had met when German-born Ernst Ramsay, an assistant philosophy professor specializing in logic at Princeton, dislocated his shoulder in a motorcycle accident. Ethel had been working a double shift in the E.R. (having fled east from the Pacific Rim following nursing school), and gently comforted the expat through the pain and the recovery. They had quietly drifted together, a distrusted German and a suspicious Japanese-American, from obligatory movie dates to dinners she cooked free of chatter and manufactured drama, and finally a Wednesday wedding in a registry office with the clerk as their witness. For Ernst (later Americanized to Ernie), it might have been a bachelor's midlife marriage of convenience. For Ethel, whose love was gradual but true, this tall, chilly, handsome man who had crashed into her life made her feel a part of something bigger than her sorrow.

All these years later, he could Google his father, Lance supposed, get an address, but that would be unfaithful to Ethel. Lance was hers. On the last day of fifth grade, Ethel had collected ten-year-old Lance in the white Dodge Dart on a sweltering Friday in late June. The high humidity weighed down on them both and quashed any urge to talk. Only bees had the energy to buzz among the blooming hydrangeas in front of the school.

The Dodge was a hot box in the oppressive weather. Lance clutched his disappointing final report card in a sweaty hand; it went unnoticed. Ethel had packed them each a blue Lady Baltimore suitcase, unused since her Philadelphia honeymoon. She put his comic books and whatever else was under his bed—no questions asked—into a cardboard carton sealed with masking tape and labeled it *Lance's stuff* in her calligraphic writing. Since it was the only container, the labeling seemed an unnecessary, but heartfelt, touch.

Driving, Ethel barely reached the steering wheel; she left behind the yellow pages she normally used as a boost. She didn't want anything to remind her of the Garden State and her cheating husband. She drove Batmobile-fast out of Princeton Junction and they were deep in Ohio before the heat broke. That was when Lance realized that this was it. This was no summer vacation. They were on the road. Ethel didn't need to explain; she knew he wouldn't ask. Besides, she never even opened his sorry report card.

On that long car trip, Lance began to think that it was the weather that had moved his mother to uncharacteristic action. If it had been May, and the white lilacs had adorned their bushes, and the peonies had risen up full-blown overnight, she might have remained. But no, he came to associate their feverish flight with the swelter of another East Coast summer. That June, Lance came to believe in the almost mystical power of weather to drive human events. Although Lance had rarely considered what he'd become when he grew up, he began to think he could become a weatherman, that in forecasting the weather he could come to understand adult motives and emotions. He discovered there was nothing that profound about the profession itself, once he entered it.

It took four days for mother and son to reach La Jolla, California, just north of San Diego; "the jewel" in Spanish. Only two days later, Ethel started work as an O.R. nurse at Mercy Hospital. They set up house on the edge of the business district above La Jolla Cove in a squalidly picturesque bungalow colony with weathered turquoise walls and splayed tile roofs. The cottages, intended for summer vacationers, lacked insulation, so their house was damp and moldy even in June.

That first summer, after holing up while his mother went to work and scaring himself reading The Exorcist, Lance went outdoors and found the ocean. Without money for a surfboard, he threw himself into bodysurfing, beginning in the sheltered cove with its busy lifeguard station, and then swimming out around the point to more dangerous waters. There, the waves were high and unpredictable. They pounded out the remaining sounds that were in his head, the dull wonderment that he had never said good-bye to his father, or heard from him since they had left New Jersey.

Lance became one of those boys who spent the mind-numbingly perfect days in swimming trunks and flip-flops, tan and casually muscled. Because of his mixed heritage, he looked Hawaiian. His California beach buddies had called him "Keanu," which meant cool breeze over the mountain, or geeky Hollywood surf boy on an excellent adventure. When Lance wasn't immersed in the Pacific Ocean, he wooed and won a stream of pale tourist girls, giving them guided tours of the tide pools, daring them to touch the anemones and then having them recoil into his arms.

Lance's vigorous good health seemed to be the only thing that pleased Ethel, who received it as a sign that blessed their move. She returned at the end of her shifts shell-shocked, with other people's blood on her white shoes. She would shed her uniform, don a robe, and fry fish while Lance slathered her shoes with chalky polish. After dinner, Ethel and Lance played cards on a folding table, while she smoked, unconcerned about longevity. Sometimes Lance returned home to find movie money taped to the front door; he would reverse course and stroll to the Cove Theater for art films that made no lasting impression on him. Ethel was never serious about the doctors she brought home, still in their scrubs, mostly married. But they forestalled some loneliness and earned her a few perks on the ward. At the hospital, the medics considered her capable, intuitive, and mysterious—until they saw the cottage. Then they knew she was a poor single mother. She might want something. And she became less interesting, which was how she preferred it. Lance became her only man.

What would Ethel have made of Lance's luxurious but weightless life now? He considered it, and decided that she would have sucked her teeth, dealt another round of rummy, and taken longer to pull out her winning cards than usual. She would have said, "Follow the path of least resistance, Lance, and sooner or later you will face a mountain you can't climb."

Ethel would also have disapproved of Lance's yoga lessons, and that saddened him, but nonetheless didn't keep him from pushing off the seawall with coffee cup in hand and leaping the barricade. If he hauled ass, he'd have time to shower. He dusted off the sand crusting his feet on his way to the Windstar.

An hour later, Lance, showered and shaved, sat cross-legged on his king-sized bed atop a bright orange throw. He felt the deep stretch along his thighs. He inhaled through his nose, filling the back of his lungs. He envisioned his rib cage as an accordion opening and closing. He exhaled, blowing the breath out his mouth toward Wren Marker, the wife of Darlene's business partner.

The naked pair faced each other nose to nose in the tantric

position called "Yab Yum" with Wren seated on Lance's thighs, as if they were meditating into a mirror. He gazed into Wren's left eye, which was brown, gold-flecked, and alive. Wren's eyes were unnaturally wide under the tended arches of her dark brows. Even at forty-four, she was still a freckled midwestern daddy's girl with high round cheeks, nose abruptly rising at the tip. (Her two sisters called her little piggy; she was the pretty one.) She carried the imprint of every pleasing smile that had ever stretched across her lips in the deep laugh lines on either side.

Wren sensed Lance drifting. "Inhale," she said, as she breathed into his open mouth, gently, as if trying to blow a large soap bubble; "Exhale," she said, placing Lance's right hand over her heart. She covered it with her left hand, the emerald-cut diamond sparkling between two sapphires on her engagement ring. She placed her right hand on Lance's chest, and he grasped it under his left hand with the dull gold wedding band.

Wren's strong straight freckled back rose and fell with her deep even breaths as she inhaled the scent of an Aveda lavender candle. Her sex was planted firmly on Lance's prick, his large feet crossed behind her ass. The English translation of the position was "cranes with necks intertwined": a position of birdlike grace. Wren nested in Lance's lap and tilted back her head to gaze directly into his eyes. She studied his left eye, which was brown-black and difficult to read alone without his laugh lines. Was it a well or a wall, she wondered, deep or shallow?

"Enflame the dragon goddess," Wren said, pushing Lance away without breaking eye contact. They arched in opposite directions like shuffling cards to become a two-headed snake (one long body with their heads at opposite ends of the bed). Lance kissed Wren's foot ("Ohm," she said with a sigh). She took what she would call his "lingam" and circled it at the gates of her "yoni." She inserted it and they made small O's, pelvis to pelvis, while she contracted her pubic and anal muscles in "bandhas."

Lance grabbed Wren's right hand, pulled her back into Yab Yum, and pressed her close, face-to-face again. They undulated and took short fire breaths, inhaling and exhaling from the nose until Lance's snorts were audible. They returned to inhaling and exhaling into each other's mouths, gazing into each other's eyes. They amped up, fire-breathed, ramped down, meditated. Over the next half hour, they repeated the sequence until Wren broke out into a full birthday party grin and Lance came while staring deep into Wren's sparkler eyes.

Wren rolled off, reversed in a gymnastic move, and leaned against the headboard on Lance's side of the bed. She twisted her sweaty dark hair up and clamped it with the butterfly clip she reclaimed from the side table, at ease in her freckled skin. "I'm worried about Max," Wren said without prelude in her low-pitched voice.

"Why?" Lance asked, lying on his back on the left side of the bed, Darlene's side. "He's a great kid—and, luckily, he has your looks."

"Max bit a girl in the turtle sandbox yesterday."

"At Encinitas Park?"

"I can never go back," she said.

"Sure you can. Kids bite. I don't see psycho killer in his future at twenty-two months," Lance said. He grabbed a box of baby towelettes and asked, "Wipe?"

Wren swabbed her "doorway of life" and continued, "Not nibbled. Really chomped. They were fighting over a plastic spoon. How pathetic is that? A plastic spoon. The girl started bawling, then her mother got right in my face and said Max needed a muzzle."

"That's drastic," Lance agreed. "You didn't bite her, did you?"

"I'm Zen enough not to bare my teeth."

"Did you comfort her kid first and then discipline Max?"

"Totally," Wren said, passing the wipe back to Lance, "and she was some mangy sandy-mouthed little girl. I pitied her— until I saw her mother. Real surf Nazi. Her kid pushed Max first, but I stayed back so they could sort out their aggression."

"You're on the right track, Wren. Comfort the victim; chastise Max. This biting phase will pass when Max can talk. It's preverbal. Now, when he's frustrated, or tired, or needy, he pulls out the fangs."

"You're telling me," Wren said. "I had this harpy in my face and I was hoisting Max out of the sandbox by the waist and he locked his jaws on my forearm. Look!"

"His teeth came in well." Lance inspected the bite ring on her forearm. "Maybe he wanted to see how you taste. I do."

Wren withdrew her arm, rolled away, and spit-snuffed the candle. "I never should have bit him as a baby, even playfully."

"I know, but I bet his toes were irresistible."

"I never bit Sam," she continued, "and Sam never had this problem. Is it me?"

"Don't play the blame game," Lance said. The phone rang beside Wren. She handed Lance the receiver.

It's Darlene, he mouthed to Wren, who hugged her knees tight to her chest and held her breath. Her worried eyes didn't leave his face. Lance continued, "I can hardly hear you . . . you're on your cell and you're what? Copulating? Oh, ovulating. No, baby, I don't know why I said copulating."

Lance rose as he talked and replaced his Ocean Pacific board shorts with his free hand without losing balance on his six-foot-one-inch frame. "See you in fifteen? Oh, ten." He paused, absentmindedly rubbing his nipple, trying to pull his head back into the present like a balloon on a string. "No, baby, I can't wait. You're breaking up."

After Lance hung up the phone, he offered Wren another wipe, unsure what to say. She declined without speaking, shaking her head no, and putting her palms up as if she were under arrest. She exhaled and released her knees. Then she rolled forward into child's pose on the bed, pulling inward as her forehead touched the mattress. She rested her belly between her thighs and stretched her hands forward, palms down.

Lance stared at the freckled curve of Wren's back and listened to her breathing become more rhythmic. He tried to regulate his own breathing to match hers; he was still so blissed out he was slow to register how busted he was. He replayed the conversation. Had he given Darlene any clue to what he was doing? Copulating. She had to know. Then again, she was so preoccupied these days he could have said lacrosse and she might have bought it. But even if she didn't know what he was doing, he did. And it wasn't strictly yoga.

He was so busted.

chapter 3

Wren sat back on her haunches from child's pose, raised her eyes to smile at Lance, and noted his clouded face, his hooded eyes. She kept silent. This was usually a pleasurable moment, but they were split by fear. Wren moved the same way, with the same grace as she normally did. She rose, pulled the orange coverlet along with her, and threw it to Lance. He balled it up and tossed it by the bedroom door. They remade the bed carefully, with nurse corners, like a married couple. Darlene's call had interrupted their charade; they were not husband and wife. The intrusion forced the pair to reflect on a situation they'd intentionally left ambiguous; it affected their intimacy but neither was sure how.

"Darlene's on the Pacific Coast Highway past La Jolla," Lance said.

"I gathered." Wren fanned her right palm, then her left, across the floral comforter to smooth the wrinkles. She felt a twinge that she was making the younger woman's bed, that it would be Darlene's hands unmaking the sure tucks.

"She'll be here in ten minutes," Lance said, "unless there's traffic."

"There will be." Wren was relieved that she had parked her car discreetly down the hill, although at the time she had felt she was being paranoid. Now her heart raced. She was afraid of Darlene, yes, but that was relatively minor. Wren was more afraid of her husband, Alec, and how she abdicated her position of higher moral ground by stooping to his level, by sleeping with Lance.

Oh, she justified it, though. She believed what she and Lance shared was no cheap grab in a Vegas hotel. Alec made those business trips alone, deducting miscellaneous receipts. She was resigned despite her anger to see him off, let him blow off steam. Sometimes she couldn't believe how much she wanted him out of the house, even if it meant late-night phone calls filled with read-between-the-lines excuses, inordinate professions of love. It would have been much cleverer if he had called and listened to her, asked her what she was doing and was curious about the details of the kids' day.

Wren had the numbers on her side. Lance was her only, well, lover since Alec. She didn't venture a count for her husband. Of course, it hadn't started out that way, the infidelity. They'd had a passionate courtship, she and Alec. One humid Sunday afternoon years before in the dying days of disco, they had declared their love for each other for the first time in New York City on the roof of her Chelsea walk-up. She left a huarache sandal in the safety door so they wouldn't get locked out, and he carried her, one-shoed, over the blazing tar beach and settled her on the ledge overlooking PS 11 and the deserted August streets. It had been an insane week for Wren. She had the lead in a low-budget horror film. Her throat was raw from screaming. She was the production's only female except for the intern who did makeup, wardrobe, and ambition-humped the director. There was always something wrong with the shot—lighting, cues, continuity—and they would add another rip to Wren's T-shirt and more snakes, boas, garters, garden. She had called Alec in California in tears, and he had flown the red-eye to New York that night to take care of her. His timing had been impeccable.

Within a month, Alec closed the deal. Wren ceded her sublet to an understudy and abandoned the only bedroom she'd ever had to herself. Alec had the stubborn confidence she lacked; he believed in her, just not enough to follow her to New York and survive on Kraft singles and saltines until she got a break. But he made her feel secure for the first time ever and she wrapped that around her like a life vest—and flourished.

Then, Alec had been Wren's rock. And, now, he was her millstone.

Besides, Wren rationalized, what she and Lance had was tantric, not fueled by drink or casual lust. They had rituals. They never touched when they were not on the orange throw.

There were no passionate clutches in dark hallways, or late-night words of love from phone booths. They had rules, as if they could contain what they had unleashed. Who were they kidding?

"Should we schedule another playdate?" Wren asked, achieving a false lightness of tone.

"The kids could get together today after school. Does Sam have soccer?"

"I meant you and me."

"Oh," he said, turning away, "right."

"Are you okay?"

"Fine," Lance lied, "you?"

"It's just sex," Wren lied.

Lance shuttled Wren out of the bedroom, down the wide steps, through the cathedral-ceilinged great room, and past the big-screen TV. The lead story was "Wildfire Watch," as the local news cadged ratings on the rising tide of Santa Ana winds. With concerned eyes, the male news anchor reported on fires burning north and northeast of San Diego. He then fanned the flames of local panic by recalling the 2003 Cedar Fire that had scorched 280,000 acres and killed fifteen, before he tossed the segment to a lantern-jawed ash blonde standing on a desolate Escondido patio beside a burnt umbrella. A careless smoker had ignited a palm tree, she reported gravely. Back to the studio, where the anchor wrapped the segment: "Check back for more news at noon for a complete evacuation schedule."

"I'm sorry," Lance said, ignoring news of a world beyond his birds-of-paradise.

"For what?" Wren asked.

"This."

"Playing around," Wren asked, "or getting caught?"

Before Lance answered, the doorbell chimed the first five notes of "California Dreaming." The pair froze, and then locked eyes. Wren took the orange coverlet and glided toward the kitchen and away from the front door. It couldn't be Darlene so soon—and she wouldn't ring the bell. After looking over his shoulder to ensure Wren was hidden, Lance flip-flopped through the foyer. The househusband was dismayed to see Coco, thirty-two, his bright-eyed next-door neighbor, a petite bombshell with a blue-black bob and magenta lipstick. Her husband John Juan and Wren's Alec were boon companions, generous alumni of University of San Diego Law School.

Coco shifted between platform mules in a fuchsia-and-orange-striped silk blouse. She matched the garden's birds-of-paradise and bougainvillea. Before the door was fully open, she announced that she wanted her daughter Jade's Girl Scout cookies. Lance, head of Girl Scout Troop #773 cookie distribution, admitted Coco into the foyer.

"Your cookies are in the pantry. Hang here," Lance said. "I'll go get them."

Lance retreated through a corner of the great room, past the single leather Chesterfield chair awaiting Darlene's return from a tough day at the office. Wren was pouring a glass of tap water, but Lance took it from her and whispered urgently, "Danger,

Will Robinson, danger." He herded Wren gently past the black granite kitchen island. When they entered the narrow laundry room, he resisted the urge to slide his hands down the back of her yoga pants, palms against cheeks. (Just the thought began to make him hard again.) Wren dropped the orange coverlet on the Whirlpool. To the right was the door to the garage; he opened the door to the left, the back door opening onto the patio and pool. He wanted to lean down for a kiss, when she said, "Hola, Paco," and he looked up to see the gardener.

"Yoga lessons," Lance said preemptively. He turned, like a duck in a shooting gallery, leaving Wren in the backyard, where she briefly discussed azaleas with Paco, then slipped around the garage and jogged to her green VW convertible parked down the hill on Jonquil Drive. If her own house wasn't uphill, she could have run the mile and a half home.

Inside, Lance tossed the coverlet into the washer and camouflaged it with a load of pink sheets. He leaned down at the dryer, opened the door, felt residual dampness, tossed in a fabric softener strip, and restarted the cycle, sending the machine into a productive thumpa-thumpa. He swiped his hands on the flaming orange and red dragons curling up the sides of his black board shorts and looked up.

Coco sat atop the kitchen counter, ankles crossed, picking the dead leaves off a wandering Jew. "I like a man who knows his fabric softener," she said.

"Downy Free & Sensitive," Lance said.

"One sheet or two?"

"One's plenty."

"And my cookies?" Coco cocked a dark eyebrow.

"In the pantry," he said. "I just needed to start another load."

"That wife of yours works you too hard," Coco said, uncrossing her ankles.

Lance shrugged. "I try to keep busy." Over Coco's head, he spied the open master bedroom door at the top of the steps. Had he and Wren left behind any clues? He hadn't done his final sweep, like a traveler checking out of a hotel room.

There was a knock on the back door and Paco entered the kitchen. The five-foot-seven, wide-shouldered Baja California native wore his longish wavy dark hair in a bandanna, tied pirate-style. "Can I please have a glass of water?" he asked.

Lance grabbed a child's Ariel the Mermaid cup and approached the sink, but stopped and turned toward the refrigerator when Paco asked, "Do you have bottled?"

"Gassy or flat?" Lance asked.

"Flat," Paco said.

Lance slipped the gardener a twenty-ounce Poland Spring and said, "Excuse, me, I have to get Mrs. Montoya's cookies," before disappearing into the pantry.

Paco turned to Coco (unlike her gardener, he didn't keep his eyes at soil level), and asked, "Here for a yoga lesson?"

"*Qué?*" she asked. "What?"

"Like *Sra.* Marker."

"So that was the girl who just left?"

"*Sí.* She's very flexible."

In the distance, the garage door slapped up and a car squealed to a stop. Darlene ran in, unzipping her pencil skirt, oblivious.

She dropped it on the laundry room floor and called, "I don't have much time," before entering the kitchen. She was camouflaged by an enormous bouquet that would have made more sense in a hotel foyer urn. The arrangement contained orange daylilies, yellow roses, freesias, and white hydrangeas and concealed her torso, which was clad only in white Wonderbra and panties.

Darlene stepped off her Coach sandals and then looked over at Coco and Paco, dumbstruck. It was the same look she'd had in her Mount Helix High yearbook photo—her ash-blond hair fell from the middle part in two sheets on either side of her round face. Her sweetheart lips revealed prominent bicuspids in a toothy smile that seemed a little apologetic, as if she were laughing but didn't quite get the joke.

Lance entered from the pantry hidden behind ten cookie boxes. Coco took them from Lance and said condescendingly, "You're a treasure." To Darlene she said, "Nice seeing you again."

"I guess you didn't expect to see so much of me," Darlene said, clutching the bouquet in front of her.

"Jade is looking forward to Isabelle's birthday party," Coco continued as if nothing out of the ordinary had happened. "Lance, let's schedule a playdate; your Isabelle is such a sweetie."

Coco sidled out of the kitchen toward the front door with her bright cookie boxes. Paco leaned his sweaty back against the kitchen island and crossed his arms over his bare chest before Coco called, "*Vayamos, el jardinero*. Help me open the door."

"Sí, señora." Paco strolled into the great room and vanished into the foyer. The front door opened and shut.

"I had no idea how busy it was around here," Darlene said, her face flushed with embarrassment. "Are they going to revoke your cookie distributorship for loose morals?"

Lance shrugged. "No one else wants to do it."

"Oh, honey," said Darlene, "that sounds so pathetic. You'll always be my cookie man. C'mon over and show this little Scout some sugar," she said with false bravado, but when he approached she sniffed: "You smell ripe, Lance."

"It's from lifting all those heavy cookies," he said. "Besides, it's hot today."

"Not as hot as Barstow," Darlene said, sweeping aside the San Diego Union-Tribune dramatically. She boosted herself up, butt first, onto the kitchen island. "C'mon," she said, "let's do it!" She snapped one bra strap down, revealing a round bouncy breast. She shimmied once and winked. She was trying hard to be spontaneously sexual for the second time that day—and the first had been, well, disastrous. She felt like hell about that and couldn't come up with a quick emotional spackle fix. Her carelessness and preoccupation had given Belle another episode to tell some future therapist.

Darlene tried to forget about scarring Belle for life that morning and live in the present. She smiled at her husband with her endearing chin-tucked smile that had hooked Lance before she even knew his name. She was more beautiful than she thought she was, not because of any single feature but because of the animated glow she never saw reflected when she looked at herself in the mirror. She held Lance's dark brown eyes, which were impenetrable, possibly sleepy, with her caffeinated green-hazel ones. The dryer buzzed insistently.

"Laundry," Lance said, "it'll just be a minute."

Darlene chilled on the granite. She rolled her eyes, and then rolled her head in small circles. She conjured up an early memory of Lance. She'd seen him around before at keg parties on the beach, but the day she remembered most vividly was when she'd been a UCSD junior applying for a hostess job at the tony Hotel Valencia. She saw Lance across Prospect Street and yelled to him, instantly mortified by her own boldness. She was more than pleasantly surprised when he dismounted his ten-speed in one fluid motion, his left leg forming a brief arabesque before setting down on the opposite side.

Lance was casually muscular, with narrow hips and wide shoulders. She liked a wide-shouldered man, she realized, as she studied him standing behind his well-maintained bicycle (an early clue that he was more guarded than he appeared). His face was open and deeply tanned beneath salt-matted, sun-streaked shoulder-length hair. He was not conventionally handsome with his deep-set dark eyes under hooded lids, and a well-defined mouth a little too Mick Jagger full, with two precise, cartoonish peaks. Still, Lance was the cutest surfer boy with whom Darlene ever thought she possibly had a chance.

Darlene could tell Lance was happy to see her, smiling and nodding on the street as if he had all the time in the world. She didn't quite know how to break the small talk barrier. She wasn't smooth. Neither was he. She twirled her hair. He squeezed the hand brakes. When she looked at him there was no bold-face headline that he was the one, no swoopy Hollywood John Williams score telegraphing big romantic emotions. And yet, with the sedate whoosh of La Jolla traffic behind her, she had the distinct feeling, a flight in her stomach accompanied by a total inability to string a sentence together, that he could be the one.

Darlene was the first to break their connection. She backed away, saying she had to return to campus. He pointed out the nearby cottage court where he lived and said, "Number seven; stop by and have a brewski."

"Number seven," Darlene had repeated, never figuring she'd have the guts to knock on his door. But then, three weeks later, she split from her current boyfriend, the controlling pre-law student Clive, and dragged her distraught ass to bungalow seven, half hoping Lance wouldn't be there. He was.

Lance invited Darlene into the cozy but damp cottage where he still lived after his mother's death. He placed her in the bat-tered wicker club chair, made her mint tea, and sat, cross-legged, on the hardwood floor. Darlene cried and vented and mourned her failed relationship. She felt no need for self-censorship in Lance's presence. It was as if everything she said was impor-tant to him because it came from her. He listened intently. Dinnertime came and he cooked her miso soup, followed by a medicinal glass of Blue Nun. Afterward, he ran a bath, lit candles, made Ivory soap bubbles, and invited Darlene into the chipped claw-foot tub. When she hesitated, he handed her a bamboo-patterned blue kimono, way too short for her five-foot-nine frame, and turned to leave. Darlene called him back and he returned shyly, slipping into the bath opposite her, their knees touching.

"Look," Lance had said, pointing to the small rectangular window on the opposite wall. Darlene was surprised to see a dinky temporary church fair set up in the distance, seemingly captured in the casing. The Ferris wheel lights were just coming out in the dusk, a sapphire and ruby necklace set against the throat of the darkening sky. She took it as a sign that she had stumbled on something magical, an unexpected treasure framed in rough wood.

Darlene and Lance never really dated: no dinners out separated by a red-checked cloth and awkward table manners; and no first movie spent holding hands in the dark. Still, Darlene had never been treated better. Lance was the caregiver Darlene hadn't realized she needed; she was the spark that had been missing in his damp cottage life. She wasn't coming from a place of disappointment and neglect; and, in his mother's absence, he yearned to stop drifting and share the company of a generous, good-hearted woman.

What Darlene and Lance had wasn't a relationship exactly, it just *was*. She never doubted that he was the one for her. She was committed to this partnering, as her parents had been to each other. She understood that marriage had peaks and valleys, but she was a realist and had no desire to stray. She still found Lance attractive even if sex on demand was no aphrodisiac.

Over a dozen years since their wedding, they continued to roll on with little analysis on the part of either partner. They'd never formed a working mechanism to hash out and resolve differences. Lance avoided confrontation. Darlene, who tended to react, had little to react against. And so, when they began to drift apart, it was as if they didn't know how to return to their impulsive beginning—that shared bath.

Back in their designer kitchen, Darlene sat up straight and tugged her bra strap, making her tit jiggle pleasantly. Not bad for a mommy, she thought, and called, "Whatcha doing?"

"Folding laundry," he said.

"Lance, baby, I have to be back at work." Darlene sighed. She had been excited by rushing in, midday, ready for action; and then there was that clownish neighbor and the gardener— how shame-making. And now Lance was ignoring her after she'd made herself as available as a prawn on a party tray.

"Were you talking to me?" Lance asked, entering the kitchen behind a load of turquoise towels, intentionally oblivious. Darlene grabbed the top towel, wrapped herself in it, and made for the stairs. When Lance arrived in their bedroom, Darlene was yanking off the bedspread. It was unclear whether she was acting out of anger, or false bravado, or both. She had entered the house feeling empowered and aroused behind her giant bouquet, and now she felt diminished. She felt uncomfortable in her own skin. She overcompensated by becoming more aggressive and so she turned and attacked Lance's shorts, grabbing inside for the drawstring.

"Whoa, Nellie," he said, "you don't want me like this."

"Like what?" she asked.

"Smelly," he said, "must shower."

Lance entered the master bath with its two-headed shower that was one of the house's selling points when they bought it ten months before. He began to lather his hair with Aveda Shampure, inhaling the scent with deep cleansing breaths. All he should have wanted to do was make Darlene happy at this moment. She was right. He was the one pushing for another child, and if he slipped, it was playing into her ambivalence about the whole process. Her initiative should have been rewarded. But he'd never been good at sex on demand, and after two transcendent hours with Wren, he was sapped. Everything Darlene did to arouse him made him feel like an avocado molested by a budget shopper.

Wren had awakened something in Lance that he hadn't anticipated. His deepening feelings for her confused him. He was becoming more reliant on their time together. He wondered whether his actions were just a coward's escape from a marriage that was no longer as easy as it had been. He couldn't parse whether the passion he felt for Wren now was any more intense than what he had felt for Darlene in their earliest, most randy days. He wasn't accustomed to analyzing his emotions like this. Lately, he and Darlene seemed so whacked: her manic dress-for-success rise; his inability to answer that most basic cocktail party question: What do you do? A query that was more urgent in Encinitas than in Barstow, where the first question at any barbecue was, Budweiser or Coors? There were so many men unemployed there, anyway, it would hardly have caused a ripple if he'd joined them.

Ambivalent, Lance tried to examine his motives for infidelity: was this just the way men signaled marital discomfort, to shed one woman for the next without examining their role in the relationship's failure? Was he a serial monogamist? That sounded like something requiring FBI profilers. What would it take to save their marriage? He gulped. Did it need saving? Would having a baby restore balance? Or was that what was throwing them off—his pressure for more kids and Darlene's reticence?

And what had Darlene done to merit his betrayal, right when she was taking the most personal risks in her own life? She deserved better than him. Belle deserved better. But that was a cop-out, too, like saying she'd be better off without him, so please, dump him, because he was incapable of initiating that action himself. What a cliché. He refused to accept or own that level of personal failure. He was better than that.

Lance remembered the first time he saw Darlene, at a keg party on the bay beach. It was clear and calm that night, the sudden drop in temperature after sundown hardly noticed by the partiers. He spotted her just after the big crescendo of fireworks launched nightly at SeaWorld across Mission Bay, as tourist families turned indoors to escape the chill. Darlene was smashed and barefoot, braless. She twisted her blond hair in a random knot on the back of her head, anchored with an oversized pink paper clip. She tried to teach Lance to polka until her boyfriend, Clive, arrived and reclaimed her. Lance shuffled backward to rejoin the single guys circling the keg. He had watched Darlene fold into her boyfriend, the vibrant light extinguished like a torch in a bucket. He had wanted to see that light again, to make her shine.

Five months later, Darlene and Clive argued over who was dumping whom. Shortly thereafter, she moved into Lance's moldy cottage with two suitcases and enough ambition for both of them. She filed Lance's junior college application and, once enrolled, he gravitated toward meteorology, a field that had interested him since the day he fled New Jersey. He studied "Understanding Weather Forecasting," "Elements of Physical Oceanography," and required a tutor to survive "Synoptic Applications of Dynamic Meteorology."

Lance's success had less to do with texts and labs, and more to do with his laid-back approach on camera; he became the least wacky of weathermen at the school station, the surfers' favorite for his ability to read tides and report the locations for the best waves. It wasn't a skill much in demand in Barstow, at least 150 miles east of the coast, but that was where he landed his first professional gig.

Darlene required an engagement ring to follow Lance to the desert backwater, figuring that she would return to graduate school after a few years of real-world experience. They'd married on the fly before the move and, afterward, he'd appreciated the stability of their shared domestic life. It was Darlene who flinched first. When Lance didn't land a job in a larger market, she began plotting their escape from Barstow. Now that she was working like a demon and he was unemployed, he didn't crave his old job. He had liked the idea of being a weatherman but not the repetition, the forced banter with the shellacked anchorman, the cardboard cutout of himself he became on camera. But he did miss how the career defined his place in the pecking order, and he was dismayed how lacking one changed the way he and Darlene related to each other. And, for that reason, he had felt compelled to keep up the job search, or at least the appearance of looking for one.

The bathroom door opened. Darlene entered naked, her shoulders rounded. "Hey, Cookie Man," she said softly. Lance opened his eyes. Suds swamped them.

"Grab me a towel, baby?" he asked, rubbing his eyes.

"Don't rub." Darlene got a hand towel and took it to Lance in the shower. While he wiped the soap from his eyes, she moved in, standing pelvis to pelvis with her husband and taking his penis in her right hand.

"I thought you said don't rub," Lance said, smirking.

"Your eyes," she replied, working his member. It just wouldn't cooperate.

"Paco can see us," he said, looking toward the shower window.

"There's nothing to see, Lance."

Lance kissed the top of her head.

"Don't get my hair wet," she said, defeated. She retreated. "I have to get back to work, baby. I'm sorry. I shouldn't have rushed home. I tried. All I do is try; I'm very trying . . . ,"

Darlene said, frantically toweling off her torso, and heading toward the bathroom door.

"Come back, baby. We've got lift-off," Lance called to Darlene from inside the shower.

"Too late," Darlene said before she left the steamy bathroom, shutting the door behind her.

Lance squeezed cream rinse into his palm and then massaged it into his scalp. He felt his hairline receding, but when he examined the crown of his head, there didn't seem to be any thinning. He'd have to double-check in the mirror. He rinsed his hair and opened his eyes and caught Paco looking up at him, making no attempt to hide his gaze. Lance did a big princess wave and then turned when he heard the bathroom door. Darlene stuck her head in for a final word: "Remember, we have dinner at Alec and Wren's this Friday. Seven-ish. Can you call Wren and see if we should bring a dish?"

"Why is there a dinner party the night before you open?"

"Apparently Wren's sister, Robin, will be in town."

"She is?"

"She will be," Darlene said. "I don't want to go. I'm stressed as it is. But Alec insists. He said we'll make it an early night and Julia will babysit. I left you a list of things you have to do before Belle's birthday party on Saturday."

"Did you check with Belle to see what she wants?" Lance asked.

"Barbie cake; balloons; presents—what more could she want?"

"Have you asked her?"

"What little girl wouldn't want a monster party?" Darlene asked, but she repressed a spasm of doubt even as she continued, "You worry about your part, I'll worry about mine."

"Yes, dear," Lance said in the subservient way he knew Darlene hated. When the door shut, he cried, "And don't forget to schedule a fuck session."

chapter 4

"A fuck session," Darlene sniffed when she was back in the Saab. She was horny. She was hot. She peeled out of the garage, turned right, and sped downhill past a raccoon road pizza. She felt a rising panic. Her worries about the diner franchise began to balloon as Saturday's opening party neared. (Had she ordered enough balloons?) The concerns seemed to color everything else: parenting, driving—and lovemaking.

Darlene liked sex. Ever since her first openmouthed kiss under the eaves in a junior high breezeway before school. She was good at it. Not slutty, and not so experimental, either. She still wanted to be romanced. She wanted hot baths and chilled champagne. She'd take cold Heineken. She remembered the first bath she'd shared with Lance, at his little La Jolla cottage, but she couldn't remember the last. It wasn't in the new house, she knew that.

Darlene ducked the Saab under I-5 and stopped for a red light. A bus blasted past bearing a giant ad with the banner head-line AMERICA'S FASTEST GROWING CITY above a picture of a pregnant San Diego Mayor Hackett. The square-jawed ex-volleyball star encircled two towheaded children with muscular arms. Below, in smaller type, was the slogan, "She can Hackett."

"I'm glad *she* can hack it," Darlene said. She felt like there was a stack of books—*What to Expect* guides, she suspected—on her chest. She had always insisted motherhood wouldn't change her. She didn't have two different faces, one for adults and one for kids. No baby talk—ever. No bullshit. Kids weren't stupid, or oblivious. Belle wasn't. Like that morning. What a disaster. "Only making love"; okay, that was bullshit. But sometimes stock phrases flew out of your mouth when you were a parent. Not that Darlene would ever have interrupted her own par-ents. Their room was off-limits at the far end of their U-shaped house. Besides, as okay as Darlene's folks were, they weren't warm. She couldn't imagine climbing in bed between them like Belle did with her and Lance.

Married couples were either lovers or parents first, Darlene figured. Hers were the former: she and her brothers had been well fed and clothed, neither neglected nor nurtured. Her folks were totally into each other, with their nature walks and solo trips to the Sea of Cortez, their Spanish lessons and *Smithso-nian* magazine subscription. They had been the loves of each other's lives from the day they met over a Bunsen burner in college chemistry when her father staged a pillar of smoke to get her mother's attention.

Darlene hardly talked to her parents now without getting a lecture on brown rice and whole grains, wild salmon the wonder-fish. Let Belle eat Lucky Charms and Hostess Sno Balls. Let her enjoy them while she was still running around enough that she wouldn't wear them on her hips. Was Darlene rebelling against her parents? Sure. She couldn't buck psychology. But she wasn't blaming them, either. It wasn't as if she was, in turn, the most responsive of parents, putting Belle first in all things. She wasn't one to get down on the ground and dress Polly Pocket dolls in little rubber disco boleros and Jell-O-orange boots, or play Clue like Lance did.

When had it become so hard just to sit still and play? Men had Peter Pan complexes, but women had the Wendy Darlings. The Wendys wanted to fly a little and be dazzled by pixie dust, but they were consumed with relationships and caretaking and what the neighbors thought. Wendy's lost boys were content to fly; Wendy had to civilize. She couldn't abandon herself to wild dancing by firelight with the Indian braves; she had to funnel them all back into London middle-class respectability. Wendy was in such haste to grow up and become the mother, that central domestic figure; to children, their mother's skirts were the world.

As skeptical as Darlene was of Wendy, it saddened her that she wasn't that safe maternal haven for Belle. Lance, not Darlene, had become the Ramsays' emotional center of gravity, the figure waiting at the window with the lit candle whenever Belle ventured outside. When Belle cried, she cried for her father. Darlene admired Lance's gift for parenting: he had a better understanding of Belle's needs just by listening, by waiting out her defenses with quiet talk and infinite patience. But Darlene was also a little jealous of it. She was somewhat confounded by her own emotional limits, like a person who thought she'd rented a spacious apartment and found, once she'd unloaded her furniture, there was hardly room to turn around in.

The truth was, Belle was daddy's little girl—something Darlene had never been and had always craved being. In the Ramsays' tight triangular relationship, the relationship of parents with only children, that left Darlene out in the cold. She reacted by distancing herself from both Lance and Belle. She simultaneously hoped they would reach out to her, and yet searched for a place like her diner, where she was central, as she had been central when it was just her and Lance.

But wasn't that an argument for having more kids? Darlene tried to visualize their next baby, maybe a mama's boy. She tried to spin out the imaginary threads of the child's life, to see his face, hear his laughter, and imagine his obsessions with Yu-Gi-Oh! cards. Howling was all she could conjure, so she unconsciously picked up speed on the Pacific Coast Highway, slaloming on the curves north of Torrey Pines. On her right, the Pacific glittered like panels of aluminum foil, distracting. Come play now. Don't plan. Let go.

Darlene remembered the first three months after she had Belle. They were the hardest days of her marriage. Everyone acted as if she was supposed to be blissfully happy, but she'd never felt so incompetent. Pregnancy was okay, but once the baby arrived, everything else failed. When she bathed Belle, she feared she'd either drop her or drown her. And the nursing. She couldn't nurse. The baby didn't latch. Her nipples were like chew toys. She went from capable wife to a motherhood wash-out. It only made her feel more pathetic that it was all supposed to come naturally.

The big meltdown occurred a few nights after Belle's birth. At two-thirty A.M., when Darlene was so sleep-deprived she would have confessed to any crime if only she were allowed a four-hour nap on a concrete floor, she begged Lance to call the lactation consultant. She couldn't breast-feed on her own, but she hated to ask for help. Ninety minutes later, a plump fairy breast mother with brown bangs arrived with her claims that even—unbelievable—fathers could nurse.

The consultant, Astrid, removed a breast pump from her macramé bag as if it were a kilo of home-grown pot. She unraveled the transparent rubber tubes and yellow suction cups while she explained to Darlene that nursing was absolutely natural. Darlene had bristled, but Astrid assured her that she'd never known one woman who couldn't master and enjoy the pleasures of nursing, potentially for two full years. If Darlene hadn't already been attached by her tits to the sucker, she would have bolted. She lay there with some stranger rubbing her own hands for warmth and touching Darlene's breasts. Astrid gave them the occasional squeeze and shift to keep the milk flowing. Darlene's sense of individuality seemed to ebb away through her own convex nipples. She had felt like a cow, as she tried to capture first one, then two ounces of milk. Astrid peered down encouragingly, as she had on countless other women with breasts large and small, nipples like Tootsie Rolls or goose bumps. While Lance had stood alongside, eager to learn, Darlene didn't think he understood the indignity of being milked to someone constitutionally opposed to domestication.

Darlene felt entirely uninspired to repeat that natural experience. Motherhood made her feel like an unnatural woman. Wasn't there a Carole King song there? *You make me feel like an unnatural woman; oh, baby, what you've done to me.* There were so many things women never sang about: Where was King's breastfeeding ballad? Or Judy Collins's miscarriage lament? Or sobwriter Laura Nyro's postpartum depression wail? Darlene had caved to peer pressure and the surgeon general, but breastfeeding never made her feel one with the universal mother. On Belle's first birthday, Darlene retired her breasts. A year later, as she cleaned up ground-in cupcake spores from the checkerboard linoleum in their Barstow rental on Belle's second birthday, she ditched her life as a stay-at-home mom—at least in her own mind.

In order to regain her sanity between Belle and Lance's weekend weatherman duties, Darlene sought out a productive outlet. She needed to escape the endless discussions of childproofing, toilet training, or how much TV a child should watch. It amazed her that it was Lance who totally dug those discussions and was more connected to the other mothers. He kept the *What to Expect* books dog-eared on his bedside table. She began to feel inadequate in comparison, swinging between delegating child-rearing duties and resentment that he was more capable. What kind of man was he? But worse was its corollary insecurity: what kind of woman was she?

Around that time, Darlene realized she needed to get out of the house. She read the want ads and wasn't surprised that there was no local demand for sociology graduates. On the other hand, she felt a pent-up demand that corporate America had yet to recognize and exploit: mothers needed a hipper place to congregate than the ball pit at the local McDonald's. She would open an eatery. She wanted to call it the Bitch-Inn. Lance suggested she try a part-time job; particularly since, he reminded her, she couldn't even cook an edible grilled-cheese sandwich.

Instead, Darlene found a shuttered Barstow diner, a pit stop on the road between Los Angeles and Las Vegas. She drained a small inheritance to rescue it from foreclosure and then, assisted by Target, remade it into a haven for Barstow moms. Darlene's Diner was born. And, having asked around, she discovered the secret to the perfect toasted cheese: simplicity, salted butter, Wonder Bread, and real American cheese that wasn't individually wrapped. Turning a challenge into an opportunity, she made good old grilled cheese, cooked to a golden brown, the centerpiece of her new enterprise.

Darlene understood that consumer culture had yet to catch on to the needs of her generation—and that was her innovation as a businesswoman. Disenfranchised mothers needed a place to vent and laugh. She knew how crappy it could be on baby watch, and that it was nobody's fault. Even getting an anthropology degree couldn't prepare liberated girls for slumping on futon couches like Zulus with their tops down. They dreaded what they would say to their husbands when they asked the inevitable question: "What did you do all day?" Answer: "Argghhh." These weren't women who could afford in-home child care, the balm of the upper-middle-class working mother who had to confess that returning to work often felt like a vacation. At least there they could go to the bathroom by themselves.

At Darlene's Diner back in Barstow, the waitresses doubled as a constant supply of babysitters, so that Belle could be with her mom when she wasn't with Lance between his weatherman shifts. And the restaurant didn't just solve Darlene's individual maternal distress. The diner's toddler corral became a favorite dumping-off point for mothers on the verge of committing hari-kari. And it was good for the waitresses, too; they tended to be single mothers desperate for a place to work where they could occasionally bring their kids when the sitter's kids had the flu.

Darlene created a spot where mothers and children felt safe. This was her contribution to motherhood in general, even if it didn't make her a better individual mother. But, hey, if she was happy, wouldn't Belle be happy, too? At the diner, they were the Underground Railroad for overeducated mommies unaccustomed to grunt work, forlorn feminists without the sense of humor to realize this was the punch line of a joke that was long in coming. At Darlene's, if a kid wanted a bread-and-mustard sandwich, she'd say, "You got it." And if that kid wailed like he'd just been beaten because the diner lacked his favorite brand of mustard, she didn't look askance at the mother tethered to his side with the unspoken comment, *You don't cut it, you're not—gasp—a good mother.*

The diner's exuberant success surprised Darlene. She walked the aisles in a pink polyester waitress uniform and fuzzy slippers, feeling competent, generously doling out free sundaes. She had a knack for making guests feel welcome and attracting good talent, and an iron will when axing slacker employees. The diner made her happy, and that, in turn, made her family happy.

The best times were when Darlene, Lance, and Belle were all there together, vibrating at their own speeds but content to be under one leaky roof. Belle would be at her corner table working the crayons or Lincoln Logs, surrounded by kids of various ages, at the epicenter of friendship, a network that spiraled out to include the playground and schoolyard. Lance sat nearby, legs outstretched, drinking bottomless cups of coffee and sharing advice with slog-weary mothers (for a feverish child, call the pediatrician within twenty-four hours if the fever rose to between 104 and 105 degrees, or visit the emergency room if it hit 105). And Darlene buzzed between the front door and the tables and the kitchen, the fact that she could never sit still a virtue in that environment.

Darlene's friendly glow was like a beacon to customers. Locals returned as much to be a part of this extended family as for the great coffee. What began with a simple grilled-cheese sandwich grew to twenty-seven varieties and a gala celebration during National Grilled Cheese Month in April. But Darlene had never anticipated that, over time, the restaurant's good vibe would start attracting a broader crowd. Hollywood drivers would stop en route to Vegas, and return, sending friends. When she went to twenty-four hours, there was a lively flow of travelers that filled the place, big tippers she welcomed back with her toothy smile.

Alec Marker entered Darlene's Diner late one spring night. He was returning from Las Vegas, disappointed by a dud business prospect, and dreading his meeting the next morning with an L.A. business partner. He was a tall, broad-shouldered Baby Boomer originally from Massapequa, Long Island, who knew how to fill a booth, the eldest brother in an Irish Catholic, Kennedy-worshipping family of boys, and thus more used to leading than to being held accountable. He liked blondes, and by three A.M., Darlene was sitting opposite him, trying to keep her long legs from bumping into his. She refilled his coffee, and brought him a second Jarlsberg, avocado, and bacon on sprouted wheat, and listened to his plans to expand her diner across the country, starting first in a California urban center, then expanding outward and upward across the West, until they became the next IHOP. She liked his deep, sure voice as much as his dream for her future—but assumed he'd never return.

Darlene was wrong; she knew nothing about Alexander Graham Marker.

Two weeks later, Alec returned with a sheaf of legal documents and became, despite Lance's reservations, Darlene's business partner and chief financial backer. He transformed her shaggy but marginally profitable dream born out of sleep deprivation and desperation into something larger. It was also more unwieldy. This past month her stomach had churned in a way it hadn't since eighth-grade algebra. In four days, she and Alec would launch the flagship Darlene's Diner on Balboa Boulevard with a big Saturday afternoon party hooked on Belle's eleventh birthday. The plan was to create a birthday mill and ice-cream parlor that also catered to adult needs, with twenty-seven varieties of grilled cheese, including sophisticated offerings like spinach, Brie, caramelized onions, and plum chutney on ciabatta. There would also be safe zones for parents to drop off their kids in order to relax in a more adult-friendly space (bar included).

Today, as Darlene sped south in the Saab, feeling stressed and insecure, she worried that she had become caught in the vortex of Alec's dream and had lost track of her own. She missed those days at the diner when she had been part of that tight triangle, she, Belle, and Lance. But she didn't miss Barstow. Not one bit.

chapter 5

All the Zen euphoria Lance had felt with Wren had evaporated with the scent of the lavender candles. He stepped out of the shower, toweled off, shaved, and padded from the bathroom to the bedroom. Glancing around, Lance considered the Danish modern furniture as if entering a hotel room. It was nice enough, but he hadn't chosen it. Darlene had. At that moment, he was entirely detached from it. He felt numb to his surroundings, as if he could exit naked and leave almost nothing of himself behind. He imagined exiting the front door into the glare off the white stucco, through the tended garden, past the birds-of-paradise and the ADP Security sign. He could stroll down the scrubbed sidewalk past new houses with Mediterranean Revival facades—and could keep walking, north or south, along the coast and start fresh. But he wondered if he would get a nowhere-paycheck beach bum job, charm a woman, maybe have a child, a dog, a cat that slept on his pillow and licked his ear, and spiral back to where he was now, appraising a bedroom to which he had no connection, a headboard, two lamps, and a copy of *The Idiot's Guide to Tantric Sex* hidden beneath a *Girl Scout Handbook* in one of the matching side tables.

And then Lance considered his Girl Scout, Belle. He couldn't leave her. She was his skin. It was as if she had come out of his body, not Darlene's. He and Darlene kept reassuring Belle the move from Barstow was good for her, but she was as adrift as he was. They had brought Belle into the land of playdates, where every encounter was staged and scheduled. On Saturdays, there was not a child roaming the neighborhood. He could hear them splash in backyard pools, see them entering SUVs with tennis gear, baseball bats, in white karate pajamas with bright orange belts, with oversized birthday presents, on the conveyer belt of packaged pleasures, parents wary that someone would snatch up their daughters or that their sons would follow a soccer ball into traffic and corrugate their dreams.

Lance grabbed his shorts (balled on the carpet, dragons deflated) and scored a hamper free throw. He walked to the adjacent dressing room where there were three walls of closets with wooden sliding doors. Lance's suits and pants filled half of one. Inside that closet, pant legs and shirttails grazed his mother's beaten Empire bureau with its scarred veneer.

The old chest had been a bone of contention when they

moved to Encinitas. Darlene had implored Lance to leave it behind; Lance had resisted. He'd stood his ground in the usual way: not arguing with her, just ensuring that it made the moving van. It was the only furniture that Ethel had shipped across country from New Jersey. It wasn't much of a legacy, but it was his.

Ethel and Lance had been marginal people in La Jolla. It was as if they were expected to disappear between seasons, to be gone by the time the Santa Ana winds arrived, but they didn't. He remembered how small she had become in their California bungalow, more sister than mother. And then, one damp afternoon during his high school senior year, Ethel cooked a pot of miso soup and retreated to her bed. He came home from busing tables at the Chart House and found the soup burned, seaweed stuck to the bottom of the pot, and his mother lying curled on her bed in her white tofu-colored shoes and a Mexican wool poncho, dead. Material goods had never meant much to his mother; they meant even less to him.

Lance dug around the second drawer of Ethel's old chest and removed his navy-blue Ocean Pacific shorts with baby-blue hibiscus blossoms flowering up the sides and stepped into them. From the drawer below he chose a light blue San Diego Zoo T-shirt emblazoned with DISCOVER THE BEAST WITHIN. As he popped the T-shirt over his head, Lance wondered what had happened to the free-range children of his childhood. During those New Jersey summers when he was growing up, the local kids had gathered on the double-wide lawn that sloped from his house to the neighbor's: a soccer field, a baseball diamond, a Slip 'N Slide dream. It rolled to a stream at the back and a jumble of pines and spruce and maple, the rambles with the best and scariest hiding spots during their all-neighborhood twilight games of hide-and-seek. The games attracted kids from four to fourteen, although occasionally the teens would pair off and disappear to fondle each other in the woods beyond, away from their parents' prying eyes, and still within hearing distance of the olly olly oxen frees, the parents' final calls once the ten o'clock news of slaughter and baseball scores had run its course.

Lance was ten the last summer he spent there. There were more fireflies than mosquitoes that year. It was easy to distract the littlest kids with stories of fairies that carried off the young and put them to work in the bowels of old oaks boiling sap into sugar syrup. That was the summer he and Carl, his next-door neighbor (who had a dime-sized divot just beneath his right eye courtesy of a missile from Lance's slingshot), had created the best hiding place ever. It was a secret bower beneath entwined lilac bushes.

One evening late in the summer, Lance saw his father appear at the top of the lawn, square-jawed, pale-faced, his tailored white shirt glowing in the ten o'clock twilight, the ice in his highball tinkling as he swished away a nonexistent bug. Carl and Lance watched Mr. Ramsay. He was half smiling, looking down at his neighbors' Colonial and at the children rising up from their hiding places like fireflies, hardly knowing what these children's names were any more than he knew the names of the garden flowers. Behind him, in the house, in the bright square of light coming from the kitchen window, his wife Ethel stood on a stool. She bent her head scrubbing pots, her face unreadable especially to children too busy running wild out of doors to study the strange stories in their parents' expressions.

Carl and Lance had run up the hill and dragged Mr. Ramsay to see their hiding place. The man resisted, disliking dampness on his leather soles, but, a little drunk, he let the boys lead him down the slope behind the two houses, down to their hollow beneath the overgrown lilacs. Lance registered his father's amazement when they pulled aside the branches and revealed the cozy spot within, with its soft bed of leaves lit by a Coleman battery-operated lantern, an old quilt, a stack of plastic-wrapped comic books. Mr. Ramsay followed the boys inside, stooping over while they sat cross-legged, one hand on the ground for balance, the other on his glass. "Good work," he said, in his soft German-accented English, "marginal but acceptable." It was his highest praise and then he left the boys to their schemes, saying come up soon, bedtime, meaning it was time for Mr. Ramsay to go to bed and he wouldn't want to be disturbed.

"Marginal but acceptable," Lance repeated now as he went downstairs. It had been ages since he remembered that phrase. He hurried through the laundry room and outside, where it was bright and hot. He watched the tentacled automatic pool cleaner slowly make its circuit, blindly bumping against the Spanish-tiled sides and inching into the next quadrant. He didn't even have to clean the pool.

Lance really had made an effort to find a job when they'd first arrived in San Diego County. All last spring he'd sent out résumés and put on his best suit for informational interviews at the handful of local TV stations. One by one, they'd rejected him. The farthest he'd gotten was an on-camera audition at one local network affiliate, but he'd failed to laugh heartily enough at the anchor's jokes, and was later told by the general manager's secretary that he just wasn't right for the mix. And that was the best experience. Another station offered him an unpaid internship on the weekend shift, telling him he needed to retool if he seriously considered a future TV career. It had been demoralizing—and he'd certainly felt like a tool.

Now he exited the side gate beneath effusive magenta bougainvillea, dangling his keys from a ring with a plastic photo of Belle riding a mechanical jousting pony at Legoland. He looked down at her joyous face framed by a mass of black curls and his morale lifted: *I'm not useless in Belle's eyes,* he reflected as he climbed in the minivan, *or Wren's.* He cranked the engine, and turned north out of the carport onto Pacific Breeze past the Montoyas' McMansion, on the way to pick up Belle at school.

To the west, on Lance's left, the Pacific was a bright glow beyond the houses. If it wasn't for the brilliant orange of the occasional Japanese maple, it could have been summer now that the Santa Ana winds were blowing off the desert. To Lance's right lay a series of raw earth terraces where a developer was planning to build four houses if he could survive divorce court with enough working capital. And beyond, to the east, over the freeway, were the endless developments with idyllic Spanish names built on the north county wildfire plain: Rancho Bernardo, Ramona, and Temecula.

Lance coasted past Encinitas Park. Before he and Wren began scheduling playdates for their kids—and then each other—they often met by chance at this sedate green overlooking Rancho Amigo Elementary School. He hadn't even known she was Alec's wife that first morning shortly after the Ramsays had moved from Barstow. Darlene had slept in after a night of manic unpacking and Lance had swooped Belle to the park to kick a ball around and keep it quiet at home. It was a gorgeous Saturday: sixty-nine degrees below a turquoise sky that only faded when it met the southbound Los Angeles smog. Far below, on the Rancho Amigo playground, the junior high school marching band practiced with no discernible unified beat. He'd confessed to Wren that he'd never played an instrument; Wren said she'd opted for the flute, but passed out during her first lesson and prematurely ended her musical career. There was nothing in that day, in their generic conversation, or in the way that Sam and Belle began passing the soccer ball between them, keeping it away from Sam's little brother Max, that boded for any bigger connection. Just two parents passing like scooters in the park.

The next time they saw each other, Lance and Wren discovered that their spouses were business partners and laughed that they were so out of the loop they'd never met. They liked each other. They talked but were just as happy sharing the Zen silence. Unlike some of the other caregivers who considered the park exile, they enjoyed themselves: the sun, the grass, the slow movement of the clouds, the children's cries. They even appreciated the minuscule dramas: the scary dog, the truck fought over, the grass burns met by Neosporin and a Sponge-Bob Band-Aid. And when Max started his hitting phase, Lance had been understanding and encouraged Belle to play with the toddler. Of course, Max never hit Belle.

Over the next few months, these chance park-bench meetings began to happen so regularly Lance and Wren knew it wasn't coincidence, but neither would cop to it. They were like teen crushes that cruised the familiar spots so that they could connect as if by chance. The pair relished those intense, familiar adolescent feelings, long gone from both their marriages. At that moment, cruiser and cruised were bound solely by their desire to see each other more than anyone else. There was no commitment, no social acknowledgment that they were a couple. It was an elaborate game of tag that could extend for miles and months.

But then their cruising phase was over. They began making indoor playdates for the kids. To pass the time, Wren taught Lance yoga in her scented meditation room on Obsidian Lane. Then, while Julia the tongue-pierced babysitter watched Max and the sixth-graders attended school, they continued the lessons at Lance's house. They sat cross-legged, facing each other across Wren's orange throw that smelled like her room, musk and lavender. They matched each other breath for breath. He learned every line on her face. She recognized the constellation of chicken pox scars that he'd gotten after roughhousing with his friend Carl when they were five and quarantined together.

Lance and Wren's yoga lessons became the most intimate part of their day. He joked that it was like sex without physical contact; she admitted she had always wanted to try tantric sex. He asked: What was that? She began to show him. They began to make playdates for themselves. Lance couldn't characterize himself as a cheating hubby, but what was he: a husband with tantric hobbies?

Lance glanced at the park in his rearview mirror. Dogs crisscrossed the hills while their owners drank Starbucks. It was dog time at Encinitas Park. The neighborhood had decreed specific hours when residents could unleash their pets in the park. Lance wanted a beagle but Darlene didn't want the hassle, even though he would assume the responsibility. ("They smell," she said. "They bark.") Ultimately, she conceded a little and let Lance buy Belle the turtle, which Darlene now insisted must be let out of his environment and walked twice a day, a convenient excuse for her to say, "Imagine if we had a dog." Lance thought, *It might be capable of displaying affection*, but said nothing.

Lance knew he relied on Darlene's vitality, her drive. They had gotten as far as they had because of her; she'd yanked him out of the torpor he'd hardly been aware of since Ethel had driven him out of Princeton Junction for the last time. He had Belle, and he had met Wren, thanks to Darlene. And he knew that somewhere there had been that same spark with Darlene that he felt with Wren now. What he didn't know was how to find the road back to that place with his wife. And did he want to?

As Lance turned left, he was aware he could get lost just picking Belle up at school. He had no sense of direction. Since the move, he hardly drove anywhere without Belle or Darlene—his human compasses. He could find Starbucks, Safeway, and Swami's Beach, but when Darlene wanted him to meet her downtown, his hands got sweaty. Once, he landed alone in the long line headed toward the Tijuana border on a Friday afternoon. It took three hours to enter Mexico and turn around. The Border Patrol pulled him over and German shepherds smelled his car down to the spark plugs because he was so freaked he appeared suspicious.

It was only two-thirty P.M. when Lance made his first pass by Rancho Amigo. The five-year-old elementary school was a maze of single-story stucco buildings with breezeways instead of internal hallways (better for control). On a dry patch of lawn, the sign said RANCHO AMIGO ELEMENTARY. A kid had scrawled RAUNCHY GRINGO PENITENTIARY with indelible marker the first week of school, and the ghost of his creativity remained.

Too early for dismissal, Lance drove downhill to the Pacific Coast Highway. He had time for a half-decaf, half-caf latte. The lot was crowded, so he parked in back by the Dumpster. He ran in, scanned for Wren, got coffee, and returned to his car. He was debating whether to return to Swami's Beach or get an early spot on the mommy line at Rancho, when there was a knock on his passenger window. It was Wren's babysitter, Julia, grabbing a chai latte before skateboarding uphill to Rancho Amigo to pick up eleven-year-old Sam. (Max was at the pediatrician's with his mother.)

The UCSD psych major had an Austrian harvest maiden's broad face. Julia was born to wear a dirndl and steal an Aryan farm boy's heart, but she did everything to thwart that look. The twenty-year-old had braided her honey-blond hair in cornrows; a beaded silver ring pierced her dark blond brow. When she thumped on Lance's window, he saw the black Maori tattoo encircling her biceps. He hit auto-unlock; to do anything less would have been considered unfriendly. His contact with the young woman had been random, crossing paths while picking up and depositing children when they were rarely alone together. He liked it that way. Chats gravitated toward the weather, or the flu, or whether macaroni and cheese was a meal or side dish. He tried to fly low under her radar, avoiding an aggressive quality he didn't care to engage.

Julia pulled the handle and paused, framed in the car's doorway, revealing all five-foot-seven of her square-shouldered, high-busted muscular body in black biker shorts and spandex tank. She raised her chin (a tick she'd picked up from her corporate lawyer father) and smiled her confident grin. She toed the back of her skateboard so its nose popped into her right hand, and climbed into the passenger seat. She pulled a cherry ChapStick from a waist pouch, stroked her lips, then looked Lance full-on and said, "You look like you haven't taken a crap today."

"Hello to you, too," Lance said, taken aback by her directness.

"I thought that was you," Julia said. "Didn't you see me inside?"

"No," Lance said.

"Give it up," said Julia. "What's wrong?"

Lance didn't reply. He inhaled, exhaled, and inhaled. He tried to align his chakras. In all the Girl Scout cookie madness he hadn't pulled the salmon from the freezer. Could he zap it to defrost? *Salmon, salmon, salmon,* he wrote on a mental Post-it.

Julia watched Lance's tan forehead furrow, carving familiar lines on it. He wasn't much older than she was, she reflected, maybe ten years. She'd fucked teachers older than that, not to mention her father's law partner. And that gold salesman in Athens last summer. And Lance seemed younger than she was in a way she found endearingly aimless but never tolerated in the boys who had attended La Jolla High with her. Maybe it was because he listened to too much Neil Young. But he seemed less mellow today than he usually did when she saw him with Belle, so she said, "C'mon. Tell Mommy."

Lance examined his left knee, the jagged bike accident scar, but couldn't resist sliding his gaze to the pliant bands of muscles underneath Julia's spandex shorts. Was she coming on to him, or was this just the way college girls behaved these days? He said, "I can't discuss it. It's a marriage thing."

"Don't bottle it up," Julia said. "I'm a psych major. I should know. Sometimes it's easier to discuss, um, difficulties, outside the marriage. Just answer yes or no. You don't have to fill in the details."

"Okay," Lance said, peeking at her thighs. The girl had no boundaries.

"Did something happen today?" Julia asked, suddenly clinical.

"Yes," Lance said, keeping it vague. Something happened every day.

"Just now?" Julia probed.

"Yes," Lance said.

"Isn't Darlene at work?"

"Yes," Lance said, and then qualified his answer, "and no."

"She came home from work?"

"Yes."

"And caught you cheating?"

"No," he said, surprised but sounding indignant. "She didn't catch me cheating."

Julia turned in her seat, leaned toward Lance, and pursued, "Afternoon delight?"

"Yes and no," he said, aware their little game had gone too far.

"You're making me crazy," said Julia.

"Occupational hazard," Lance said, struggling to keep the tone light, "when you're a psychologist."

"Okay. Darlene came home. Why?" Julia asked. She paused to consider the possibilities and then pounced: "She wanted action."

"Yes." Lance sighed, the need to talk overcoming his reticence to talk to Julia.

"Right there," Julia said, "right then."

"Yes."

"And you couldn't deliver."

"No," Lance said. "I mean, yes. I didn't deliver."

"Of course not," said Julia.

"Is it the weatherman thing?" Lance asked.

"What weatherman thing?" Julia asked.

"Never mind," Lance said, taking renewed interest in the scar on his knee.

"You're a weatherman?" Julia asked. "I didn't know that."

"At least I was a weatherman back in Barstow." It struck Lance how lousy unemployment made him feel when he was talking to others. What frustrated him was that people judged him by his profession. And, apparently, Darlene did, too. He'd never defined himself by what he did—a busboy, a body surfer, a stay-at-home dad. (The mental Post-it note popped up: *Salmon*. What would Darlene say if he was home all day and didn't manage to defrost dinner?)

"So, our weather isn't good enough for you?" Julia teased. "Today's perfect, tomorrow's better?"

"It's perfect until it isn't," Lance said, sidling into a weather report to evade Julia's personal questions. "With high pressure out of Nevada right now, if those northeast winds coming through the mountains start blowing over fifty miles per hour we could be in for some fierce heat and fire activity."

"There are Santa Ana winds every year," Julia said dismissively. "They blow over."

"Well, this year they're blowing faster and harder, on top of a western North American heat wave that began last June. It's hardly rained since last March. Conditions are aligning to create a perfect firestorm."

"Hey, I'd hire you to be my weatherman."

"You'd be the only one, Julia. Apparently I'm not pro enough for the major stations here; I've already been dinged by all four. San Diego is a bigger market than Barstow. To them, I'm a hick. And the computer graphics I learned are obsolete."

"That would keep me soft," Julia said sympathetically. "You know who your neighbor is, right?"

"Coco's husband?"

"He's the general manager of a local TV station."

"Mr. Gold Chains?" Lance asked with renewed interest. "Which station?"

"I don't know. Ask Coco next time she comes around for cookies, weatherman."

"Jade has to sell more first," Lance said.

"Right, Dad, it's all about those cookies," said Julia sarcastically. "Anyway, your problem with the wife isn't the weatherman thing. It's the sex-on-demand thing. The 'Here's my fish, now fry it' thing. Never works after the first six months. This is what you need," she said, pulling her knees under her butt, turning toward Lance, and, yes, popping his seat belt, "you need coaxing."

"No, I don't, thank you very much. We're parked behind the Starbucks."

"You need someone to hunker down next to your dick with lips that speak its language."

"You know the lost language of dick?" he asked.

"Lean back," she said, "I'm the dick whisperer."

Lance wanted to laugh, but Julia's hands were on his

drawstrings. His throat tightened. It was as if he were in the safe center of the Encinitas free love society. Could it be that if he took no action, he would get more sex (not that it was worth sacrificing his marriage for, because it wasn't, and he knew it wasn't, damn it!) than he had ever desired in the horny frustrated days of his teens?

Yes . . . but.

"Thanks, Julia, but no thanks," he said, and brushed her hands away.

chapter 6

Lance pulled up at Rancho at three-fifteen P.M. with Julia beside him, joining the Volvos and Saabs and occasional dusty-
blue Valiant waiting behind the school buses in front of school.
He was the only father in the pickup line. He glanced to his
right. He wished Julia would exit the minivan. Now. But that
would draw more attention than if she stayed. If the babysitter
had seen him at Starbucks, who else had? And which other
parent parked in the line made the same coffee run and saw
him there? He was getting paranoid.

Across Julia's chest, through the passenger window, Lance
saw a flock of Girl Scouts separating from the main building,
walking side by side toward the cars. They were tall and short,
pressed and raggedy, in green skorts and white blouses and
green sashes, sneakers and platform sandals. Coco's daughter

Jade held the middle—blondes to her left, redheads to her right—her blue-black Apache hair swinging down her back. She had wildly outgrown her peers—and she bore the training bra to prove it.

Belle wandered behind, sweaty and neglected. Her dark curls clustered beneath a green felt beret tilted at a drunken angle, her white shirt half untucked, the eczema twining her forearms exposed. With only the troop number and Girl Scout insignia sewn on, her sash was a bare canvas awaiting badges—Aerospace, Adventure Sports, Art in the Home, and Being My Best; and, someday, Becoming a Teen, if she lived that long.

Belle flunked Jade's finely calibrated scale of playground fabulousness. Her Keds and Lee jeans were fashion crimes. No pink. No sparkle. No flair. Jade had skewered and categorized Belle swifter than an entomologist with a moth: geek. In her low-slung jeans and beaded chunky Target mules, Coco's daughter was leading the troop on a hormonal rush out of girlhood. When she tossed her Apache mane, otherwise repressed male teachers feared for their licenses. The sole factor that stemmed her quest for dominance was her disinterest in the opposite sex; she still wanted to be a star among girls, rather than join the experimenters behind the science bungalow.

Watching Jade and Belle from the relative safety of the van, Lance sympathized with his daughter; the move had been hardest on her and he felt at a loss for a way to ease the transition. He had no nostalgia about being a kid—elementary school was a tough job with intense politics. But the Belle walking toward him today wasn't the daughter he had brought from

Barstow last January, the cheery little soccer-playing cowgirl who always met his eyes with a smile, whose mouth rounded upward even when he woke her for breakfast and she gave him a sleepy hug and whispered, "Lucky Charms," or "Fruit Loops." She used to laugh in her sleep; he loved that. Now she didn't want to get up in the morning. Sunday night after bath was the week's bleakest hour.

The flock of Scouts scattered. Girls broke off in twos and threes. Belle slunk toward the pickup line, alone. "Hey," Belle said with a sigh to Julia when she reached the van.

"Have you seen Sam?" Julia asked.

Belle jerked her head backward to Sam, who had rushed out of school and leapt on his skateboard, despite flattopped sixth-grade teacher Everett Baumgart yelling, "No skating on school property." The eleven-year-old landed curbside, six inches shorter than Belle, with scabby knees and his mother's russet hair in a mullet; Wren's eyes looked out from his freckled face, overlarge, thickly fringed with lashes, trusting.

"Must have food," Sam said.

"How about a playdate?" Julia asked, exiting the van to make room for Belle.

"I don't do playdates," Belle said. "I'm in sixth grade."

"Got any food at your house?" Sam asked.

"Every flavor of Girl Scout cookie," said Lance.

"Coolness," Sam said to Julia, and pointed his board toward Lance's house.

"Let's ride," said Julia, pulling her skateboard from the minivan, and they hit the pavement. Lance flicked his eyes up as he keyed the engine. Julia and Sam appeared like two dolphins in his rearview mirror.

"It smells in here." Belle rolled down her window. "What were you eating?"

"Nothing," said Lance. "How was school?"

"Fine," Belle said. She pulled the Harriet Tubman biography from her backpack, feigning interest. Here came the third degree. "How was home?"

"I did some exciting laundry," Lance said. "I discovered the lost underwear of King Tut."

"Smelly, I bet."

"Luckily I found them after the wash cycle." Lance made a three-point turn that halted traffic in both directions. "What's happening at Rancho, amigo?"

"Nada."

"Who'd you sit by at lunch?"

"No one."

"No one?" Lance said, prodding her gently to tell him more.

"Nobody," Belle said, with a shake of her head. "If the invisible man went to Rancho, he wouldn't sit next to me, either."

"You're exaggerating."

"Only the invisible man part; he graduated."

"What's the deal?" Lance asked. Peripherally, he saw dark clouds crossing Belle's brow, occasionally broken by a look of evil genius defiance. Her anguish hurt him, not only because of the guilt he felt at leaving Barstow. He knew that wherever they were, a parent had to cope with a child's unhappiness as an individual navigating the real world. If he asked Belle her thoughts she would say nothing, but that was because she couldn't verbalize her feelings, at least not without summoning levels of emotion and rage that frightened her. She lacked the benefit of adult hindsight, knowing that "this, too, shall pass." Hell, most adults couldn't manage that perspective, either.

"I want to surrender my sash," Belle said. "I look like a git in this getup."

"You can't just quit Girl Scouts," Lance said.

"Why, Dad?" Belle asked. "Because you have a garage full of cookies?"

"Well, that, yeah," Lance agreed, thinking of the brightly colored cookie boxes filling the pantry, and the dunning calls he still had to make and dreaded. He pushed those thoughts aside and said, "And you haven't given it a chance."

"I'm a conscientious objector."

"Where did you learn that term?" Lance chuckled, impressed.

"Sam."

"Smart kid, Sam."

"And he's not a Girl Scout."

"He's not a girl," Lance said. "What's the deal? Why weren't you eating with the troop?"

"Jade told the scouts that if they ate with me, they could never eat with her again."

"Cold," Lance said.

"The coldest," Belle said.

"Their loss."

"Right," Belle said, looking out the window at the anonymous fancy houses. There were no children on the street. No bikes tossed carelessly on the front lawns. No litter. "And I'm sure they're feeling the pain right now, when they're hanging out with each other, working on their badges. Look at my sash: it's totally empty. I'm ten years old and I'm an outcast."

"A pariah in a ponytail."

"A loner in loafers."

"A Girl Scout without a cause," Lance said, slowing down the van to avoid a tabby housecat on the prowl. "What set Jade off?"

"If I said the word, you'd charge me a buck."

"Okay, you get one free pass—if you tell me what happened."

"She's a bitch."

"Feel better?"

"No."

"Okay," Lance said, "spill."

"It's a badge thing. You wouldn't understand," Belle said, waving her right hand dramatically and then scratching at her eczema-crusted elbow beneath her shirt.

"Try me."

"We were working on our career badges and we're supposed to say what our father does. . . ."

"Comedian," Lance said. "Peanut butter spreader."

"Loser," Belle said.

"That hurts," Lance said.

"And you're not even surrounded by a coven of scout-witches."

"Why would you say that to me?" Lance asked with an ache in his voice.

"Jade called you a loser," Belle said.

"She's a bitch."

"That's what I said. I told her you used to be a weatherman, but now you stay home and take care of Mom and me."

"And do the laundry and cook the meals," Lance added.

"Okay, Dad."

"And buy the birthday cards," he continued, "and register the cars."

"This was about me, remember? Me," Belle said, touching her chest. "How was my day?"

"It just flames me. I fold your underwear as well as any-body."

"Better, Dad, but it's not cool for your father to fold your panties."

"Guess not."

When Belle was one, she'd tried eggs for the first time—followed by three hours of volcanic vomiting. Tired of changing his clothes, Lance had stripped to his boxers, sent Darlene to bed, and hunkered down with Belle. They shared a plastic chair in the living room, watching a James Bond TNT marathon, naked except for her diaper and his boxers. He needed to cradle Belle close to comfort her (she was too young to hold her head over the toilet), so he just let her shudder and vomit. Drenched in yellow baby lava, they stuck together, chest to chest, occasionally stepping into the shower, then back for *Octopussy* and *Dr. No*.

Later that night, Lance laid Belle between him and Darlene on a waterproof flannel sheet. Dressed in a fresh onesie, Belle conked out immediately next to Darlene, her cheeks flushed with sleep. Before he drowsed—trying to stay awake in case there was a relapse—Lance felt a new unaccustomed sense of wholeness that extended beyond his own body to include those of his daughter and wife. They were one. This was his family: he and Belle and Darlene, not the family his father had traded up on at the used-car lot of love. They were the Ramsays: rock-solid in the dead of night and into the butt crack of dawn.

"So," Lance said after a pause that Belle declined to fill, "did you stand up for me?"

"I told Jade that Girl Scouts don't discriminate. I quoted the handbook: 'People who respect themselves also respect others.'"

"How did that go over?"

"That's when she called you a loser."

"And what did you say?"

"Nada. I stopped listening to her, like the handbook told me. But it didn't say how to get her to stop talking once you stop listening. If you figure that out, Dad, tell me."

"I will," Lance said as they approached the house. He opened the gate with a remote and parked the Windstar in the garage. "This bums me out. I need a cookie."

"Me, too."

"Do you think my thighs are getting big?" he asked.

"Get outta here," she said. And then, "Race ya."

"You are so toast," Lance said, chasing Belle into the kitchen, "I'm gonna butter you."

Ten minutes later, Sam and Julia skated to the front door. Lance had cookies and milk ready and the kids disappeared into Belle's room, leaving Lance and Julia behind to fill up the time. In Belle's room on the sunny southern side of the house, she plucked Boxy the turtle from her Barbie Dream House where he'd thrust his bucket-shaped head against the kitchen window. Sam used a Kleenex to remove a black turtle turd from the painted lavender oval area rug of the otherwise pristine living room. He walked to Belle's adjoining private bathroom, with its pink toothbrush and row of bubble bath bottles beside the tub. He wanted to stop and examine each one—rose scent and lilac, Ariel the Mermaid. Instead, he dumped the poo in the toilet and flushed. He used that noisy moment to pop open the Barbie toothpaste and zap it on his finger for a quick, forbidden taste. Bubble gum. Yum.

Sam was crushing on the new girl, but he was quiet about it. He'd never had a girl who crushed back on him, so he was waiting for Belle to reach out to him. Even that close, surrounded by her pinkness, he felt invisible. When Sam came back into the bedroom, Belle had reclined on her canopy bed wearing a flouncy hat and moth-eaten marabou mules. "Let's play house," she said, with a twist of plastic pearls. "It's

Saturday, and I've just returned from a day of beauty at the spa."

Sam glanced wistfully at the Barbie Dream House, in awe of its perfect simplicity. He wanted to touch the modified Queen Anne structure, to work the mechanical elevator that rode between two floors in a jelly-bean-pink turret. Sam could never admit pink was his favorite color; blue, he said, when asked, or green. Could he trust Belle with his secret? Could he confess how he felt about pink? Because deep down he understood you couldn't fake the color that was your favorite, because then it was *not* your favorite.

If Sam's father, Alec, knew Sam was near anything Barbie, the former varsity football player would have gotten uptight. His father would have said, *Let's go outside and kick the ball around, buddy-o.* And Alec would have been extra rough, knocking Sam around until there was nothing playful about the ball going back and forth, just Sam's father making it harder on him and then chewing him out for missing the ball.

"I've had a rough week," Belle said, dramatically clutching a hand to her pearls. "I had to fire the whole design team."

"Oh, honey, that must have been so hard on you."

"You have no idea," she said, "their sad little faces; it was so shame-making—their tales of hardship; the tears. They have children. Can you believe it—children? But I had to do it. It had to be done."

"You had to," agreed Sam. "But wasn't it even harder on the workers?"

"You just don't understand business, sugar." Belle sighed.

She lifted her dark eyes to the frilly canopy and raised wrist to forehead in a Garbo-esque gesture that underscored her isolation.

"Here's a chamomile tea," Sam said. "What else can I get you, my love?"

Sam fluffed Belle's pillows and hovered. He wondered, if he promised to play only with G.I. Joe in the dollhouse, if he filled the working oven with plastic grenades, whether his Dad would buy him one. Girls—he sighed—got these marvelous mini-worlds with tiny utensils in the cupboard, a teeny mantel clock, and books to scatter on the shelves, as unread as the ones in his father's study.

"Did you vacuum?" Belle asked.

"No, dear," Sam said, "just dusted."

Sam cheerfully turned, pausing to ask Boxy if he'd finished his geometry (yes, he assumed), and then grabbed the play vacuum cleaner handle in his callused right hand. He reversed, and pushed the toy to the middle of the floor, pretending to move the nonexistent cord out of the way with his left hand as he walked. "What do you want for dinner, my love?" he asked. "Pizza?"

"Divine."

"I know what you like."

"You missed a spot by Boxy," Belle said. She propped herself up from the pillows, pointed, and then flopped back as Sam followed her lead. Belle loved having control. The entire day she had none: not with Jade or her teacher; nor her parents, who seemed like satellites without fixed orbits since they'd left Barstow. She tried to block out what she'd seen that morning: Darlene's flushed scowl, Lance's legs jutting out like a misassembled Lego Bionicle. Belle had thought she was beginning to get this sex thing, but the naked wrestling, the groans, and the sweat—what was up with that?

Belle wouldn't discuss sex stuff with Sam. She was *so* not into boys, and had yet to make that first simple connection—the exchange of secrets—although he would have welcomed it.

Meanwhile, in the formal living room at the front of the house shaded by the bougainvillea-draped portico, Julia and Lance drank Perrier. Lance avoided discussing what had *almost* happened in the van, although Julia's lips were playing a tune on the bottle's mouth ("Harvest Moon" or, possibly, "Stairway to Heaven"). This was the house's adult retreat with two downy, impossibly white overstuffed sofas set at right angles. Darlene called it her sanctuary. It mirrored the classy, in-control woman she aspired to be. To Lance, it felt unfinished, impersonal. He winced if any guest entered with red wine. Juice boxes were verboten.

"How's Belle adjusting to Rancho?" Julia asked.

"Fine," he said, "fine." The repetition gave him away.

"She was wobbly today when she got in the van, Lance. What was that about?"

"You know kids," he said, "it's hard to get them to talk about their problems."

"I know you." She dipped the tip of her tongue into the bottle. "I bet she spilled her guts."

"Why do you say that?"

"You're the father every girl wishes she had, Lance, the cool dad who listens."

"That's not the gospel according to Girl Scout Troop Number 773," Lance said. "I'm the loser stay-at-home dad. That makes Belle different, and that's bad in sixth grade."

"Girls can be so cruel," Julia said. In sixth grade she had been as hard as Jade. She had never suffered an awkward period. She would have eaten Belle for lunch and discarded her on the cafeteria floor like a yellow burger wrapper. "How are you adjusting, Lance?"

"The sixth grade is rough," he said, and laughed.

"Don't deflect me with humor," she said.

"Was I?"

"Yep," she said, a dark spot stretching on the pale couch. "How are you adjusting, Mr. Mom?"

"The girls are no problem," he said, "but I can't get the other little boys to play with me."

"I'm not sure I can help you with that," Julia said, leaning forward and preparing to pounce. "But we can make a playdate anytime. I'm not put off by your feminine side."

"I didn't know I had one. Shit!" Lance said, jumping off the couch. "I forgot to pull the salmon out of the freezer. How long does it take to defrost?"

"No clue, Lucy," Julia said in frustration. "I'm going to go check on the kids. Maybe they're having more fun."

She got up from the couch, walked through the formal dining room and the two-story great room, and then headed down a short dark hall toward the private areas of the house. When she entered Belle's bedroom, Sam asked her, "What's up?"

"Take that apron off," Julia snapped. "Your father will shred me."

"Are we going?" Sam asked, removing the apron.

"Soon," Julia said, flopping on the bed and shoving Belle over with her hip. "How's the birthday girl hanging?"

"Dunno." Belle shrugged, twisting her pearls.

"You do know," Julia said, "in your heart. You just don't want to discuss it."

Belle nodded, absentmindedly flicking an elbow scab. Julia leaned toward Belle and raised the girl's chin; Belle's eyes were labile. "Do you have the birthday blues?"

Belle shook her head no.

"Okay, you know what's bugging you," Julia said. "You just don't know how to string the words together, right?"

Belle nodded assent.

"This is what we'll do: shut your eyes." Julia said. She readjusted the pillows behind Belle's head and examined an eczema reef before clasping the girl's hand. "We're taking a trip, Belle. I'm your guide. It's like we're in a cave. It's dark—"

"Oh, no, bats," Sam joked.

"Zip it, Sam," Julia said, "or you get liver and cauliflower for dinner."

"I'll be good," Sam said.

"Here we go, Belle," said Julia in the low, calming voice that she'd been learning from Wren. "I'm leading you, and I know where we are, and I'm wearing a miner's lantern on my forehead so I can see where we're headed."

Belle outstretched her free hand, sleepwalker-style. She felt like a slumber partier playing Ouija board who hoped the spirits would finally speak.

Sam studied Belle's face. Like Lance, he saw thoughts cross her forehead and twist her lips; but, unlike her father, Sam didn't absorb Belle's tension. She was not a reflection of him; she was separate and beautiful. He wanted to smooth those two prominent brows pinched close in concentration. The microwave buzzed in the distance.

"What are you feeling, Belle?" Julia asked in her serene Swami's voice.

"My stomach's tight."

"Why?"

"All the people. . . ."

"Which people?" asked Julia, "Where?"

"Strangers on Saturday," Belle said. "At Mom's diner."

"At your birthday party?"

"It's not my party," Belle protested. "I didn't pick the place; I wanted the Rollerama. And I didn't invite the guests. All my friends are in Barstow."

"Not all of them." Sam sulked.

"I don't even want to go. If it's my party, that's nuts. Who's it for anyway?"

"That's the big Q, girlfriend," Julia said. "You know this party isn't for you."

"So, who's it for?" Belle asked.

"Your mom and Sam's dad are throwing it."

"It's not their birthdays," Belle said indignantly.

"Right," Julia said. "It's your birthday—their party. They're using you, Belle. They claim the event is for kids, but it's really adults launching a business. You're a prop, Belle, a pretty girl in a party dress. Like many capitalist enterprises, Darlene's Diner exploits the market's real desires. It exploits Californians' utopian yearning for validation as perfect parents with perfect children. It's an opportunity for families with messy soap opera lives to fake Hallmark card memories for their children's mental albums. And it's all really just to squeeze money out of little girls' pocketbooks."

"If this chat is supposed to make me feel better, Julia, it is *so* not working."

"Sometimes we need to feel worse to get better, Belle."

"Please," Sam said, "don't say an oyster needs sand to make a pearl."

"An oyster needs sand to make a pearl," Julia said. "Belle, you need to reach a point where it's more comfortable to overturn the current state of affairs than suffer present indignities."

"I can't," Belle squeaked, not entirely sure that she'd fully absorbed Julia's message. "I can't do anything."

"You can whine—or you can take back the party," said Julia.

"I'm way too scared. I don't even want to get in front of my class for my oral report tomorrow," Belle said.

"You think I'm not scared?" Julia asked. Okay, she wasn't. She rarely was. "Work your fear. It's complacency turning to power."

"Huh?" Sam asked.

"Fear creates adrenaline, a drug that makes you work harder, faster, better," Julia explained. "Belle, harness your fear. Parents only have as much power over you as you give them. Take back this funky party. If you want to own the day, stop crying and start flying. Now, whose party is it?"

"Mine," Belle whispered.

"What are you going to do?" Julia said.

"Take it back?" Belle asked.

"Take it back!" Sam said.

"When?" Julia asked.

"Saturday," Belle said.

"Why?" Julia asked.

"I have the power?" Belle asked.

"You have the power," Julia said. "Whatever happens at the party, there's one moment rightfully yours as the birthday girl. It comes right before they sing happy birthday. Seize it. Don't let me down, girlfriend."

Now Belle's stomach really hurt.

part II

friday

chapter 7

The causes of the Witch Creek Fire were diverse and in some cases unknown: a power tool shot a spark into the brush; a boy played with matches in the canyon behind his tract home; a semi overturned, spilled gas on the road, and the fuel ignited. State troopers shot and killed a suspected arsonist. The county sheriff told the press that the number of citizens (and illegal aliens) evacuated in San Diego County was greater than those dispatched from New Orleans during Hurricane Katrina. True or not, the latter seemed to reflect the county's general inferiority complex; when the weather tended to be ideal day in, day out, it was hard to be taken seriously.

As the work week waned, the Witch Creek Fire grew. The blaze hopped Highway 15 and burned west, scorching acres in Del Dios and Rancho Santa Fe. Temperatures were still rising. It was eighty-nine degrees by the coast, and in the high nineties in east county, where the fires raged. But, down at the frosty, air-conditioned Marie Callender's restaurant on Balboa Avenue (160 locations across the country and growing), Alec was so concentrated on his business trajectory that he ignored the fire's potential dangers. He was personally unconcerned about evacuations, as no wildfires had ever reached Encinitas.

"Here's the deal," Alec said to Darlene as they shared an early lunch and a second plate of hash browns with cheese and bacon. "Who the hell was Marie Callender?"

Darlene shrugged. "Beats me." Her black jacket was off, and her white blouse was open deeply at the neck, her frilled French cuffs dangling over her narrow wrists in a vaguely flirtatious way, ruffled corporate. On some level, she knew her outfit would keep Alec's attention. She enjoyed Alec's laser focus on herself. He was handsome in that confident Kennedy clan, Ivy League, thick-head-of-hair, wide-shouldered way that made her talk a little faster and laugh louder. But she considered the mutual attraction a contact high; she had no intention of taking their relationship into physical intimacy.

"You don't know. Who the fuck cares?" Alec teased, taking another forkful of hash browns from their shared plate. "She baked pies in Southern California in the thirties, when everybody and their mother baked their own pies. Big deal. Marie could make a good apple, French apple, Boston cream—who cared? Who didn't?"

"My mom didn't bake," Darlene countered with a smile.

"Good for her."

"She could knit, though."

"Pay attention, Darlene," Alec said with mock sternness, the older man mentoring the younger woman in the secrets of business. "I'm going somewhere with this. Thanksgiving came and the old man patted Marie on the butt, but that was that."

"That was where you were going: a dirty story about Mrs. Callender?" Darlene asked. She had a willingness to laugh and take the piss that could be confused with an easygoing nature.

"Listen and learn: Then came the forties. War erupted. Pops shipped out, and everybody and his brother sailed into San Diego and San Pedro. And they all missed their mothers' pies. Suddenly women were working, homemade pies were scarce, and—bingo-bango—little Marie starts selling pies to restaurants in Southern California, pumpkin in midsummer, peach in winter. You didn't have to wait for Aunt Martha anymore. This was progress. She was no longer a little girl selling lemonade from a refrigerator box turned upside down."

"When did she do that?" Darlene smiled, playing dumb.

"Stay with me, Darlene," Alec said, appreciating the easy game between them, the sensei-and-grasshopper power dance. He stretched out his feet under the table so that they touched Darlene's. She didn't pull away. Footsies were not infidelity. "Old Ma Callender was no longer scraping for the minimum dollar. She wasn't doing that typical insecure woman thing: love me, love my pies, still worried that her pies weren't good enough for mass consumption and always afraid that someone would figure out she was a fraud. Not Marie. She knew she had something people wanted, and she was going to mass-produce them for love and money."

"Are you making this up?" Darlene smiled flirtatiously at Alec, her cute-chick smile. She enjoyed the little harmless high that accompanied their playful interaction, a cheek-flush that was absent in making-baby sex. "I bet there wasn't even a real Marie Callender. This was all a pretext to lure me into this swanky boîte for a cheap assignation. I bet they don't even sell pie. Waitress, oh, waitress. . . ."

"They have pie, Darlene." Alec smiled back, flashing his even white teeth. "Believe me, plenty of pie: lemon meringue; Mississippi mud. Hear me out. Marie never maximized her potential. It wasn't until the seventies that her son came along and opened a bakery restaurant in his mother's name. That—the franchising, the branding, the frozen food—is where the money is."

"How much money are we talking?" Darlene asked, leaning forward.

"I knew I'd get your full attention sooner or later," Alec replied, removing a stray strand of her blond hair from the hash browns. "This is the point. Marie Callender, Famous Amos, and Colonel Sanders: there's the individual and then there's the image. Picture yourself as a Gap ad. This is not about capturing your personal sensibility, but building a bridge between who *you* really are and consumer desires. In Barstow, you were the kooky mother in the pink waitress uniform and fuzzy slippers, hanging out with the customers. You were the cool mom that actually listened—maybe not to your own kid, but to your customers. That was your shtick. When you called them *honey* or *sweetie* it was italicized. But that doesn't play everywhere—in Seattle, in Santa Barbara, in Eureka."

"Why does it have to, Alec?" said Darlene, the playfulness absent from her voice. She sat back and tucked her feet under her seat. "Let's survive this weekend and see what happens. We still have to pull off the opening tomorrow at the diner, and I'm not sure if the staff can handle starting out at capacity."

"Darlene," Alec said with a sigh, "this weekend is already over except for counting the cash."

"Then there are openings in Orange County and Encino," Darlene said tautly, buttoning her top button. "And I think the fire is a real threat. We should make a plan B in case we have to cancel."

"It's just a Santa Ana, Darlene," Alec said, bristling with impatience. "The sky is not falling. Stop thinking small."

"I'm not thinking small. I'm already over my head."

"We're not over mine." Alec pushed away from the table to get breathing room. His attention wandered. At a back booth, a crush of dark-suited men circled a table, shielding the broad-shouldered blonde they clustered around. Alec recognized her whooping, quarterback's laugh; it was the kind that rallied the team even when they faced insurmountable odds. It wasn't about joy; it was about projection.

Alec had known the Right Honorable Mayor of San Diego Hackett when she was less honorable. They had first met when Joan was a brassy blond Amazon with muscular thighs (and a little lesbian problem) interning in her father's legal office. It was the summer before her senior year at UC Santa Barbara and Alec was Judge Hackett's fixer. Joanie had been the women's volleyball team captain—they went all-state the following year under her stewardship—and that summer she was just coming off three months of furious sex with the team's star spiker. She was ready to come out—and rabidly horny, separated from her ladylove. She wanted to make a big splash—daughter of conservative judge licks ladies, etc.

And then along came Alec, the suave older man. He introduced her to the Flame on Park Boulevard, the city's reigning dyke bar, just to get the edge off, and then went to work. They played a lot of two-man basketball that summer and had their share of hash browns at Marie Callender's, their place. She wasn't the kind of girl who had to be impressed by cloth napkins and fresh pasta. After Labor Day, Joanie returned to school, sublimating her sex drive into political ambitions even greater than her father's; and Alec convinced Wren to scrap acting in Manhattan black-box theaters after a particularly brutal summer and join him in San Diego. He claimed to have an in at the Old Globe Theater, but the connection fizzled and Wren never returned to the stage.

"If I had to market myself," Darlene said, "I'm the next generation of mother—I enjoy my work, my daughter, my husband—"

"In that order?" Alec challenged.

"I didn't say that."

"Did, too, Darlene," Alec said, leaning forward and covering Darlene's left hand with his right. "First, we scrape off the bull, then we spackle on a new coat."

"I'm just not a mother-first, wife-first chick," she said, retrieving her hand to take up a forkful of hash browns.

"Then, in the eyes of America, you're a 'me-first' chick," Alec said. "Gong!"

"Jesus, Alec, there are plenty of women like me. Work isn't just an economic necessity; it's crucial to our sanity. Nothing's harder than being a stay-at-home mom."

"You're exaggerating," Alec said dismissively.

"Have you ever watched your boys twenty-four/seven for a week?"

"No," Alec said, "but I've seen Wren do it. No problem."

"Either you're delusional or you'll say anything to win an argument," Darlene said, scooping up another forkful of hash browns and leaving it in midair. "Seven days straight in sweats and you'd be screaming for one decent unstained Brooks Brothers button-down."

"Are you going to eat that or fling it?" Alec asked.

"I'm thinking," Darlene said, lightening up. She put the potatoes in her mouth as if to answer his question, chewed, and swallowed. "The freaky thing is that Lance loves staying at home," Darlene continued, shaking her head. "He's a domestic goddess. He gets in a groove and he's an unstoppable laundry machine. You should see the care he takes wrapping birthday presents; he's a whiz with curling ribbon. He's so damned capable, grocery shopping, paying bills online, keeping on top of permission slips and class projects, recycling, recycling, recycling—all that endless, unrewarding crap."

"And your problem is?" Alec asked.

"I don't know." Darlene sighed, slipping off her sling-backs under the table. "Uch. What is my *problem*? What *is* my problem? I'm trying to figure it out."

"Don't sweat the small stuff, Darlene," Alec said, putting a strand of her stray hair behind her right ear and softly grazing her cheek on the rebound.

"I know. I should be happy. I should reward Lance for scooping up all the shit so I don't have to. I haven't washed a dish or bought milk in months. But something makes me feel iffy—and it may just be that he's a better stay-at-home parent than I ever was."

"And you say I'm competitive," said Alec.

"You are competitive," said Darlene.

"Lance buys a quart of milk and you're keeping score."

"I am so not keeping score." She sipped her iced tea and puckered: it was powdery, not fresh-brewed. Okay, so Alec was right: she was keeping score. She held her gaze on her glass but conjured Alec in her mind's eye. Alec knew how to wear a suit, not let the suit wear him. He was old school in a good way. He even carried a handkerchief. Who carried a hankie anymore? She used to get seventy-five cents a bundle for ironing her father's into submission—the only item she could ever aptly iron. Steam, fold; steam, fold. Alec was a full-grown man like her own father, Darlene thought, not a father in flip-flops like Lance.

Darlene looked up. Alec was staring at her with concerned blue eyes beneath strong brows. He put his hand across the table on top of hers. He was linebacker-solid, but not linebacker-dumb. He had plans. He initiated. He took charge. He went whoosh and things happened. And, for Darlene, who was weary of being the initiator, that energy was attractive.

"When Belle was a baby," Darlene continued, pushing away the disappointing iced tea, "I dreaded being asked what I did all day. It didn't matter if the question was posed with concern or just as a conversation starter. 'Nothing and everything,' that was the answer. I know what Lance does all day. I know how crowded those days are. And, still, I can't keep from asking him when I come home, and my head is buzzing from work, and deadlines, and launching this diner: Damn it, what did you do all day? And then there is silence. Because, really, what is there to say about the decision between broccoli and cauliflower? Or filing insurance claims?"

"So what's the problem, Darlene?"

"I miss the connection," Darlene said. "There's this big gulf growing between us—and he doesn't seem to feel it. I'm engaged in the outside world and he's clipping coupons. It sounds so Lucy and Desi in reverse—I'm out beating the bongos all day and he's burning the roast and bonding with the girls. And I feel guilty about that."

"You have nothing to feel guilty about," Alec said, his voice softened to a deep reassuring hum.

"Hey, Alec," Darlene said with a sigh, "thanks for being such a good listener."

"My pleasure," Alec said with a warm, intimate smile that seemed to convey that Darlene was the only other person in the universe who mattered to him at that moment.

Darlene continued, "I should support Lance but, instead, I resent him. He seems so Zen and unassuming. I don't trust it. There must be something else going on."

"Like what?"

"I don't know." Darlene laughed. "Embezzling Girl Scout cookie money?"

"Maybe he's eating the profits? Listen, marriage is a marathon, not a sprint. You don't have any reason for concern."

"Well, there's Belle. She's walking around like a sulky teenager."

"What could Belle possibly have to sulk about?"

"She's been moody since the first week of school. I guess it was the move."

"It's not like you're living in Calcutta. Everybody moves."

"We didn't."

"We didn't, either. But that's not the point: Belle's a kid. She's resilient."

"I don't even know if it's the move that bothers Belle or something deeper," Darlene sighed and fidgeted with her cuffs. "She confides in Lance, not me. When she cries, she cries for him. She falls and he picks her up. And I resent that, too. He's the more nurturing parent. Ever since we moved to Encinitas, I've abdicated my role. I feel like I'm not even the mom anymore; Lance is."

"You're the mother, Darlene, believe me," Alec said with

his deep voice of experience. "Lance is the father. You're stressing about the opening, but we have that covered. I keep telling you: tomorrow is already a done deal. What you need to do is keep your professional life and your personal life in perspective. Parenting is easier than you make it sound. You didn't abdicate your role as mother, you delegated. You're a businesswoman now. It's all about outsourcing, letting whoever is best at raising the child do the work. Belle has your genes, your love, and you're putting a terra-cotta-tile roof over her head. That's the big picture."

"You want the big picture?" Darlene asked. "Lance wants another kid."

Alec nodded. "That's a big step, and proof positive that you're the mother."

"What do you mean by that?" Darlene asked, scrunching up her forehead.

"He can't get pregnant by himself," Alec said. "But I can see why he'd want more children with you. The question is: do you want a baby?"

"Not really. Not right now. I have too much going on—"

"And maybe Lance has too little," Alec said. "Maybe he has a gap in his life to fill that you don't have."

"On the other hand," Darlene said, "Lance may honestly want another kid. And what's wrong with that? Part of my fear is that he's simply a better parent than I am."

"Maybe he is—and you're a better breadwinner."

"I'm not entirely comfortable with that, either. I'm happy to earn a living, but it's another story to be financially responsible for the entire mortgage. I don't want to get all life insurance on you, but what happens to them if something happens to me?"

"Welcome to my world," said Alec, pulling out his wallet. "It's not so easy being the patriarchal oppressor."

"Poor baby," Darlene said in mock sympathy.

"I have the burden of responsibility. I'm the older brother, the rock. Do I get to surf New Zealand?"

"No?"

"Do I get to go off and find myself?"

"Have you ever lost yourself?"

"That's another question," said Alec, grabbing the check. "I take a risk if I wear a yellow tie. I'm the bread-and-butter guy who bails the little brothers out at midnight. And damned if I don't get dissed for that, too, as if being a breadwinner was a slam-dunk and being emotionally accessible was the hard road. A little respect for the paycheck guy would be appreciated."

"Consider yourself respected, Alec," Darlene said, reaching out and touching his arm. In the background, Mayor Hackett cranked out her hearty rallying-the-troops laugh. Madam Mayor, in an American-made canary-yellow pantsuit, and her all-male kitchen cabinet entourage rose and filed through the aisles toward the exit. She paused at Darlene and Alec's table.

"How were your hash browns?" Hackett asked, placing a heavy, ringed hand on Alec's shoulder. "Did you have them dry or wet?"

"You know how I like them," Alec said.

"Not anymore," said Hackett, appraising Darlene with a

glance. Without turning back to Alec, she asked, "So, how's Wren?"

"Very Zen," Alec said, opening his wallet and palming a gold card to place on the check. "She's still into the yoga."

"I have enough trouble saying downward facing dog, much less doing it," Hackett said with a laugh.

"Yeah, but she never had your thunderbolt serve," Alec said. "What's the word on the fires?"

"Containment," Hackett responded. "We've got Mexican firemen coming all the way from Tijuana and Tecate. We've got the U.S. Army and the National Guard and three thousand allegedly nonviolent convicts to douse the flames. Next thing you know, that movie star governor will move on us and we'll have to rig a makeup tent. But there's no reason to press the panic button. We're all about life going on around here."

"That's reassuring," said Alec. "Hey, while you're here, let me introduce my business partner, Darlene Ramsay."

"Alec has told me a lot about you," Mayor Hackett said. Noticing Darlene's forehead furrow, she added, "All good. I've known Alec since I still had baby fat—my own, and not from having those damn rug rats. So, Darlene, I'm gratified you came to San Diego to grow your business. Let's get together and split a plate of hash sometime and discuss how the city can help."

"I'd love to," Darlene said, stunned by the mayoral attention—and by Hackett's bawdy familiarity.

"I'll have my people call your people and set up a date after your opening," Hackett said. "So, Alec, we'll see you tomorrow unless this turns into a *Towering Inferno* sequel. I'm bringing the brood. I'm expecting the kids to eat too much sugar, run around until they turn into pudding, melt down, and then barf in the SUV. The great thing about being mayor is you don't have to clean up after them. That alone is worth the campaigning."

As the mayor's wide yellow back receded, Darlene leaned over the table and hissed, "The mayor is coming to Darlene's Diner? Tomorrow?"

"Sure. Little Missy Hackett."

"Are you kidding?" Darlene asked, furious at Alec's secretive behavior, but unsure how to confront him without appearing like a raving hormonal bitch. "You must have skipped that detail, partner."

"I told you about it."

"No, you didn't."

"Yes," Alec said with absolute confidence, rising from the table, "I did."

"Did not," Darlene said, trying to tick back in her mind to some point where the news of the mayor attending the opening of Darlene's Diner would not have registered.

"Sure I did. It was a Tuesday. Your office," Alec said. "Trust me."

"Why do men say that at just the moment when they can't be trusted?"

"You're so suspicious. I'm not any man," Alec said. "I'm your business partner."

"I'm still furious."

"You'll get over it."

"You better hope so."

Alec laughed. "I'm scared, Darlene." He stretched his right arm around Darlene's waist possessively as he guided her out of the restaurant.

chapter 8

At Rancho Amigo Elementary School, Belle's sixth-grade teacher, Mr. Everett Baumgart, stifled a yawn and, with it, the urge to scream at a student chiseling his name on his desk. Baumgart was a man who would rather be feared than loved. He wore his Navy buzz cut above a pale, pockmarked face with deep-set black eyes and a thin mouth. He despised the ascendance of social studies over chronological history; and had been testy since the new female principal entered his classroom, and declared that he could no longer teach the domino theory. Several parents had complained that Mr. Baumgart's reactionary notion of communism spreading south from Vietnam through Australia and New Zealand and implanting itself in San Diego—where the conquerors would confiscate all Xboxes and TVs—was the political equivalent of telling their precious sixth-graders that bogeymen existed.

Parents had grumbled before the advent of Principal Hickock, M.A., PhD, and it had never mattered. But it was a new era of political correctness where frogs could no longer be dissected for fear of Kermit's feelings and the tenderness of these elementary students, a fact that any teacher of these young hellions would have heatedly debated in the faculty lunchroom. Sadly, Mr. Baumgart, twelve years and counting until retirement, could not afford that level of frankness. So he had to keep his hard-won conservative worldview to himself, as well as his opinions on such radically inappropriate matters as gay marriage. Personally, he believed, and still told his male colleagues at the Rounders Room on Friday afternoons, if Heather had two mommies, she should be ashamed.

Mr. Baumgart's was the grim face of authority that greeted Belle each morning. His all-knowing, unsmiling, pockmarked visage had ground down Belle's natural good spirits, assisted by the smirks and stage whispers of Jade and her posse. Belle sat in back-row exile, where she had trouble keeping her attention on the blackboard and Mr. Baumgart's high, droning voice. She was essentially a front-row, shooting-arm-raiser, teacher-pleasing A-student stranded among the slackers and shirkers, in the zone of the children that the school refused to leave behind no matter how little attention the kids paid. It was there that Belle had taken to gnawing her Ticonderoga No. 2 pencils like corncobs, tapping her foot in pent-up boredom, and tormenting the red blisters of her eczema half hidden beneath her sweatshirt sleeves. When she had argued about her seating, Mr. Baumgart had decreed that a Barstow honor student was likely no more than middling in Encinitas.

Mr. Baumgart's sourpuss face awaited Belle's presentation on Friday as lunch loomed, following an endless run of oral reports on such career topics as seal trainer, professional baseball pitcher, and submarine captain. "Are you prepared for your oral report, Isabelle?" Mr. Baumgart asked.

"Yes, Mr. Baumgart," Belle said, with a curtsy in her voice. She diffidently plodded the long aisle from the back of the classroom, carrying a book and a pink gym bag. An echo rose behind her, "Yes, Mr. Baumgart," in a fruity voice, followed by muffled laughter. She reached the podium and turned, feeling a breeze and worrying that the hem of her short pink plaid skirt might be stuck in her underpants. She didn't know why she tried to fit in; she was more comfortable in jeans. She stood, looking small, in front of a red-white-and-blue-painted banner that ran the length of the blackboard and read AMERICA: FIRST IN WAR, FIRST IN PEACE, AND FIRST IN THE HEARTS OF OUR COUNTRYMEN.

Belle put the backpack on the edge of Mr. Baumgart's desk. She was the day's first student to bring a visual aid. As she yanked out her Girl Scout sash, she knocked a plastic snow globe from the corner of his desk.

"Just leave it," Mr. Baumgart said impatiently from where he stood by the windows, his pale hairy arms crossed over the chest of his yellow Habanera. This was torture, for them both. Despite him, she retrieved the faded souvenir; OKINAWA, it said. She wasn't sure where Okinawa was. Given Mr. Baumgart, perhaps Vietnam? There might be a little crack; she didn't know if she had caused it. She set it gently on the desk, near where it had been but away from the edge.

Belle cleared her throat, stretched her red sweatshirt over her wrists, and began in a whisper, "For Career Day—"

"Louder, please," ticked Mr. Baumgart.

Belle boomed out, "For Career Day, I looked at the Girl Scout Careers badge."

A student named Gordon called out in a Speedy Gonzalez voice, "We don't need no steenkin' badges," and the boys laughed without knowing the *Treasure of the Sierra Madre* reference.

"Enough, Gordon," Mr. Baumgart said, "Isabelle, the topic was: what do *you* want to be when you grow up?"

"I know," said Belle. "That's always the question."

"To be or not to be, *that* is the question," said Gordon, to less laughter.

"Gordon," threatened Mr. Baumgart. "Isabelle, continue."

"I didn't want to give a bogus answer, like I want to be a nurse. Right! Give kids shots. I don't think so. I want to be a teacher and never, ever leave school? Not me! I was like, whoa, be what? What's a career? Is it the same as a job? So, I grabbed the trusty handbook," said Belle, raising the heavy Girl Scout guide in her left hand while trying to keep her wrist covered. She read the boredom in the room but didn't know how to dispel it, so she plunged ahead: "The Careers badge pictures a chef's hat, a wrench, a gavel, and a magnifying glass. It's not a pretty badge, but I'm curious why our parents are so into their careers. Do we really know what our parents do for a living?"

"I know what my dad does," Jade said. "He's a general manager."

"So what do managers do all day?" Belle asked. "What does it mean to manage?"

"He orders people around. He hires and fires people. And he goes to lunch," Jade said to silence, "a lot, at fancy restaurants. He has an expense account."

"And what does your mother do?" Belle asked.

"Belle, this is your report, not Jade's," said Mr. Baumgart.

"Okay," said Belle, "but there wasn't a single ad for a general manager when I looked in the newspaper, my first Careers badge assignment. There were no classified ads for archaeologists or mayors. There were just ads for secretaries and drivers and housekeepers and waitresses—none of them paying very much."

Belle looked up and followed Mr. Baumgart's glance outside. The sun glinted dully off the monkey bars in the smoky haze. Was it getting hotter in the classroom, or was she just flushed?

"Thank you, Isabelle," Mr. Baumgart said as he marched toward the podium.

"And teachers," Belle said, completing her list. "There were no ads for teachers."

"Thank you, Isabelle," said Mr. Baumgart.

Belle hated this man with his dandruff-dusted shoulders, his little piggy eyes. She imagined a raggedy house twisting in the sky, and then landing smack on Mr. Baumgart's head. All that was visible afterward were his black socks poking out from beneath the porch. She imagined his toes curling backward and continued, "I'm just getting started. It's like, you know, my father's career wasn't there at all."

"Loser," Jade coughed into her hand. She tossed her tresses over her shoulder.

"Ouch," said Belle. "Why call my father a loser—thank you, Jade—based on work? The handbook didn't explain why people judge grown-ups based on what they do, like Jade here."

Jade looked daggers at Belle, who had temporarily forgotten the lesson she learned in the Barstow desert—poke a rattlesnake and it will strike. For a moment she was back at her old school, where the other girls flocked around her like they did Jade here. In Barstow, Belle had sway. She was the cool one with the cool mom and her dad appeared on the TV bigger than Barney.

Those days were over. Belle was now in Jade's merciless sights. She felt helpless against such a rival. It had been the older girl's mission since the second day of school to squash Belle like a bug—all that sunny disposition and "Can I help you with your geometry?" stuff. As if geometry mattered to girls. Like that was what it took to be popular at Rancho Amigo. Being nice. This was Encinitas, girlfriend. The goody-goody with her perfect math scores posted on the board for all to see would have to get by Jade first, and that was never going to happen. It was so uncool to be good at school.

At the front of the classroom, Belle continued, "In Barstow, Dad was a weatherman, but in the *San Diego Union-Tribune*, there were no ads for weathermen. What's he supposed to do?"

"Get a new job," said Mr. Baumgart.

"But he has one already. He's my dad. Why can't somebody be judged on the kind of person they are, not their paycheck? Shouldn't it be as important to be a good parent as a good provider? Besides, as a stay-at-home Dad, he has bunches of jobs." Belle reached into her gym bag, removed a new Darlene's Diner chef's hat, and said, "He cooks dinner. His lasagna is my favorite."

Then Belle removed a wrench and said, "When the washing machine breaks, he calls the repairman." In the middle of explaining her carefully selected props, Belle eyed her audience and realized her tactical error. She should have just tattooed FREAK on her forehead. She had been worried about the kids finding out about her dad, so she blabbed. Now everyone knew. But she couldn't stop. She plucked a wooden hammer from the bag and said, "When I have a fight during a playdate, out comes the gavel and Dad decides justice. And when Mom loses her keys, Dad the detective finds them."

"Thank you," Mr. Baumgart said.

"He just doesn't get paid," Belle interrupted.

"Next time, answer the assigned topic. If you're confused, consult me first."

As if Belle would voluntarily have gotten any closer to her teacher. He'd done it again. He'd made her feel small, as low as a penny flattened by a Hummer. And yet, for a frozen minute, unable to find her sneakered feet and accept total defeat, she stared at him, with his piggy eyes and pockmarked face, and had a realization. Given who Mr. Baumgart was, he could never be a teacher children loved. Even his rare smile had a killing effect. Maybe he had tried to be warm and fuzzy in the beginning, had failed miserably, and decided to go with his strengths. It was natural for him to inspire fear, so there it was: maybe it was better to be feared than loved, especially if no one loved you. Maybe he was just another outcast, like she was—but that didn't make her hate him any less.

chapter 9

As Belle shuffled back to her seat with hunched shoulders, Lance—chef, repairman, detective, and judge—chopped onions in Wren's kitchen in the combustible hills overlooking Encinitas. He was helping his neighbor prep for that night's party. He sliced off the root, cut the bulb in half, and crinkled off the skin. Next, he sliced each half parallel to the cutting board, then, holding the victim lightly together with his fingertips, he began a row of even chops across the crown. He swept the bits into a mixing bowl and repeated the process.

After five onions, Lance rubbed the board with lemon and switched to carrots. Maybe he could get a job as a chef, but he liked to make what he wanted to make, at his own pace. He probably couldn't get a chef job these days anyway. Professional cooking had become competitive. And he despised work politics, and the pressure to rise through the ranks. Had he talked himself out of another profession, even before he applied?

Lance marched the big blade along the surface, his right hand balancing the handle, the left seesawing near the point. He was in the zone. He chopped and his root vegetables parted. He and Wren had spent the morning, while Belle and Sam were in school and Julia accompanied Max on a playdate, intently practicing tantric poses in Wren's yoga room downstairs until they were completely spent. Now, after a recess of lounging, Lance was nude beneath a red cotton velvet robe monogrammed A.G.M.

"Darlene said I want more kids because I don't want to leave the nest myself," Lance said. "She thinks my reasons are selfish."

"Are they?" Wren turned from blending hummus at the food processor.

"No," Lance said. "I love children, and being a father. Why not have more kids? Especially now that we have a big house. I'll admit it doesn't hurt that Belle is on the verge of becoming her own person with a life outside the house."

"It'll be a while yet," Wren said. "Belle needs you now as much as she ever did."

"After interrupting Darlene and me in bed the other morning, she may need a therapist, too."

"Shit happens," Wren said. Just not at her house.

"Wren, I'm scared of going back to being on my own in that way, kicking around in my own life without little kids. I don't want to hang out and shoot the breeze with the guys over brews. I don't want to figure out what I'm going to be when I grow up if this weatherman thing evaporates. Being a weatherman wasn't how I saw myself; I didn't define myself as a weatherman. How egotistical would that be? I report the weather; therefore I am—as if it didn't rain or shine without my announcing it on TV."

"You're being too hard on yourself."

"I don't think so, Wren. Maybe the truth is I don't have much ambition, but Darlene has plenty for both of us."

"Wasn't your father a professor? He sounded pretty ambitious."

"He was, always worried about getting tenure; worried about rising in the department; worried because my mother didn't fit in with the other faculty wives."

"How did he treat you?"

"Relegated me to Mom; he wasn't a kid person, at least not with me. Later, he might have been different. I don't know. I remember him as being formal, always asking questions as if I were a stranger he'd just met. No kisses, just handshakes, the occasional ruffle of my hair, or a hand placed awkwardly on my shoulder. He called me 'son' a lot, as if he couldn't remember my name."

"I bet he could remember your name," Wren said with a laugh.

"Maybe," Lance said. "There wasn't much of a connection, or at best it was faulty. Then it frayed altogether. Compared to him, I'm a slacker. Except I want to kiss my kid. I want to know what's buzzing in her head. I don't want to sit around watching the game or dump Belle in front of the TV. I love being a father."

Wren smiled. "I can see that."

"What I don't see is why I can't have the joy of having more children, of growing a family, of becoming part of an organic thing that you can't map out. . . ."

"That has a random beauty of its own," Wren said, expertly removing the container from the Cuisinart and guiding the mixture into a brown Japanese ceramic bowl with a white rubber spatula. The distant sound of John McLaughlin and Shakti rose like incense from her downstairs meditation room, the smallest in the house. Alec called it her cave, and rarely entered. That was why she and Lance made love there.

"Darlene doesn't miss the baby days," said Lance. "Me, I hated the sleeplessness, and the ache of not knowing what was wrong when Belle cried. But I miss that middle-of-the-night clarity. When I was up with Belle at three in the morning watching *Walker, Texas Ranger*, and I had to hold her with the delicacy of an egg because one shift could restart the shrieks. I had a sense of being one with her, and with the night, and all the other dislocated folks, the night workers and insomniacs. I felt a heightened awareness because there was no other place to be but with Belle—or unconscious. I knew my place in the world—and it was on that couch."

"I agree," said Wren. "I'd be sitting up with Max on the deck and I'd see the moon set and the sun rise. I felt totally centered. I'd wonder where I'd been for all those other days when the world was giving a light show and I was looking the other way. Sleep is highly overrated."

"Not according to Darlene. And she hates nursing. She already told me she never wants to be that in tune with her bodily functions again. Besides, she's content with Belle—and why shouldn't she be? But I don't share her fears that if you have one great child, why push your luck. That, to me, is selfish."

"Did you and Darlene talk about having a big family before you got married?"

"We never discussed the future, because the present was so great. We felt like each other's family then, and it seemed like enough—more than enough."

"You realize you're talking in the past tense?" Wren said.

"Am I?"

"Is it just because you're talking about your life before Belle?"

"No," he said. "Not really. The pathetic thing is that I say I want another kid so it will bring Darlene and me closer together. . . ."

"And that desire may be the thing that pulls you apart?"

Lance looked up at Wren from the celery stalks he was slicing. He loved her freckled-girl face, the way he could see Sam in the rounded cheeks, the deep smile grooves at either side of her lips, the cleft chin, the heavily fringed brown eyes so large they gave him vertigo. He fixed on her left eye, the receiving eye, and watched it dance with sunspots of color, until her pupil fixed and he found stillness there. That was the rapport he wanted, nothing you could spin table talk about, washing vegetables, chopping in the kitchen, making something together that would quickly be consumed, a castle-in-the-sand partnership. Children.

Wren blinked first, and looked away. She gazed through the adjacent glass-walled living room at the distant glittering Pacific. The view was pure soul food, but the house was too large for her. An architect had designed the seventy-two-hundred-square-foot southwestern-style trilevel for a pro basketball forward. Late one night, the Rockets star dribbled a rival's head and sold the house to pay legal fees. The sacrifice was worth it: he traded one big house to avoid another, and returned to playing ball in the Midwest after enrolling in a court-mandated anger management course.

Anger management would consume her life, Wren thought, Alec's fury, not her own, if she left her husband. There would be endless repercussions with their sons; Alec would ensure that there would be no peace. Still, she wanted to be true to herself, the self she was now, not the younger one who had met and married Alec. She wondered whether there should be a time limit on marriages; if, like real estate, she could have leased rather than bought this one. As for Lance's wife, Wren didn't bear any grudge against the younger, more ambitious woman. There was absolutely nothing wrong with Darlene that a few years and some success wouldn't fix.

"I wish I'd started having kids earlier," Wren said.

"I didn't know until Belle was three that this is what I wanted. It's not like before Darlene and I got married I knew I wanted a big family. I had a taste and I'm hooked."

"I would have had seven," Wren said with a laugh. "I would have been one of those awful women who are pregnant all the time, nursing twins, carrying a baby, toilet-training a toddler, reading to one kid, and coaching the soccer team. But what I really want is a girl." She pressed the puree button. Sixty seconds later she said, "And that *is* selfish."

"I'll lend you Belle," Lance said.

"I'll share her." They continued preparations for the night's dinner party. Wren gently moved Lance from one project to the next as they crossed chores off the big list she had attached to the refrigerator. "You'll meet my sister tonight. Robin's a trip."

"Why do you say that?"

"Sisters, blisters," she said.

"What?"

"Robin wrote a poem about us in high school. It began, 'Sisters, blisters.' It was hardly an auspicious start for a writing career, but it nailed her attitude toward me. She's written three books and claims the current one is bestseller-bound."

"What's it about?" Lance asked.

"Something about marriage and relationships," Wren said, "as if she's an expert."

"Does Robin have kids?" he asked.

"No. Her husband wanted them. He worked at the university day-care center during college, but Robin had no use for children. He knew that from the start—she always said if they came out fully formed, like Athena, she'd have one—but he hoped to change her. He thought she'd mellow, give in because it was what he wanted. I could have told him that wasn't going to happen. Anyway, she prefers adults—especially men. She adores Alec."

"Who doesn't?"

"You'd be surprised," Wren said, adding another drop of fresh lemon juice to the tabbouleh salad she was preparing, and then tasting it. "But don't mind me. It's hard to be a little sister at forty-four. Look at all this food: I'm still trying to impress her."

"I'm impressed," Lance said.

"You're easy," said Wren.

"You never complained before."

"I'm not complaining." She approached with the spatula and said, "Taste this."

"Orgasmic," he said.

"Have you ever thought—" she began, and then the front door flew open. They looked up. Due to the house's open floor plan, the broad pass-through between the kitchen and dining area (shuttered only during dinner parties) revealed Julia and Max as they entered the living room beyond.

Julia stood framed in the massive distressed-wood doorway, balanced between the balls of her feet like an adrenalized Amazon warrior. She dragged Max behind her like a pelt. He squirmed to escape a grip that had become too tight, raising a red band on his pale forearm. Julia's angry smirk, and the way she braced her legs in the doorway like a bobcat preparing to pounce, indicated that she had spied Lance and Wren through the windows, but hadn't decided how she would work this discovery to her advantage. She was unsure what enraged her most. Was it the stripping away of Wren's holier-than-thou, yoga-teaching condescension, the passive-aggressive gentleness of her master's voice when the woman clearly wanted to scream? Or that she was bullshitted by Lance's sad-sack impotence act? Or that this was another domestic drama she thought she understood, and she turned out to be the child left outside in the dark again?

Julia half dragged, half slung Max through the living area, the child screaming, "Mommy, Mommy, she mean to me, Mommy." The babysitter dumped Max in the television room beyond, with its sixty-inch plasma screen and state-of-the-art sound system. She flipped on PBS and planted him in front of The Big Comfy Couch, where a Raggedy-Ann-costumed actress sat on a super-sized sofa with her Mini-Me dolly, and began to address Max directly. The toddler abandoned all struggles and receded into the sofa like an anesthetized pit bull. The title song—a bouncy anthem to the security of the couch potato lifestyle—boomed out of the speakers.

"Didn't you have a playdate?" Wren asked when Julia entered the kitchen.

"Max bit Alfredo as if he were fettuccine and—surprise—we became unwelcome. Here," Julia said, proffering a slip of paper, "Alfredo's mom wrote down their child therapist's number."

"Max is a kid," Wren said, crumpling the paper in frustration. "Kids bite."

"They grow out of it," Lance said, attempting nonchalance, as if Julia had walked in on any two mothers helping each other out in the kitchen while the kids were at school. "No one ever sent a son off to college still biting."

"Good," Julia said. "Then set up a playdate with Alfredo when Max comes home freshman year, because that's the next time they're going to want to see him."

"Lance," Wren said, in a voice even gentler, and more impersonal, than usual, "I need cayenne pepper. Could you run down to Safeway and get some? And chervil."

"What does chervil look like?" he asked.

"Small, dark green ferns," Wren replied. It would take him a while to find it. Lance washed his hands with antibacterial soap and wiped them on a dish towel before heading out the kitchen door in Alec's red robe.

"You look like Hugh Hefner," Julia commented flatly.

"You need your street clothes, Lance," Wren said, swallowing the *dear* she normally would have punctuated the sentence with, and scooping up veggie scraps from the granite with nimble, agitated hands. She ran the tap, flipped on the disposal, and watched celery tops jostle for position, then disappear. She wanted to toss a fork into the hole, just to hear the awful noise, to create a diversion. But she couldn't risk breaking the disposal today in anticipation of the dinner party, and she didn't want to have to explain to Alec how one of their precious Reed & Barton forks got mangled.

Behind Wren, Julia prowled the fridge and scored a Diet Coke. She snuck cut celery stalks out from beneath the cellophane where they were aligned in anticipation of the party, turned, and straddled a barstool beside the granite kitchen island.

"Back in a bit," Lance cried out as he exited the front door in hastily thrown-on shorts, T-shirt, and flip-flops. "See ya, Maxaroni."

Julia dipped a celery stick into the hummus. "It's missing something," she said, licking her finger, "but it's not cayenne pepper."

"Lemon juice?" Wren asked.

"Does Alec know about mother's little helper?"

"What do you think, Julia?" Until that moment when Julia entered the room with Max, Wren had viewed her relationship with Lance as integral to a healthy life. It wasn't about love, exactly. It was about union—the spiritual union she lacked with Alec. Her time with Lance filled a gap in her own marriage, where love's first bloom had been ground down to something more mundane and institutional. Lance made her unspeakably happy, and that joy balanced the rest of her life, the sweet to counteract the bitter. It enabled her to hold her tongue about her unmet needs and Alec's business trip excesses. With Alec, tantric sex was impossible: he didn't have the time or patience, and he saw himself as the teacher, never the pupil, when it came to their relationship.

"Alec has no fucking clue, does he?"

"Unless you say something," Wren said. She surveyed the young woman she'd chosen to watch her boys, whose confidence had initially charmed, then threatened her. Wren had no prior experience with postfeminist bullies. She was just realizing that Julia exploited dogma to justify amoral behavior. It was possible Sam and Max were unsafe on Julia's watch because everyone she encountered was a pawn in a theoretical social experiment. Now Wren could no longer fire Julia, given her own infidelity. And Wren's suspicions about Julia were tricky to articulate; they weren't in the accepted realm of sexual abuse, theft, or feeding the kids nutritionally suspect marshmallow Fluff sandwiches on Wonder Bread. Wren continued, "And you are going to say something, aren't you?"

"It's up to you," Julia said.

"What do you want?" Wren asked. "More money?"

"That wouldn't cost you anything." Julia paused, considering. "Give me Lance."

"He's not mine to give."

"He's yours to give up."

chapter 10

Lance never found the chervil and Wren called to tell him she'd found more cayenne in the pantry after he'd bought it at the Safeway. They didn't discuss Julia. He drove home, shelved the pepper, and avoided making the dunning calls to mothers who hadn't yet paid for their Girl Scout cookies. He flipped on the TV, but the news was all bad: the Witch Creek Fire had burned 770 square miles, razed 1,780 homes, and caused double-digit human deaths and countless scorched animals. He switched it off and played solitaire on his computer until it was time to pick up Belle.

At 2:50 P.M., Lance approached Rancho Amigo. He scraped the curb in the Windstar. The windows were rolled up and the air-conditioning was blasting to stave off the unseasonable heat. It was October but it felt like late August, inching toward ninety degrees. Lance joined the mommy line of cars waiting in front of the school for the 3 P.M. bell. He wanted to avoid Julia at all costs, but spied her leaning against the Rancho Amigo Elementary sign while Max streaked back and forth on the sidewalk in his Big Wheel.

Julia, barefoot, was smoking a cigarette, wearing biker shorts, a sports bra, and her tattoos. Lance sensed she'd been waiting for his van, as she slowly bent from the waist and squashed her cigarette butt in the turf. He figured she could not only touch her toes, but probably flatten her palms on the ground in front of her. But, hell, Wren could do that, too, and more. He tried to censor this thought, and assumed Julia knew he was avoiding her because he'd never arrived to pick up Belle this late before.

Lance considered how visible his schedule was. At least five people must know his morning Starbucks routine, how often he drank coffee with Wren. Some might even presume she was his wife. He never went there with Darlene. Then he realized Wren had been an Encinitas resident for years. Even the Starbucks baristas knew her existence predated him, knew Alec, who never entered a place quietly. It chilled Lance to realize how little privacy he had in this quiet surfside hamlet. It was suddenly not lost on him that it was Alec who had steered Darlene to Pacific Breeze and to a house a little too ostentatious for revenues expected rather than earned.

Julia approached Lance's car, cheetah-like, the way a predator pretended to ignore its prey while circling closer. Her advance was delayed by a mother in an ice-blue Lexus shrilling, "Hey, you with the tattoo, would you mind not smoking in front of the kids?"

"Right, lady," Julia said, "I forgot. Your kid smokes behind the school. I bummed the cigarette from him, Salem menthol, right?"

By that time, Lance was slumped behind the wheel, pretending to look for Neil Young's *Harvest Moon*. Julia neared, crossing behind Max as he careened along the sidewalk. She banged on the passenger-side window. Every mother was craning her neck to watch the action. "Hey, Hugh Hefner," Julia said, banging again, "roll down the window."

"Miss Julia." Lance tried to smile breezily but could only lift one side of his mouth. He silently ran the mantra, *Step away from the van, step away from the van, step away from the van.* He pushed the window button on his door, unrolling his window, then the rear back, and then the one beside Julia. She stuck her head in the car, invading his cool bubble with a blast of hellish heat.

"You really *are* avoiding me," Julia said. "Unlock the door."

Lance complied. He was a plodder, not a schemer. He was at a loss at how to play Julia. He stared at her mouth. Her lips were flat, large for her face, and naturally hyacinth-pink. Any lipstick would gild the lily. She said something, but he was looking, not listening. "Can we hitch a ride with you?" she asked.

"Sure." Lance welcomed the safe question. "We'll put Max's Big Wheel in back."

"Do I make you nervous, Hef?"

"Calling me that doesn't help."

"Why, Hef, does it bother you?" When Lance didn't answer, Julia stretched her feet up on the dashboard and flexed. Then she coughed and said, "The air quality sucks."

"Smoking doesn't help," Lance said. "And it's so unhealthy."

"Is that true, Hef? That's the first I've heard of it." She looked at him and actually winked. "So what do you make of the firestorm, weather dude?"

"A disaster," Lance said. "And it's far from over. When those winds gust to one hundred miles per hour almost anything can happen. Scan the radar maps. These are the most concentrated smoke plumes I've seen since I started working weather."

"I'll make sure to scan those radar maps," Julia said. "But, c'mon, we're not in any real danger by the coast, are we?"

"We haven't been evacuated yet," Lance said.

"What put you in such a panic, Hef, as if I didn't know?" Julia said. When Lance remained silent, she continued, "Hey, we're not living in a Temecula trailer park. This is Encinitas."

"Agreed," said Lance, "but with winds this strong and forty-foot-high walls of flame, anything can happen. Given the dry conditions, all it takes is one cigarette tossed out a car window by a babysitter and a new neighborhood starts to burn."

"It never spreads this far west," said Julia. "We're not even in the fire plain."

"You're probably right," said Lance. "But there's a reason they call these fires wild. High winds can carry embers randomly. Have you ever heard of fire tornadoes?"

"You're making this stuff up just to freak me out," said Julia. "You should know me better than that. I don't do freak-out."

"I'm not trying to freak you out," said Lance, "but here's

the deal: these fire whirls, or firenadoes, are like flaming dust devils. Heated by the fire, powered by high winds, they spin, and spit embers. They're like flaming kites. They can rise thousands of feet in the air, get caught in the wind, and land far away, starting another spot fire and beginning the process all over again. That's why you can have two houses right next to each other and only one burns down."

As Lance extended his explanation, Julia stretched her leg over the gearshift and onto Lance's thigh. She flexed her foot and said, "You're making me hot."

"Back up, Julia," Lance warned.

"Do I sense a cold front, weather dude?"

"The forecast is chilly."

"I predict a thaw," Julia said, undeterred. "That little man wants to come out and play."

"No way, José."

"Yes way, José. You need me."

"Do not."

"I've got your number, little boy lost," she said, bending her knee and inching her bare foot up Lance's thigh. "You've jumped from emasculating wife to unavailable mother figure, without facing the big money question: what do you want to be when you grow up? Do you know, Hef?"

"Don't call me that," Lance said. No, he didn't know. He didn't really get what it meant to grow up. In one sense, he became a little adult when he left New Jersey. His mother hadn't the strength to preserve his childhood from one coast to the other. And he didn't associate maturing with becoming a weatherman. Lance scanned the row of cars. He glanced at the sidewalk. He checked his rearview mirror.

"Where's Max?" he asked.

"Right there," Julia said, gesturing with her thumb to the sidewalk as she turned her head. When she didn't see the boy or his bike, she leapt out of the car, landing flat on the sidewalk, knees flexed. Heat blasted into the car through the open door. Julia looked uphill and down. The school bell rang. Students burst out of the buildings like water pellets at Hoover Dam. She whirled in a panicked circle, her toned arms pinwheeling around her body. The blue Lexus driver honked three times and pointed downhill. Lance watched Julia race west toward Interstate 5 with her ferocious cheetah's stride, panic vanishing into determination. He felt relieved, despite Max's disappearance. Max was tough. But then Lance came to his senses: tough enough to think he could ride his Big Wheel into traffic.

Shouldering his door open, Lance leapt to the ground. He caught the toe of his flip-flop on the running board and narrowly avoided being clipped by an agitated mother racing in late and low in her Chevy Cavalier, one eye on the wailing infant in the car seat behind her. He righted himself, kicked off his thongs, and ran downhill on the asphalt in the Chevy's wake. He swung his head and saw Belle and Sam walking together, Belle dejected and Sam elated.

"Max," Lance yelled, and pointed downhill. The kids dropped their packs and followed, Sam leading and Belle struggling to keep up despite longer legs. Lance sprinted down the street for six car lengths, sweating, then jutted onto the sidewalk between two Saabs. He adjusted his stride to the cement. He felt the panic that was absent from Julia's face. How could they have let this happen?

The anxiety of his situation rose in his throat, which was already feeling scratchy from smoke blown all the way to the coast by the Santa Anas. He was playing with fire. *How could he be such a dick?* How could he get so distracted he lost sight of the most important thing in his care: their children? Nothing was more important than the kids.

"Dad, wait up," Belle called from behind, but Lance kept running, gaining speed on the slope. The harsh air burned his lungs. He envisioned Max, his fair skin not nearly as freckled as it would become, already a scar segmenting his right eyebrow after cracking into a glass coffee table. He pictured Max racing off the sidewalk, swaying with the curb's impact, his rump rising and falling on the big plastic seat. He pictured him pedaling fiercely into the flow of traffic, arcing toward the freeway entrance like a surfer catching a wave. And then a truck fender obscured Lance's vision. And he pictured the same face, older, more freckled, the nose finer and the lips pinker: Wren's face.

He loved that face. Had he really let his heart roll this far from Darlene? He had no time to follow the thought any farther because at that moment he saw Julia. She was at the bottom of the hill, two football fields away, walking toward him. She carried the Big Wheel in her right hand, and Max like a football on her left hip. The red-faced boy screamed and cried, his arms pinned to his sides. His feet kicked wildly. Julia's head was bent as she lectured Max, not hollering, but more frightening for her quiet intensity. Lance felt a breaker of relief crashing against a crest of anger like a physics experiment in wave dynamics. He could not believe the girl's arrogance. She was like Max on that Big Wheel, careening among the adults, smashing into their lives at midstream, aware only of her power, but ignorant of the damage it might cause, and which would, given karmic reverb, eventually wash back on her.

But the Julia who strode uphill toward Lance was remorseless, Amazonian under her blond cornrows, her head now held up beneath the leaden sky and her back straight despite her burden. When she reached Lance, she handed him the Big Wheel. She said nothing, so he also said nothing and turned around, moving into step as they neared Belle and Sam. The kids stood side by side, ruddy-faced, their hands on their knees, leaning over and breathing heavily.

"Run and get your packs and meet us in the van," Julia ordered over Max's continuing wails.

"What happened?" Sam asked.

"Where was Max?" asked Belle.

"Get," said Julia.

"In the van," said Lance.

"Are we having a playdate?" asked Belle.

"Can we, Julia, can we?" asked Sam.

"One thing at a time," Lance said, wiped out.

By now the pickup was mostly over except for the stragglers. A few mothers lingered in their sandals and shifts, tight-eyed behind year-round tans. The women were locked in a battle of competitive moaning about the rising firestorm, secure that it would never reach Encinitas. Fires happened to the east, north, or south, but never near the shore. His neighbor Coco Montoya was saying that to the east, across I-15 in Poway, her husband's golfing partner had lost his house, along with two purebred Weimaraners he was putting out to stud. Residents had to evacuate, Coco said, repeating what she had seen on news teasers between soap operas. The willowy frosted blonde standing beside Coco was saying that she'd attended Point Loma High School with the wife of the helicopter pilot downed while covering the Ramona blaze. Amid clucks and snuffles, a third claimed the official death toll—one—was intentionally underestimated. She went on to blame global warming and runaway development and George Bush. The willowy blonde said it was just burning bushes and don't make every thing political. Burning bushes like in the Bible, Coco pointed out.

The discussion stopped as the women let the small procession pass: Lance, Julia, Belle, Sam, and the squalling Max. The mothers channeled the spirit of Madame Defarge: Guillotine! Guillotine! Guillotine! These were the same parents who had excluded Lance from their clique, who couldn't make room in their calendars for playdates with Belle if her mother didn't accompany her, who left him standing solo at the birthday parties to which she was occasionally invited. Even Coco, standing small and tailored among the mothers, a dahlia among tulips, said nothing, but Lance detected a raised eyebrow as he passed. Was she on to him?

At the van, Lance opened the hatchback and secured the Big Wheel. He padded to the passenger side, feeling the tenderness of his bare feet, and the reflected shame that he feared no amount of distributing Girl Scout cookies would absolve. He climbed in the back and helped Julia settle the squirming trio in the rear seat, boy, girl, boy. As he strapped and buckled the kids (a concern that seemed belated from the sidewalk mob's perspective), Lance strained to avoid physical contact with Julia, refusing to participate in their unspoken game of Twister. He didn't have to worry. Her movements were now mechanical. She wasn't someone accustomed to fucking up.

"How far did Max get?" Lance asked.

"Too far," Julia said, without offering any specifics. She buckled up beside Lance. Through the windshield, orangey haze filtered the glare off the Pacific. She stretched her legs out against the dashboard with a runner's pride in the body's ability to respond to a sudden demand for speed. Disaster averted was no disaster.

In the back, Max cackled. To entertain his little brother, Sam was singing a song he'd learned in kindergarten: "Juggle, juggle, juggle, juggle, pie in your face," miming first the motion of tossing balls in the air and then smacking his forehead to catch the pie. Max opened his plump petal mouth in big baby laughs and revealed his even seed-pearl teeth—those aggressive fangs that so alarmed his mother. His pudgy untried hands wildly pumped the air in ineffectual imitation and then smacked his freckled forehead hard, leaving behind a red mark above his segmented brow.

Belle joined in, her voice at first tentative, slipping in beneath Sam's strong chant, and singing, "Juggle, juggle, juggle,

juggle, cry." All three wailed like colicky babies. Max laughed and said, "Again."

Sam and Belle sang, "Juggle, juggle, juggle, juggle, pie in your face," and slapped each other's foreheads. Max said, "Jugger, jugger, jugger," while the older kids started another verse. "Dance, dance, dance, dance, pour water over your head," shaking their hair wet-dog wildly. Belle's shimmering dark ringlets boinged like a Koosh ball; for the moment all thoughts of her teacher Mr. Baumgart had evaporated.

"Running, running, running, running, good night," Sam sang, pumping his wiry, muscular arms, and then he put his head on Belle's shoulder and started to snore. She patted his head as if he were a baby, and cooed. For the first time since he awoke that morning, Sam felt just right. The action wasn't elsewhere. He was there, in the moment, dancing, in the glow of Belle.

"Again," said Max. Sam and Belle sang, "Juggle, juggle, juggle, juggle . . ."

The Windstar pulled into Wren's driveway. Lance started to undo his seat belt and Julia stopped him. "I've got the boys," she said. "See you tonight?"

"We're bringing Belle," Lance said. "You're watching the kids?"

"I drew the line at Jade."

"Didn't want the competition?"

"B-I-T-C-H," she spelled.

"Bitch," Sam said from the backseat.

"You owe Sam a quarter," Belle said.

"Why?" Julia asked.

"Saying a bad word," said Belle.

"I didn't say it," Julia said, finally exasperated. "I spelled it."

"Same difference."

"Out, dudes," Julia ordered. "Pop the back so I can get the wheels."

"It's unlocked," Lance said.

The hatch swung open, then slammed shut.

"Can I sit up front?" Belle asked.

"Climb on up," Lance said as Julia called through the passenger window, "Don't tell Wren."

"Tell Wren what?" Belle asked.

Lance sped off without answering, and then paused at the stop sign at the bottom of the hill where Obsidian met Overlook.

"Tell Wren what?" Belle repeated.

"Swearing in front of the boys," Lance said, turning right.

"It wasn't the first time," Belle said. "Where are we going now?"

"Home," he said.

"It's a left, Dad," Belle said. "Not a right."

"Seat belt," Lance said, "now."

Belle peered over the dashboard at the horizon. The eastern fires supercharged the sunset: Tang orange melted into raspberry sherbet. Belle could see that Encinitas was pretty, even today, and maybe the sunsets were better than Barstow's. But pretty only went so far. She didn't measure up to this landscape; she was not a pinky, peachy girl. She missed dust and rust and the ticky-tacky Barstow bungalows. How could she explain that she was a desert girl born to bake under the big blue sky, snug in a small inland crisscross of blacktop where everything she needed was just a bike ride away?

Belle missed zipping down to the playground against the warm wind, pretending her secondhand bike was a motorcycle tearing up the asphalt, until she slung it down next to the metal merry-go-round that got almost too hot to touch in the summer. She would join the throng already in motion, little kids in the middle and the big kids running in the dusty circular track before they leapt on board. They all laughed for the sheer dizziness of it as the shabby parched-grass park spun around them. And, as long as they were moving, they were beyond thoughts and rivalries, boys and girls, toddlers and big kids, spinning at the center of the universe, Barstow-variety.

Barstow was less than three hours north by car, but it seemed impossibly far to Belle. She even missed her hometown's volatile, four-season weather: dry heat, gusty northeast winds, crackling wildfires, shattering thunderclaps, javelins of lightning, muddy flash floods, snow. She loved freezing star-speckled midnights followed by blazing noons. She wanted those three-digit days, so hot she waited eagerly for the sun to set. Looking at her father biting the inside of his cheek, his sloe eyes squinting at the road as if navigating a sandstorm, Belle knew it wasn't a moment to say she'd rather be in Barstow. It just bummed him out, like all the things that bugged her that he couldn't change or fix. Mommy needed to be here in Encinitas, that had been explained. On a good day that was enough. But today was not a good day, thanks to Mr. Baumgart and Max's wild ride. At least she and her father shared the same funk at the moment.

"How was school?" Lance asked dutifully.

"Rough," Belle said. "My oral report was a disaster—*Krakatoa, East of Java*. Baumgart's going to flunk me because I raised a question that I couldn't answer."

"He probably couldn't answer it, either," Lance said sympathetically. "What was it?"

"Why are people so into their careers? And why do adults judge each other based on what they do?"

"Beats me," Lance said with a shrug. "But it makes people feel comfortable if they can slot you by what you do."

"What's the difference between a job and a career?"

"You do a job just to make money," Lance said, pausing to give the question some thought. "Flipping burgers at McDonald's is a job, managing one is a career. But plenty of people start out in careers and end up in jobs. And then there are the lucky few who make money at something they love to do. Find one like that—a profession that makes you happy, even if it drives you crazy."

"Have you ever found one, Dad?"

"Not yet," Lance said, shaking his head. He looked over at Belle. "But we have to help you find yours someday. It's tricky. It only works from the inside out. I can't make you love being a doctor, even though that's a good career. If you want to be a singer, I can't promise you'll be the next Taylor Swift. Lots of folks want singing careers but end up waiting tables, and that's a job."

"What about Mom?"

"Your mother would never have said that opening Darlene's Diner was a career—but that's what it's become. It's something she backed into."

"And your mom was a nurse, right?"

"She was an operating room nurse," Lance said. "And Dad was a professor."

"Those are careers."

"I guess so," Lance said, thinking that his father had been a career asshole. He remembered his mother's face that late November Sunday, as she staggered uphill beside their New Jersey house, her eyes wide, her black hair flying behind her. He ran down to meet her, but she raised her hands in a gesture that said *Don't touch me* stronger than a slap. Lance let her pass and looked down the hill through the twilight gloom at Carl. His best friend stood at the entrance to their bower-clubhouse, his arms crossed and his feet planted wide. Lance began to skim down the slope, moving sideways so he wouldn't take a header in the muck, but Carl stopped him as he approached the edge of the woods with a forbidding shake of the head and said, "Your pop, my mom, you bastard."

When Lance and Ethel moved west, they had been fleeing something. Belle interrupted his memories, asking, "Is your dad still alive?"

Lance shrugged. "I guess so."

"How can you stand not talking to him? I'd go crazy if I couldn't talk to you."

"Thanks, spud." Lance extended his right hand and took her left. It was reassuring that it was still childlike, a reminder of how young she was despite the way she talked.

"So," Belle said, "is being a stay-at-home father a job or a career?"

"So that's where you've been going with this, you little weasel?"

"I may be a weasel," Belle said with a laugh, "but I'm your weasel."

"True," Lance said. "Being a father is what you make it. With me, I guess it's my passion, even though I don't make any money at it. I save us money—because we don't pay a sitter, or a house-keeper, and Mommy can work like a maniac. But raising you is the opposite of the goal-oriented career path: it's the day-to-day stuff that matters, not some future gain. And I have to be ready to change course at a moment's notice."

"Does that mean we can move back to Barstow?"

"Don't push it," Lance said. They sat together in silence. He didn't want to go down that road again.

"Daddy," said Belle, changing directions, "if I don't know what I want to be when I grow up yet, is that okay?"

"Sure, baby," Lance said as the van climbed Jonquil Drive. "You have time. Even I have time."

"What if being a stay-at-home dad is what you were meant to be—and no one in Encinitas is cool enough to get it?"

"Nah," they said together, and laughed.

"Look out," Belle shouted as a shape scuttled across the road. "Raccoon."

"Big cat," said Lance.

"Raccoon."

"Bigfoot."

"Bigfoot," Belle said. They were in agreement again. It felt good.

chapter 11

Wren had been watching from the immaculate living room when Lance's van disgorged Julia and the boys, wondering where her kids were and why they were late, and worrying about leaving them in Julia's care. She wore a periwinkle kimono and leaned pensively against the picture window frame, eating nacho soy chips. A tiny golden crumb dome formed on the ledge. Three houses uphill, a Mexican gardener mowed the lawn, sweat-slicked in the unseasonable warmth beneath the apocalyptic sunset, the sun a bright eye straining to see beyond the smoky haze. Wren was sure there was no cause for alarm; fires never came this close to the coast.

She thought she recognized the gardener, but she had no idea who owned the house. Although she'd lived on Obsidian Lane for seven years, her neighbors were strangers; what she knew were their cars. The last time Wren saw everyone without their vehicles was an April night four years before. Two Torrey Pines High School juniors in a Mercedes four-door sedan sped up the hill from Swami's Beach looking for a party that didn't exist and collided with a midnight skateboarder practicing moonlit slaloms. The driver pinned the stoned athlete against a gardener's parked Chevy truck and the grinding sound of metal against metal had attracted the whole neighborhood. Young and not-so-young ran into Obsidian Lane in shorty pajamas and plaid robes, wondering what had happened, and relaying the news of the accident to whomever arrived on the scene next. The neighbors had remained outside until the last emergency vehicle left, the teens sitting conspiratorially on the curb, the littler ones playing tag in the street, and the longtime residents appraising the new arrivals. It was the closest Obsidian Lane had ever come to a block party.

Isolation in a crowd wasn't what she had expected to feel when they'd bought the house and she fulfilled her domestic fantasy of her own home. She had been born in rural Illinois, near the farm her maternal grandparents and great-grandparents had struggled to maintain with a spirit of stubborn pride and a fierce atheism that frightened the neighbors. For her first ten years, Wren and her FBI agent father, mother, and sisters (Robin and Paloma) moved frequently. Then they rented a series of anonymous suburban Maryland ranch houses, where they lived on the verge of a flight that never materialized. Now she owned the kind of house—okay, a little grander—that she had admired from the family Valiant. She reached out and touched the glass

window, leaving behind a nacho smear. Being on the inside
didn't feel much more secure than she had felt in her father's
car, elbowing her sisters out of the way for the sweet spot, the
window seat behind her mother that was nearly invisible in her
father's rearview mirror. And tonight she would have her sister
Robin to contend with, too.

When the massive rough-hewn oak front door opened, the
boys raced to the TV room and missed their mother entirely.
"Snacks," Julia said brightly. She walked directly to the kitchen,
although she knew her back was to her boss. She was aware of
Wren's watchful gaze from the very first moment the van pulled
up, and the look of reflective upheaval was as distinct on Wren's
face as her cleft chin. The two women were calibrated differently: Julia was energized by the prospect of conflict, and Wren
avoided it at all costs. And yet Wren couldn't resist asking,
"Where were you?"

"Oh, hanging with Lance."

"Hanging?" Wren asked, following Julia into the kitchen.

"Yeah," said Julia, opening the door of the snack cupboard
and gazing at the variety. "We were in his van. Listening to
tunes. Chatting."

"Was Belle with you?" Wren asked, tight-lipped.

"What do you think?" Julia said, pulling out a new bag of
tortilla chips from behind the previously opened bag with its
bright blue plastic clip.

"Where was Max?"

"On his Big Wheel."

"What did you and Lance chat about?"

"The weather—drought, sparks, smoke flumes, fire torna-dos, high winds, the Witch fire torching ten thousand acres," Julia said as she turned from the cupboard, ripping open the new bag of chips. "It's heading toward Escon-dildo."

"Escondido," Wren corrected.

"Right," Julia said with a condescending smile. "It's funny what they say about weathermen, because Lance is so *not*."

"What *do* they say about weathermen?" Wren asked, taking the bait.

"Gay," Julia said, sitting down on a barstool beside the kitchen island. "But we both know that's not true."

"What do you mean by that?"

"He's married," Julia said, but her tough level look ac-knowledged what she had seen that morning in the kitchen. "Not that that's proof positive. Is there any salsa?"

"No," Wren said tersely. A row of unopened hot sauce bottles sat on a cupboard shelf, but she had no intention of serving Julia.

"Lance seems great in the kitchen," Julia said, crunching on a chip. "It's funny, too, because he's so damn sexy when he cooks. He's, like, all flexed, ready but relaxed. The way he holds that knife, confident but not macho, with just the pressure he needs, you know he knows where to put it and how to move it. How's he hung?"

"Hung?" Wren asked, removing wineglasses from a rack overhead and wiping them with a wet paper towel, then align-ing them on the kitchen isle.

"Hung," Julia repeated, louder and more roundly enunciated. "You know: zucchini or radish?"

"You're not really going to talk to me like this, Julia," Wren said in a quiet steady voice that Julia recognized as an attempt to control her temper and the situation—a sign that Julia was nearing her target. "We're not intimates, although I had hoped we could be friends. And I don't talk about men that way."

Sam entered the kitchen and asked, "What way?"

"This is an adult conversation between adults, sweetie," Wren said, in a less steely but still quiet tone.

"Then why are you talking to Julia?" Sam asked.

Wren smiled and Julia asked, "Carrot or sprout?"

"I don't want carrots for snack," Sam said. "Can't I have chips, too?"

"All right," said Wren. "Julia, would you get the boys chips and juice boxes?"

"They're in the pantry, Sam. Go get 'em, and then back to the TV with your flat butt."

"Julia!" Wren chided the babysitter.

Sam interrupted, "All Max wants to watch is Barney."

"You used to love Barney," Wren said.

"I used to poop in my pants, too—and you don't want me going back there," Sam said. "Besides, Barney is so faggy."

"Yeah," Julia said, "he could be a weatherman."

"Sam, where do you learn this stuff?" asked Wren.

"I don't think Barney has sex, Sam," said Julia. "They didn't give him reproductive organs."

"Julia, you're not helping," Wren said.

"No sense in denying his curiosity," Julia said.

Sam was only really curious about snacks right then, so he collected the chips from the cupboard and juice boxes from the refrigerator and left the kitchen, oblivious to his mother's disapproving looks at Julia.

"You know, Wren," Julia said, breaking the heavy silence Sam had left in his wake, "you seem a little edgy."

"I wonder why," Wren replied in clipped tones.

"Maybe you need to go downstairs and meditate."

"Maybe you need to drag the kids away from the TV, go upstairs and see if their rooms are in good shape for tonight, and bathe them. You can give them supper in an hour. Nothing from a box, please. There's some tortellini and broccoli in the fridge."

"One last question," Julia said. "Zucchini or radish?"

Wren made no attempt to answer as Alec's confident, heavy footfalls were heard on the steps leading to the bedrooms. He entered the kitchen looking fit and relaxed in crisp khakis, a Brooks Brothers navy-striped shirt open at the neck, and Topsiders without socks. "How are my beauties tonight?" he asked with a broad smile.

"We were just discussing Lance," Julia said.

"Short subject," he responded congenially.

"Not as short as you think," said Julia.

"Did you two dip into the wine already?" Alec asked.

"No," Wren said. "I'm going upstairs to get ready."

"Why change? You look beautiful in that kimono." Alec

caught Wren by the shoulders as she walked past. He spun her against his body facing away from him and slid his hand down the front of her kimono, his fingers with the cold gold wedding band moving across her nipple and then cupping the breast. He looked at Julia, catching her gaze and holding it, acknowledging that the moment was as much for her as it was for his wife, then wincing as Wren elbowed him in the ribs and removed him like a scratchy sweater.

"I'm going upstairs," Wren said. "You two behave."

When Wren's soft footfalls receded up the stairs and a distant door closed, Alec asked, "Red or white?"

"Red," said Julia. "How about a syrah?"

"Good choice." Alec removed a bottle from the rack and suavely opened it. He poured them two healthy snorts in the crystal glasses Wren had set out for company. He continued to uncork red wine to let it breathe for the guests—and so Wren wouldn't be able to keep track of how much he'd had to drink.

"Your wife's way touchy, for someone who's so Zen," Julia said.

"Marriage is a flawed institution." Alec sighed, hiked his pants, and sat on the barstool beside the babysitter.

Julia leaned her elbows on the granite, put her chin in her cupped hands, and asked in her best breezy young-wife voice, "So, how was your day?"

"Good," Alec said. He took a swig from his glass and considered the day and the wine: "Pretty good."

Alec and Julia in the kitchen were like Sam and Belle in the little girl's bedroom, Julia thought: trying on surface roles for the sheer comfort they brought, unencumbered by reality. It was easy to play the game without the weight of history. Julia found her boss attractive in a Bill Clinton, alpha-male woman-izer way but knew she could never acquiesce to Alec, who would demand it. She valued her pleasure too much. And he, for his part, had no feelings for her—she was too fierce for his taste. Her relative youth didn't concern him. He'd had younger, but not so close to home. For Alec, Julia was a backboard for his displays of robust masculinity. She was a practice chick. So their exchange was pleasantly cozy in its falseness.

"What's on your mind, honeybunch?" Julia asked.

"It's not so easy to brand Darlene," he said, scratching his head.

"I guess the hog-tying would be tough," she said with a laugh.

"You've got to catch them first," he countered.

"I imagine she's got a kick to her, cowboy."

"And the heifers go crazy when they smell the branding iron," said Alec, taking another swig. "And, of course, there's the scent of burning flesh from the other cows."

"And people say you lack a sense of humor," she said, sip-ping beside him.

"Do they?" Alec said, turning his big, square head to look directly at Julia.

"Only behind your back," Julia responded. "So, branding . . ."

"It's not as easy as you might think," Alec said. He paused to consider the process, taking out his handkerchief and blowing his nose. "Mrs. Fields Cookies wasn't born in a day.

Darlene is pretty quirky and she's resistant to being homogenized."

"Is that worse than branding?" she asked with false naïveté.

"Milkier," he said, replacing the handkerchief in his pants pocket. "See? I made another joke."

"It's a record." Julia pushed her empty glass toward Alec. He smiled, filled it, and refilled his own. Then he took the empty bottle and hid it deep under the sink. "So, what you're trying to do," she said, "is create, like, the Bob's Big Boy figure of Darlene—something even the drunkest driver can recognize from the freeway."

"Basically," said Alec, nodding his head.

"I can see where she wouldn't want those Big Boy hips."

"She's already heading in that direction," he said confidentially.

"Is not," she said dismissively.

"She's hippy," he persisted. "Have you ever watched her walk from behind?"

"Obviously not as much as you have."

"From what I can get from Darlene, if working moms like her have anything in common, it's that they bitch all the time."

"That's hard to package," she said. "How do you market a spot where the whole family can complain?"

"Call it the Whine Bar?" Alec asked.

"Another joke, Alec; you're on a roll." Julia laughed. "I vote for Susan Smith's Homicidal House of Pancakes."

"That'll pack them in," Alec said as Julia yanked at her

sports bra. She pulled down the sides and reached inside the scoop neck to adjust her cleavage.

"That's a neat trick," Alec said. "Need help?"

"I can find my own boobs, thank you very much. So," Julia asked disingenuously, "what did Lance do before the Ramsays came to Encinitas?"

"He was a weatherman."

"That explains it," she said definitively, raising her glass to her mouth and drinking slowly for Alec's benefit.

"Explains what?" Alec asked, momentarily distracted by her full lips.

"You know what they say about weathermen."

"What?"

"Gay."

Alec smiled. "I guess that's why Darlene's so needy."

Darlene stepped out of the upstairs shower adjacent to the master bedroom. She wrapped her hair in a towel, eyes down, naked except for the terry-cloth turban. Lance entered and gently caught her around the waist. He cupped her chin, raising her face to see her murky green eyes, and brushing away an island of foam from her cheek with the heel of his hand. The unexpected anger her eyes flashed startled him. He immediately dropped his arm from her waist. He had wanted to drink in her eyes and what he got was scalding tea.

"Don't even go there," Darlene said in response to his physical affection. "I'm so beyond uptight."

"Are you worried about the opening tomorrow?" Lance asked.

"That," Darlene spat, wrapping her torso in a second towel, "and surviving tonight! Attending a dinner party for Wren's sister is the last thing I want to be doing."

"Then let's skip it," Lance said.

"We can't. I already said we'd be there," Darlene said. "It's just that I feel like everything's out of control."

"Nothing's out of control, baby," Lance said, fighting his desire to reach out and embrace her. He tried, instead, to caress her with his voice: "Everything's going great. Tomorrow's going to be a breeze—it's just a party. You're the party girl. And, look, we've escaped Barstow. Isn't that what you wanted? You've got a great house, a great kid, and, hey, you have me. I'm not much, but I clean up well—"

"Isn't it time for your shower?" Darlene interrupted.

"Not until you tell me what's eating you."

"Alec announced at lunch that the mayor is coming tomorrow."

"Terrific," Lance said enthusiastically.

"More like terrifying," Darlene said. "It's so over-the-top. And, then, now the fires are raging uncontrollably. If there are evacuations, shouldn't we cancel?"

"I don't know." Lance shrugged. "What does Alec think?"

"Postponing is unthinkable to Alec. He thinks delaying because of wildfires is as ridiculous as saying we can't open the restaurant because there might be an earthquake. So, there's that. And we had another stupid chat about branding. He wants to turn me into the next Marie Callender, the pie lady. The more we talk, the more I feel like dough."

"I guess that's why I knead you," he said, touching her shoulder.

"Hands off, please," she said. "I got Darlene's because I was Darlene."

"You are Darlene."

"That's kind of my point. I feel like I'm losing touch with my inner Darlene."

"Your Darlenitude."

"My Darlenitude."

"Well, I'm very in touch with your Darlenitude," Lance said, stepping closer.

"I'm so not in the mood," Darlene said. "This is the deal: at work, I feel pushed into being some sacred representative of working mothers, Our Lady of Manic Multitasking. And at home, I feel like sex is work. I keep thinking about getting pregnant, and wondering if I'm ready for another baby, and sleepless nights, and all that worry."

"You said you were ready, baby," said Lance, his hands falling limply to his sides. "You're just freaked about tomorrow."

"Maybe, but I have real doubts about having another child," Darlene said, looking down and away from her husband. She readjusted the towel on her torso and then looked up at Lance. "We're so lucky with Belle. She's perfect. Why risk having Damien, the demon seed? And what if the second kid has birth defects—how would that affect Belle's life?"

"Darlene, you're jumping the gun," Lance said, trying to stem the rising impatience in his voice. "There's no reason to believe that a second child would have problems—and Satanism doesn't run in our genes. Belle is proof that we make great babies together."

"Lance, maybe we should quit while we're ahead?"

"I didn't realize we were ahead. I thought we were still in the middle," he said as Darlene put on a robe and opened the bathroom door to release the steam. He felt stung. This was bad news for him. It was suddenly harder to be supportive of Darlene's work anxiety, to function as ballast for her, and to control his rage and impatience. At times like this, he was even clearer about wanting more kids.

"I'm not sure I want another child." Darlene followed the steam out the door.

"I do," Lance said quietly as he turned on the shower, thinking, ironically, those were the words of his marriage vow. Was it that Darlene didn't want to have another child with him? Or that her love for him wasn't big enough to make that kind of sacrifice? "I do," Lance repeated to the shower head. "I do."

chapter 12

"Another?" Alec asked Julia, raising a second wine bottle ready to pour as the babysitter finished her second glass.

"Three glasses this early would be asking for trouble," Julia said.

"Begging for it," Alec said with a broad smile. He refilled his glass. "The night is young. It's Friday."

"The best part of the evening is already over for me, boss."

"I'm flattered."

"You're not babysitting," Julia said.

"You haven't met Wren's sister Robin," Alec said, gazing up and seeing his wife in the kitchen doorway. She wore pollen-yellow cheongsam pajamas, her hair swirled into a chignon anchored with teak chopsticks. "Look, it's my golden geisha. Wanna walk on my back?"

"Yes," Wren said curtly. "What are the kids doing, Julia?"

"Legos upstairs," Julia said, pointing to the ceiling with her thumb.

"Could you check?" Wren asked, although it was an order. "I wouldn't want Max to choke on one."

Alec laughed. "What doesn't that kid put into his mouth?"

"Broccoli," Julia said. She slipped off the stool and gave Alec a peck on the cheek, saying, "Thanks for the memories, boss."

While Wren took stock of the refrigerator's contents, Alec gave Julia a backhanded slap on the rump. His wife turned, walked to his side, put one hand on his shoulder and picked up the wine bottle with her free hand, examined it. It was more than half full, so she bit her tongue.

"One glass of wine won't kill her," Alec said, acknowledging the unspoken question. "Cut the girl some slack."

The doorbell rang, followed by forceful knocking. The front door opened and Wren's older sister, Robin, stepped through, leading Dave Corning, a relatively hesitant younger man in a dark suit, by the hand. She left the door ajar.

Robin was four-foot-eleven-and-a-half in stocking feet, although she generally wore four-inch stilettos; even her slippers had a three-inch heel. She was a plump, pink, doll-faced brunette with a thinning bob she wore teased to add a tuft of height. Tonight she wore a black skirt suit of undistinguished cut, short enough to reveal her rounded, dimpled knees and a pleasingly firm length of calf. The minimal scarlet satin acetate tank underneath revealed a shelf of jiggling cleavage bracketed by a Victoria's Secret corset.

"Come on in," Wren said after the fact, gliding forward to embrace her sister.

"Don't you look ethnic," Robin said. Wren stiffened mid-hug. "I dragged David with me against his will. He's profiling me for *Newsweek*."

Dave followed Robin in a charcoal Hugo Boss suit that was the first giveaway he was Ivy League gay. It wasn't because he was effeminate in his boyish, confident stance, but because few straight men under thirty had the attention to sartorial detail he had and weren't on-air talent. He had heavy brows, a square chin, a flawless nose, and even white teeth under a full head of well-mowed hair with just a hint of a widow's peak.

"Hail the bestselling author," Alec said, raising both arms in welcome, "*Househusbands—and the Women Who Love Them*. What a great title. Who knew there were so many of us?"

"How's my favorite brother-in-law?" Robin asked, giving him a copy of her new book.

"Your only brother-in-law," Alec said, "since Paloma dumped Fred for that Italian soprano."

"Alec," Wren warned.

Robin laughed, spreading her arms wide and beckoning with scarlet, pointed nails. "Come and give your sister some sugar." They embraced with the vigor absent from her hug with Wren.

"How did your workshop go at Orange Coast College today?" Alec asked.

"A total ambush," Robin said. "They booked some bogus doctor pushing a self-helper called *Back to the Ironing Board:*

Rediscovering the Joys of Housewifery. Who buys this crap? I'd rather join a Wiccan coven!"

"I'm sure they'd be happy to have you," Wren said.

"Wine?" Alec interrupted.

"Vodka," Robin replied, turning toward her brother-in-law. "Do you have Absolut Citron on the rocks?"

"Would you take Stoli with a twist?" he asked apologetically.

"Stranded on this desert island?" Robin said, raising her hands palms up in mock disappointment. "If I must."

"And, Marvin, what can I get for you?" Alec asked.

"David," Robin corrected.

"Dave," Dave corrected.

"Dave," Alec repeated, as if practicing a foreign language. "So, Dave, are you holding out for Absolut?"

"No," Dave said, hanging back by the entrance and observing the ostentatious setting. "Diet Coke, please."

"Must have been a hard week, Dave," Alec said with a laugh.

Dave laughed agreeably, adding a bit of locker-room banter: "An afternoon with your sister-in-law is heavy lifting,"

"That's what all her old boyfriends say," Alec said with a wink.

"You don't know the half of it," Robin replied in a gravelly voice. "Now, who do I have to fuck to get a drink around here?"

"Don't worry," Wren said sourly. "He's prefucked."

"Breathe, yoga girl," said Alec, putting his hand on the small of Wren's back as she passed him on the way to shut the front door. "Breathe."

"Are you still doing that crap?" Robin asked.

"Ohm," Wren replied. She turned to Dave and said, "We have a beautiful view from the deck. Coming?"

"Love to," Dave said, and the pair exited through the sliding glass doors.

Alec steered Robin to the bar. She asked, "What's that smell?"

"Meat, I guess." Alec dropped ice cubes in an old-fashioned glass with a pair of silver tongs and then poured the vodka with a heavy hand. "How's your publisher treating you?"

"Best ever and, even better, I've got Dr. Phil on the line," she said, taking the glass from Alec and swirling it so that the ice tinkled pleasantly within. "We're pitching a segment on breadwinner wives and the challenges of finding domestic balance. Did you know that one in three wives in American families is the primary breadwinner?"

"No clue. That's some stat, Robin. You're a branding dream," said Alec appreciatively. "How's the little hubby back in Cleveland?"

"Not so little. The doctor diagnosed Eamon with type two diabetes. He's been hissing and spitting ever since we put him on the all-salad-all-the-time diet," Robin said, then sipped her drink. "The downside is there's a complete ban on alcohol."

"What's the upside?"

"He can eat as much tofu as he wants."

"Do people in Cleveland eat tofu?" Alec asked incredulously.

"No," said Robin with mock seriousness. "He's the first. In the meantime, he's keeping busy at the East Cleveland Playhouse. This season he's lighting *Long Day's Journey into Night*. He hardly notices I'm gone, but he sure wants whiskey."

"Does he make any money doing that?"

"Last year he grossed fifteen thousand, up seven hundred from the previous year."

"You're a saint, darlin'," Alec said, resting his large hand on her shoulder, "a saint."

"That's what I keep telling Eamon," Robin said, smiling with the pleasure of having her biases confirmed.

"Wait until you see the househusband we have for you tonight," Alec said, watching Wren and Dave laughing as they returned from the deck. "This guy Lance is a total loser. Isn't that right, honey?"

"Right, honey, what?" asked Wren as she turned to slide the glass door shut behind her and checked to see if the latch caught.

"I said Lance is a total loser," said Alec, "right, honey?"

"Why would you *ever* say that?" Wren asked, taken aback.

"How else would you describe a guy whose biggest responsibility is distributing Girl Scout cookies?"

"That's awfully judgmental. The way you portray him, Alec, sure, he sounds like a washout," Wren said, readjusting the chopsticks in her hair as she approached Alec and Robin, with Dave following in her wake. "Look at him another way: If you consider Belle his primary responsibility—and that raising children right, and with careful supervision, is something of value—then what Lance is doing by staying home while Darlene works is incredibly worthwhile. Not the least of it being that he frees up Darlene for your schemes. And if, in addition, he's the only daddy involved in Scouts, how great is it that he's taking an active role, instead of just dumping Belle off at the weekly meetings—"

"And sewing on her badges," interrupted Robin. "This goes right to the heart of my book—"

"C'mon, you women's libbers, we're talking about a guy who hasn't worn long pants in seven months," Alec said disparagingly. "If you ask him what he did today, he'll say, 'Made a right turn.'"

"That's unfair," Wren said, perturbed. "He was a TV weatherman back in Barstow."

"And you know what they say about weathermen, Robin," Alec said.

"They do it in showers?" asked Robin with a shrug.

"Gay," Alec concluded.

"Not David Letterman," said Dave, taking a sip of his soda.

The doorbell pealed like rain falling on lily pads. "Is someone outside, or are we getting a massage?" Robin asked. "Ohm," she hummed as she strode to the enormous oak door and yanked it open.

"Hello," said Darlene, riding a wave of harsh, warm air. The Ramsays made a handsome couple. Lance looked taller and leaner in a khaki linen suit with a burgundy-striped button-down oxford shirt and burgundy tie, his hair slightly slicked back from his tan face. To Lance's left, Darlene wore a retro burgundy polka-dot dress with a full knee-length skirt, a tight waist, and a sweetheart neckline. Her sun-streaked blond hair was twisted away from her face in a high ponytail. She had emphasized her carefully lined mouth with Russian red lipstick, keeping the rest of her makeup matte and understated, except for lashes thick with black mascara. Belle walked five steps behind them, a condemned prisoner.

"I'm Robin, Wren's sister. And you must be . . ."

"I'm Darlene and he's Lance, and our daughter, Belle."

"Oh," said Robin. She made a sweeping motion for them to enter while vodka splashed out of her glass. She rubbed the spot into the rug with her toe.

"Here's the birthday girl now," Alec announced, drawing Belle into the living room. He put his arm around her shoulder and gave her a big unwelcome squeeze, saying, "Happy birthday, girlfriend."

"I'm too young to be your girlfriend," Belle said, retreating beneath her curls, chin down, appalled by the adult attention.

"True enough," Alec said.

"Only just," Robin cracked.

"Alec has such a way with children," Wren said tartly, stepping in before Robin's words had a chance to soak in like the vodka on the carpet. She reached out, separating Belle from Alec, and asked, "Could you take chips and dip upstairs to the boys?"

"Sure thing," said Belle, desperate to escape the parents. "Is Julia here, too?"

"Yes."

"Hurray!" said Belle.

"Hurray," Wren said, with less enthusiasm. The door chimed again. Wren pointed Belle toward the stairs while Robin opened the front door, having wasted no time adopting the hostess role. Coco Montoya entered, dwarfed by the oak doors and her husband, John Juan, who stood beside her. He draped one large arm over her shoulder, across her chest, and hooked a hairy hand onto her waistband. She could have been his ventriloquist's dummy.

In addition to wearing her husband, Coco had on a red halter dress and matching high-heeled sandals. Large golden chandelier earrings bracketed her hopeful, dramatically made-up face. John Juan, a once-handsome thick-necked man with heavily lashed large brown eyes that suggested the beautiful child he must have been, was casual in khakis. His deep blue Ralph Lauren dress shirt was unbuttoned to reveal a robust crop of chest hair.

After they made their introductions and Alec offered drinks, the guests chatted and Robin gave Dave a tour of her sister's house. Wren talked to Darlene and Lance about the vile Mr. Baumgart, and the rumor that he had thrown a blackboard eraser at the head of one sixth-grader during social studies. Lance said it had happened in math, and was only a pencil eraser. Wren asked if she could still order more Thin Mints, and acted pleased to discover it was still possible, since those were Alec's favorites. Alec, hearing his name, came over and agreed, and asked if it was only him, or did the cookies seem to be shrinking?

Wren excused herself, feeling ridiculous and false and shallow standing beside Alec and making small talk with Lance and his wife. She walked over to the open dining room to putter with last-minute arrangements while her guests continued prattling away. She lit blood-colored tapers at the large rough-hewn oak table that had enough room for the night's eight, plus another eight. She refolded napkins and aligned cutlery. Her hand brushed against one bunch of the abundant pink-throated, cream-tipped lilies she had set along the table's center to counteract the room's maleness. She closed her eyes and breathed deeply: the blooms were disturbingly fragrant; when she had bought them their sweetness seduced her, but en masse they produced a heavy perfume edged with an undercurrent of kindergarten paste.

With a sigh, Wren went into the kitchen and returned with the salad course, setting one plate down on each charger. She returned to the kitchen twice to finish the task and then stepped back, absentmindedly wiping her clean hands on her thighs. She admired the way the red cabbage and dried cranberries picked up the lilies' rose-pink throats. She couldn't delay any longer, so she dimmed the electric lights and invited the guests to come in and take their seats.

"What is this in my salad, a cockroach?" asked John Juan, assuming the spot at the head of the table that Wren had set aside for Robin.

"A walnut," Wren said.

"See, Coco?" Juan laughed. "I told you they were going to serve us nuts and berries."

"Juan," Coco cautioned.

"Am I embarrassing you already, *hijita?*" John Juan brayed.

"Alec," Robin said, cutting John Juan off and seizing control of the seating, "drop your butt at the other end."

"Yes, mistress," Alec said, and set his full wineglass at the foot.

"Wren, stop futzing with the flowers," Robin said. "They're beautiful, but we're not eating them. Plop down next to John Juan so you'll be near the kitchen. Then, let's see, how about Lance next to you. And Darla—"

"Darlene," Wren corrected.

"Right," Robin said, pointing to the empty seat next to John Juan. "Darlene, hunker down next to . . . which is it, John or Juan?"

"My friends call me John Juan. I was born Juan. I came to this country and they called me John. But John Juan rhymes with Don Juan, which is closer to the real truth."

"I'm sure it is," Robin said. "Dave, honey, could you sit on my right, please? Are you sure you don't want anything stiffer than a Diet Coke?"

"No, thanks," Dave said. Yes, he did want a stiff one, but he was on the clock. He locked eyes with Lance to acknowledge they felt like Ken dolls manipulated by an overbearing girl. Dave got a vibe that Lance had some secrets, but he wasn't sure what that meant. Was he gay? Maybe, but unlikely. Dave wondered whether he would have time to connect with an old college friend at a Hillcrest bar before the town rolled up the sidewalks.

Meanwhile, Coco stood for a moment like the last child out

at musical chairs, until Wren said, "Coco, you sit next to Alec."
Coco brightened when she realized Lance was on her left—and
they were far from her husband and his reflexive dinner-table
domination.

"Vegetarianism mystifies me," John Juan said. "If God had
wanted us to graze, he wouldn't have put cows in our path
and sharp bicuspids on our palate. I spent my life working to
afford steak, but then I'm just a reactionary old patriarch, right,
hijita?"

"Right, mi amor," Coco said. She spread her napkin ostenta-
tiously across her lap. "And that's why I love you so much."

"So, Robin," John Juan said, "tell us about this little book
of yours."

"It's about working women who earn more than their husbands."

"All two," John Juan said.

"All twelve million, thank you very much," Robin said
with authority. "The book addresses who these women are,
what their husbands do, the pitfalls they face inside and outside the home, and how these couples can achieve domestic
balance."

"What's the title?" Coco asked. She slipped her hand beneath
her napkin and moved under the table toward Lance's lap with a
swimmer's suave muscle control. From what she had glimpsed
in his kitchen when she'd dropped by to pick up her Girl Scout
order, she figured the box was already open and he wouldn't
mind sharing his cookies.

"*Househusbands—and the Women Who Love Them*," said Robin.

John Juan snorted. "More like *Losers and the Suckers Who Marry Them*."

"Spoken like a true alpha male," Robin said dismissively.

"Nothing wrong with that," Coco said, drumming her nails on Lance's thigh under the table.

"Here, here," said Alec. He raised his glass, toasted, swigged, and returned it to the table. Lance and Darlene shifted uncomfortably. They didn't make eye contact across the table. Darlene ferreted out a walnut in her salad. Lance glanced down the table at Wren, catching her discreetly switching wineglasses with Alec.

"You get paid for writing this fiction?" John Juan pushed aside his half-eaten salad.

"Very well," Robin said. "More than my husband earns."

"At my house, I earn the dough," John Juan continued. "I've never met a woman who makes as much as I do. Never! *Nunca!* If a man earns less than his wife does, then he must be really low-paid. What kind of freeloader would let this happen?"

"That attitude makes househusbands the last taboo—and keeps breadwinning wives quiet about their accomplishments," Robin said, a little louder than the intimate setting required. "When a working woman admits she outearns her husband, she rarely gets approbation. Instead, she gets her man dissed."

"Forgive my husband. He didn't mean to be personal." Coco walked her hand, slowly and lightly, up and up and up Lance's thigh. He inhaled and tried not to panic. Maybe her husband was a TV honcho, but another inch and Coco would know he was no impotent weatherman. He covered her hand with his and gently returned it to her lap.

"Robin's a big girl," John Juan said. "She understands rhetorical arguments."

"Personal reasons inspired the book. I slipped onto the fast track writing how-to books for working women. At the same time, my husband, Eamon, wanted to leave Cleveland to see if he could make it as a theatrical lighting designer in Manhattan. I convinced him to stay in Ohio, where our standard of living soared on my salary. Meanwhile, Eamon pursued his art without stressing over money, while taking over the shopping, cleaning, and cooking. The downside is that he's a better chef—the proof is in our waistlines."

"I like a woman I can grab on to," Alec said.

"With two hands," agreed John Juan, making a grabbing motion with both arms outstretched. "What about you, Dave?"

"Three hands," Dave said, looking up from his salad and picking up his cue. "I'm curious, John Juan, what you expect from a wife and whether that corresponds to what Robin expects from her husband."

"Sex on demand," John Juan said.

"Sounds good to me," said Robin.

"It's a wife's obligation to look after her husband," said John Juan.

"Yes, mi amor," Coco said as she crossed her leg over Lance's.

"Did you say lick her husband?" Alec asked with a smirk.

Wren pushed her chair back in disgust. She rolled her eyes at Alec as she rose and began to remove salad plates.

"Look," John Juan said, "but lick is okay, too."

"Let me help," Lance said to Wren. As she retreated into the kitchen, he stacked Robin's plate on his own, then backed his chair away from the table and awkwardly rose. Coco took her napkin and delicately wiped the corner of her mouth; her salad was untouched. Lance held the plates low on his lap as John Juan said, "A wife should cook, clean, and care for the kids."

"You could be describing Lance," Alec said with a laugh, looking up at Lance, who stood at his left, collecting the host's empty salad plate.

"So, Lance, what do you do all day?" John Juan asked, as the man in the khaki suit backed against the swinging door and followed Wren into the kitchen.

"Maybe you should ask your wife," Alec said.

Darlene looked at Alec, then at Coco, and then back at Alec, puzzled, and said, "Ask your wife what?"

Coco swiftly responded, "The husband should earn enough to hire a nanny, a cook, a housekeeper, and a personal trainer so his wife has the muscles to heft her gold card."

"That wasn't Alec's question," John Juan insisted. "Why should you know what Lance does all day?"

Darlene cringed and stared at Coco, waiting for her answer.

"Christ, he lives next door, John," Coco said.

"No wonder I didn't recognize him. He's wearing pants," John Juan said, laughing.

"He's in charge of cookie distribution for Jade's Girl Scout troop. If you could put down the Thin Mints, I wouldn't have to go over there so often," said Coco.

"He's the cookie man?" John Juan laughed heartily. "Oh, hijita, I knew you had better taste."

"I married you, no?"

"I thought I married you!"

"That's what I wanted you to think," Coco said smugly, "that you had chosen me of your own free will."

"Well, you weren't my ex-wife's choice," John Juan snorted.

In the kitchen, Lance scraped plates and Wren placed them in the dishwasher. "Thanks for all your help," Wren said.

"What do I do all day?" Lance grumbled to Wren. "I try not to feel like a loser just because Darlene earns more money than I do."

"I know what you do part of the day," purred Wren, "and you're no loser."

chapter 13

Alone in the kitchen, Wren and Lance stared at each other over the open door of the Miele dishwasher. Wren wiped her hands on a dishrag and studied his dark brown receiving eye. He looked confused and harried, flushed. She read the weariness of disappointing others who had unrealistic expectations. Then she looked past that and saw his passion for her, unfiltered. She knocked it back like a shot of tequila. She was dizzy with the emotion and, in the moment, fired back a look of pure affection, romantic and platonic, that he clearly understood.

Alec stumbled in, tossing a comment over his shoulder ("Market domination") as he shoved the swinging door with one hand, an empty wine bottle in the other. The door, typically left open when there wasn't company, rebounded and clipped him on his broad forehead. The banging sound, along with the laughter that pursued Alec into the kitchen, didn't break Wren and Lance's concentration. Alec watched for a moment, dizzy from the knock on his head. He looked from Wren to Lance and back, as if he'd channel-surfed onto a Middle Eastern soap opera and couldn't gather the narrative thread. For a moment he saw them separate from him, as the evening's host and hostess, but ignored that instinct and cracked, "So now Wren's giving you the silent treatment, eh, buddy? You've got to watch out for those sudden cold fronts."

Wren turned. She saw Alec over her shoulder, saw him in full like no one else could—not even his mother, who had a lock on the baby years, but hardly knew the man from annual visits. Wren saw the handsome big brother of five she had fallen for, with his linebacker shoulders and square forehead, his Irish blue eyes and feathered hair. He was the fixer, the class president type she had never aspired to, with his five-year plan, his ten-year plan, his lists in a cramped but careful hand.

Wren eyed him, aware that silence was her greatest weapon. He was defenseless without her reaction; he had no traction. He was still a big, boisterous, handsome man with a full head of sandy brown, slicked back, Kennedy-scion hair—she could see that. She could. She could see it in how other women reacted to him—Robin, Darlene, and Julia. How he attracted them. But she also saw his face ruddy with drink, the way laugh lines crisscrossed anger lines and his right eyebrow arched in amused mistrust of anyone's intelligence but his own. His reddish cupid's mouth had shrunk, the top lip thinning in contrast to the sensuous bottom lip. She saw the bully, the bullshitter, the cheap desperate flirt. And she knew her power over him, his great need for her. To be strong for Wren meant not confronting his own weakness. She'd only seen him cry once, at his father's funeral. Alec was a walled city. And Wren realized that her long siege of his heart was nearly over. She was no longer trying to scale those walls. She had almost turned away from him, but not quite, and she suspected that it would be at that very moment when her back was turned that she would be most vulnerable to him.

"Robin wants more wine," Alec said, raising the empty bottle.

"Leave that bottle with the empties under the sink," Wren said. "Lance, can you carry the couscous in that orange casserole?"

"The Creuset?"

"Uh-hum," said Wren. "Here's a pot holder."

"Toss it," Lance said. Wren flung the oven mitt and Lance caught it one-handed. He had removed his jacket and draped it on a barstool. His sleeves were rolled up; he had skipped tying on a half apron, although he considered it. "Do I need a trivet?"

"On the sideboard," Wren said.

"Are you two starting a catering company?" Alec asked.

Wren and Lance looked at each other. "Nah," Lance said, as he neared the dining room. "I'd rather slack off."

"I'm right behind you with the leg of lamb," Wren said.

"So that's what that smell was," Alec said, running his hands through his hair.

"That's the smell." Wren's voice rose melodically. She was

trying to be Zen and remember if she had laid out the carving knife. "Is it a good smell or a bad smell?"

"It's a lamb smell," Alec said.

"Can you carry the moussaka?" she asked Alec over her shoulder.

"Is it animal, vegetable, or mineral?"

"Forget it," Wren said. "I'll come back."

Left alone in the kitchen, Alec opened the wine case and scanned the bottles like a scholar at an antiquarian book fair. He uncorked a French Merlot and poured himself a fresh glass. He considered seeking the moussaka, but didn't know what it looked like. He congratulated himself on his ignorance, on being a red-blooded steak-and-potato guy. He had a vague recollection that Moussaka was the patriarch in The Lion King, and laughed aloud. He was nobody's stiff.

The door to the kitchen banged open and Darlene entered, her cheeks flushed. She had been sitting at her place at the table near Coco and John Juan (neighbors she routinely avoided when she walked down her driveway to get the newspaper), steaming in silence ever since Robin had announced her book title. "Where are the carving knives?" Darlene demanded.

"Is it safe to tell you?" Alec asked with a smile.

"You knew about this, didn't you, Alec?"

"About the carving knives, Darlene?"

"No," she said, banging drawers in search of silver. "This. This ambush."

"What ambush?" he asked, sounding genuinely concerned.

"Loser husbands and the women they marry."

"You're overreacting," Alec said.

"Men get angry," Darlene said, rummaging through drawers. "They kick garbage cans. That's okay. They smash their hands into doors. Fine. You invite me to your house and I'm a fucking specimen and you don't even give me a heads-up? Shit, Alec, we're supposed to be partners. We see each other every day."

"That's a good thing, right?"

"Of course it's a good thing, Alec, but this isn't about you. Here they are." She turned toward Alec, a large knife in one hand and a larger one in the other. "Which knife?"

"Do you have a license to carry?" Alec jokingly took a giant step back. "Here, Darlene, have a glass of Special Alec Reserve."

Darlene returned the smaller knife to the drawer. She approached Alec, her back to the kitchen door, and said, "Look at my tongue." She inched forward within the circle of Alec's winey breath, the large knife in her right hand, her tongue extended.

"What am I looking for?" he asked, off balance. "You smell nice; what's that perfume?"

"Don't change the subject, Alec. See any scars?"

"No," he said, confused. "Why would there be a scar?"

"From biting my tongue," Darlene said.

Wren entered silently behind Darlene and said, "I see you've found the carving knife. I meant to use it on the lamb, not the host, although I can understand the motivation."

Turning toward Wren, Darlene realized how she and Alec must have looked from his wife's perspective. Intimate. Who would have believed Darlene, her cleavage raised so close to Alec she was almost touching his chest, was just sticking her tongue out, or that her dominant emotion was rage, not desire? What Darlene saw in Wren's marsupial eyes was a studied blankness. The hostess stood in an annoying sea of calm and perfect posture. She tipped her head slightly in an attitude of patience, her hair upswept except for a wispy escaped spiral, her silk pajamas revealing her curves better than any low-cut blouse.

"I was just coming out with the knife," Darlene said.

"I'll take it," Wren said, extending her hand.

"Do you need any help?" Darlene asked, handing over the knife.

"We've got it covered," Wren said, holding the blade point down at her side. She left the kitchen: we; she and Lance.

"C'mon," said Alec, walking toward the door and placing his hand gently but firmly on Darlene's bare arm to move her along with him. "Chow's on."

"Just cop to it, Alec. Admit you ambushed me," Darlene said, pulling away from his touch. "You knew about Robin's book. You not only concealed it, but you delivered Lance and me as Exhibit A of her thesis."

"It doesn't apply. Lance is a weatherman," Alec said back, gentling his voice as if she had gone off the deep end, in a way that just provoked her more.

"An unemployed weatherman," Darlene snapped.

"We're working on that," he said, herding her forward with his hands on her ass. "Now march."

"What's that smell?" Darlene asked, swatting his hands away.

"What smell?" Alec asked.

Upstairs, in Sam's room, Julia read BOMB, outstretched on his bed, a heavy Adirondack twin of rough-hewn branches that looked like it had grown out of the floor. With her muscles, golden cornrows, and robust features aglow, Julia resembled a Botticelli Diana of the Hunt, a flawless beauty perfectly able to shoot, skin, and flay a lesser animal, then wear its spotted pelt while still warm. As a vegan, she would censure the idea, but the image's ferocity would secretly delight her.

Sam's bedroom was self-consciously boy: Persian-blue walls with a constellation-painted ceiling, a blue comforter sprinkled with images of rocket ships and comets in full gassy spray. An array of modest-sized trophies cluttered a curio cabinet. Given pride of place was his father's high school quarterback MVP award, a gaudy cobalt-blue column supporting a gleaming golden figure of a player in Statue of Liberty position, arm back, ball firmly in place, eyes focused on the inevitable future touchdown.

From the next room accessible through an open door, the TV blared and Max conversed unintelligibly with Wyle E. Coyote. Adjacent to Sam's bed, under a homemade mobile of the sun and planets (oops, there were only seven), Belle knelt on a rocket-shaped area rug. She assembled a Lego Bionicle warrior piece by piece, occasionally consulting the diagram to her left. Sam sat on the foot of his bed, painting Julia's toenails the color of Merlot.

"What's that smell?" asked Belle, looking up.

"Nail polish?" Sam asked.

"That icky meaty smell," said Belle. She looked skeptically at the Bionicle's head. "It makes me want to hurl."

"Need a bucket?" Sam asked.

"It's the lamb," Julia explained. "That's what the alleged adults are eating."

"Eew," Belle gagged. In the next room, beyond the connecting bath, Looney Tunes ka-bangs inspired Max's gleeful laughter. The toddler had found his first vocation: demolitions expert.

"What is lamb, exactly?" Sam asked.

"Baby sheep," Julia said, laying aside her magazine. "They slaughter them before they turn one year old, or before they lose their baby teeth."

"So, downstairs our parents are eating dead baby?" Sam asked.

"That is so gross," Belle exclaimed. "Why would anybody do that?"

"Don't shoot the messenger," Julia said, taking a long luxurious stretch and flexing her newly polished toes. "I don't eat anything on hooves, but the flesh is more tender when they're young, according to carnivores."

"What's a carnivore?" Belle asked, looking up from the Bionicle at Julia.

"A meat-eater," Julia explained.

"I thought it meant a carnival worker," said Belle.

"Like a clown?" Sam asked.

"Only scarier," Belle said.

"Clowns are scary enough."

"You don't like clowns, either?" Belle asked.

"They creep me out," Sam said.

"They're just freaky adults in makeup," Belle said, attempting to insert the toy's legs into its torso. "Why do parents think kids want clowns?"

"I'd rather be in a room with a vampire," Sam confided. "At least then you know what to expect."

"Do you know what veal is?" Julia asked.

"No," Belle said.

"Baby cow," Julia said.

"Why don't they just call it baby cow?" Belle asked.

"No one would eat it," Julia said. "That's why they pass it off as veal."

"Then what's tofu?" Belle asked.

"Soy protein," Julia said. "No animals harmed. No baby teeth."

"Well, that's a relief," said Belle. "I'd become a vegetarian, if I liked vegetables."

"You just need someone to cook them right for you," Julia said.

"There isn't a right way on the planet to cook peas," Sam said.

"I eat them straight out of the freezer," said Julia, "like green pellet pops."

"Lamb is starting to sound good," Sam said.

"So, Julia, could you explain something I read to me?" Belle asked.

"It depends on what it is," Julia said.

"What does 'like lambs to the slaughter' mean?"

"That means they're innocents, Belle. They—the lambs, the people in that position—didn't do anything wrong, but they're being led to their doom."

"Doom?" asked Belle.

"The slaughterhouse: the babies don't have a clue what's coming. And, because they're ignorant, they don't even resist."

"Resistance is futile," Sam said.

"Reminds me of my birthday party," Belle said.

"You could change that, my little lamb," Julia said, sliding off the bed and sitting on the rocket-shaped rug facing Belle. "Whose party is it?"

"Mine," Belle said halfheartedly.

"What are you going to do?" Julia said.

"Take it back?" Belle asked.

"When?"

"Tomorrow."

"Why?" Julia asked.

"Because I have the power," Belle said.

"Okay, my lioness, don't wimp out on me," Julia said, pulling her knee to her chest and inspecting Sam's polishing. She gave a long, slow blow on her toes, then stretched her foot out again and rose to a standing position. "Well, you guys are no prob. I'm going downstairs to make sure the adults are behaving."

"Do you need to take my bat?" Sam asked, gesturing toward the closet.

"No, thanks," Julia said, stopping at the door to do a karate pose, "I have my fists of fury."

After Julia left, Belle stretched out on the carpet with her legs raised on the side of Sam's bed. The masked Bionicle monster dominated her chest, anticlimactic and inert now that she'd assembled it. The lamb smell (and her new knowledge about baby sheep) twisted her stomach but if she stayed still she might not actually throw up.

"Cool," said Sam about the completed Bionicle as he approached Belle with two bed pillows. He tossed one on the rug beside her and the other onto her face; she repositioned it under her head. Sam lumped down next to her and placed his legs on the bed, less successfully, given his lesser height. For a while they stared at the ceiling, until Belle felt compelled to break their silence.

"There are eight planets," she announced, looking up at the mobile dangling above Sam's bed, "not seven."

Sam was silent for a moment and then he said, "Not in my world."

"Your world *is* my world," said Belle.

"No," said Sam. "It's not. In my world, there are seven planets, plus an invisible one ruled by the legendary Zondor and his evil onions."

"There's no such thing as an invisible planet," Belle said. "And if Zondor was so legendary I would have heard of him."

"You don't know everything," Sam said.

"I never said I did, Sam. But there *are* eight planets."

"It's really stupid to always act like a know-it-all and correct people and stuff. It makes them feel small."

Belle paused in response to the hurt in Sam's voice. "Does it make you feel small?" she asked.

"I am small."

"No, you're not," Belle said. "Max is small."

"I'm the smallest boy in our class."

"Really?"

"Really," Sam said. "Welcome to my world."

"Thanks for inviting me," Belle said.

"Just don't bump your head on the way in."

They reclined in shared silence until Belle asked, "Do you want to play house?"

"Not really," Sam said. "If Dad caught us, I'd be roadkill."

"Forget it. I'm sick of moms and dads anyway. Let's play desert."

"How?"

"We're two snakes lying on a warm rock in the moonlight . . ."

". . . listening for field mice . . ."

". . . to eat for dinner . . ."

"You can take the first one," Sam said.

"No, it's yours. I'm not so sure how I feel about eating live meals."

"It's the bones that worry me," said Sam.

"I worry about the wiggling as they go down."

"Yuck. I wish you hadn't said that. What if they scream as they're going down?"

"Okay, so let's say we just ate our dinner, and we're feeling fat and lazy . . ."

". . . and we have big bumpy things in the middle of our stomachs . . ."

". . . and we're looking at the moon," Belle said.

"Is it full?"

"The fullest. It's ginormous and yellow . . ."

". . . but not cheesy."

"I love the moon," Belle whispered. "When I was little, I thought it was following me. We'd go driving at night, and there it would be, riding along in my window. Or it would play hide-and-seek, crossing from one side of the car to the other, but always coming back. It was my moon. And when I saw the moon in the daylight it meant that it was hanging around to watch over me and good things were coming. 'Look, Dad,' I'd say, 'it's my moon.'"

"If you can have a moon, then I can have an invisible planet."

"Why not?" Belle said, acquiescing.

Belle and Sam lay side by side, breathing slowly like snakes, watching the moon and seven planets, hearing cartoon ka-booms and John Juan's booming bass, Aunt Robin's tinny laughter. Sam snaked his right hand over to Belle's left and covered it. She didn't pull away, she just said, "Snakes don't have hands."

"They do in my world," said Sam.

"Fine," Belle said. "We could be salamanders."

"You put the Bionicle's head on backwards."

"I thought it looked weird, but I couldn't tell."

"No big deal," said Sam.

chapter 14

"You never answered my question, Lance," John Juan said, shoving away his plate and easing his belt. "What do you do all day?"

"Tell us Cro-Magnon hunters what makes you new age gatherers tick," said Alec.

"Back in Barstow——" Lance began.

"I bet you sleep in every morning," Alec interrupted.

"Yeah," Julia said from the perch on the sideboard she had assumed when she came downstairs from Sam's room, "with your wife."

Darlene, mortified by the subject of Lance's daily routine, had been picking at red candle wax from the table. Now she looked up at the freakish babysitter, not sure what she had actually heard because it came out of left field. She looked over at Alec, missing Lance's covert glance at Wren. (He had a bungee jumper's gut fear that the world was about to fall away from him, yet a small part of him wanted their secret blown, wanted their domestic worlds exploded so they could reconfigure.) Eyes down, Wren studiously worried a table-cloth spot with her napkin while Alec paused to read Julia's face. The babysitter's predatory blue-gray eyes stared back into Alec's above her raised, defiant chin. Alec had a flicker of the scene he had interrupted in the kitchen; it registered like a déjà vu and was immediately ignored.

Julia unwrapped her Chiclet-toothed smile and said, "Just yankin' your chain, boss."

"And I pay you?" Alec asked.

"Not nearly enough," said Julia, glancing over at Wren and raising her eyebrows. Wren looked away.

"Don't expect a raise anytime soon," Alec said.

"Always thinking with your checkbook," Robin said.

Alec laughed. "Not always."

"Lance doesn't need to justify himself to you throwbacks," Robin said, ascending her soapbox once more. "This kind of knee-jerk external criticism impacts these marriages. Even if Lance excels at home—and I bet he does—where's his recognition? Instead, he becomes afraid of socializing because he can't answer that softball question: what do you do?"

"You're not afraid, are you, buddy?" John Juan asked.

"No," Lance began, gearing up to pitch John Juan based on Julia's intel that he managed a TV station. "I have a profession—"

"And consider the internal strain of the couple balancing

household responsibilities," Robin interrupted. "Who vacuums, carpools, and schedules the pediatrician? It even affects who takes the lead in bed."

"I do," Darlene said.

"Only on Tuesdays and Thursdays," Lance said. He sensed the window of opportunity to approach John Juan for a weatherman job sliding shut. Maybe Coco could help him later. He gave an inward groan; what would that cost? "I've got Wednesdays and Fridays."

"On the weekends, it's freestyle," said Darlene.

Alec said, "If you're getting it at home six days a week—"

"Seven," said Lance.

"Then I'm quitting work!" Alec said, decisively putting down his fork. "My only question is, how will Wren support me?"

"I'll open a yoga studio," Wren said, rising from her seat. "Does anybody want more lamb?"

"We all have plenty, Wren," Robin said. "Stop fussing and sit down. Now, nervous kidding aside, I'm curious to see John Juan's reaction once Lance reveals how full his days really are."

"Typical day?" Lance asked.

"If there is such a thing," Robin said.

"I get up before everyone else, put on my shorts."

"Spare us every detail," John Juan said.

"I start the coffee, walk outside and get the papers, check the garden's progress: what's bloomed, what's peaked. Then I do my crunches and give Belle a five-minute warning. I nudge Darlene, return to Belle, get her breakfast order and hope it's something we have. I go back and rattle Darlene's cage again and make sure she puts two feet out of the bed—otherwise she just rolls over."

"I do not," Darlene protested.

"Darlene, why not use an alarm clock?" Robin asked.

"Lance is awake, and he always gets me up in time," Darlene replied.

"The point is, Lance is reliable. He isn't contributing the bigger paycheck, but he's the one who keeps the household rolling. He's the pulse," Robin explained.

"What next, Lance?" Dave prodded.

"Make breakfast," Lance said.

"I can open a box," John Juan put in.

"He makes me eggs," Darlene said in her husband's defense. "French toast if I'm stressed."

"Then I help Belle get ready for school," Lance continued. "I find the lost sock or rescue the homework from the turtle. We negotiate Belle's bag lunch: I try to veto the Fluff sandwich, but don't always win. Meanwhile, I comment on the newspaper items Darlene reads aloud from the dining room. I empty the dishwasher, shift a load of laundry to the dryer, or start a presoak. I water the kitchen plants and take a pass over the family room for the obvious piles of shoes, toys, and last night's wineglasses. By then Darlene is ready to go, so I help her locate her keys and sunglasses."

"And he reminds me how fab I look," said Darlene, looking at her husband.

"That's easy, babe," Lance said, making eye contact. "Then

I grab coffee and Belle gets a juice box for the road and we hit the minivan. We'll have our morning chat—the birds and the bees, global warming, the secret rituals of the Girl Scouts, free trade, how to spell logorrhea. Then I brake in front of the school and she leaps out. I try not to notice as Belle's skirt flies up that even in gag-green and knee socks my daughter's total perv bait. After I check the bushes, I realize there's zip I can do about it except make sure Belle has a good head on her shoulders, and a keen eye—mine—watching her back."

"Then back to bed, right?" asked John Juan.

"First I attend Underachiever's Anonymous at the local Presbyterian: my name is Lance and I'm a shirker. Then I hit Starbucks."

"Coffee-klatching with the girls to discuss child-rearing techniques?" Alec asked.

"With your wife," Julia said. Alec pulled his checkbook out of his back pocket and waved it at her. She made a motion to zip her lips. Darlene looked at Lance. He shrugged.

"I maintain a man is what he does," said John Juan obstinately.

Darlene, desperate to shift the focus away from her husband, asked, "So, then, John Juan, tell us about your typical day."

"Lance could always get a job at Starbucks," Alec said, ignoring Darlene.

"He already has a job . . ." said Robin.

"In Barstow—" Lance began.

". . . raising Belle," Robin concluded.

"Kids are like plants," Alec said dismissively. "You water them and they grow."

"As if you know," Wren said, raising her voice for the first time that night.

"Why are you so hostile?" Alec asked.

"I'm not hostile," Wren said defensively, as the diners' attention shifted to her. "I'm just impassioned."

"Oh, so that's what it looks like. I haven't seen it in a while."

"Not at home," Wren said. Lance studied his empty plate.

Blushing, Darlene wrongly suspected that Wren was referring to what the hostess had seen in the kitchen between her and Alec. She watched Alec top off his glass. They'd all had too much to drink. She was deeper into the Markers' marriage than she cared to be. She suppressed a rising tide of jealousy tempered by embarrassment. She had always felt in control of her playful banter with Alec, but their partnership was not strictly businesslike, as much as she protested to the contrary. The realization made her want to shower off the Coco Chanel perfume (sophisticated but so not her) she had spritzed in anticipation of tonight.

Darlene felt saturated with the older couple's antagonism, queasy from the lamb, and dizzy from the wine that filled her glass even before she emptied it. Alec's flirtatiousness curdled into reflexive machismo at his own table, between the tension Darlene sensed in Wren's terse responses to his teasing and the overbright looks Robin tossed Alec's way while touching her own cleavage whenever she scored a point in the dinner-table debate. Darlene wondered about Alec resting his hand on her ass—and where else that hand had wandered tonight.

Walled in between John Juan and the slick eastern reporter, Darlene simmered. She hadn't wanted to come tonight anyway. She wanted to be recharging and getting ready for tomorrow's big event, spending some quality couch time with Belle, maybe taking a walk to watch the sunset together as a family. All this awkward talk about Lance was the last thing Darlene wanted to discuss with strangers. And what was reflexive bullshitting for some jackass like John Juan caught Darlene off guard. The topic pushed her buttons, heightened her latent career and sexual confusion. Maybe she was just PMSing, she reflected, or obsessing about worst-case scenarios for Darlene's Diner rather than visualizing an equally possible future of success and ease and continuous cotton-candy cash flow. But there it was, the nagging question: what did she really know about what Lance did all day? And she was his wife.

She flashed on last Tuesday when she'd run into the kitchen half dressed and ready for sex. What was Coco Montoya doing perched on the counter? Until that moment, Darlene could have sworn the despised neighbor had never been in her house, and yet she looked pretty comfy. Darlene realized she had been so self-consumed with the business that she'd lost touch with Lance, something that was no less true just because she tried to rationalize it as temporary.

Shaking her head, Darlene looked left and Dave caught her eye. He smiled sympathetically, projecting an air that he shared her embarrassment. She wondered if he was picking up the undercurrent of sexual tension that wasn't quite explained by all the tippling. Dave seemed polite, she thought, but she didn't trust him. He was a reporter, after all. They must have looked like sodden hicks. All she wanted to do right then was rage at Alec, but she would never have confronted him in front of strangers and a Newsweek reporter and, worst of all, Lance. Her husband had always been suspicious of Alec's motives. She'd championed the entrepreneur, because Alec's schemes coincided with her own dreams of escaping Barstow and achieving a lifestyle that seemed almost possible now.

Darlene pushed back her chair and considered Lance. She remembered when just looking across the keg at a party and catching him looking at her had made her feel sexy and connected down to the soles of her feet. Neither of them could slow-dance worth a damn, but sooner or later they'd end up on somebody's patio or in the sand climbing that ridiculous stairway to heaven. Lance was the only man who had ever listened to everything she said. He got her to tell him every secret fear and hope. And it was that articulation that had put her on the road to realizing her dreams. He paid attention; she took action. He would talk endlessly about everyone but himself. It gave her the false impression that he was content, she realized. But he was just closed off, an open facade hiding a locked vault.

"The trick is selling the stay-at-home-father idea to people like Alec and John Juan," Robin continued after an awkward pause. "Working men who are convinced that a man is what he does, as validated by the income declared on his W-2."

"Sounds to me like a sucker who lacks a good accountant," said John Juan.

"Stay-at-home fathers are the gay men of the new millennium," said Robin.

"Is that because they're unemployed weathermen?" Alec asked. Lance winced; what a way to introduce his real profession to John Juan.

"No, you goose," said Robin, "because of the stigma. They face social prejudice just for being who they are. Even as America becomes more aware of their presence—like people with disabilities in the nineties, gays coming out in the eighties, or the civil rights and women's movements of the sixties and seventies—these men are still rare enough to be considered a Jay Leno punch line. And, like anybody else who works, like any stay-at-home mother, they want respect for what they do. They want acknowledgment that raising kids is important, even if they don't get that paycheck validation."

"Lance, do you see yourself as part of a larger movement?" Dave asked.

"I'm no househusband," Lance said, loosening his tie. "I'm a weatherman between jobs."

"Is that what you'd really like to do," asked Dave, "be a TV weatherman?"

"Maybe I'll get another crack at it someday," Lance said, evading a straight answer as he glanced at John Juan. "For now, I'm just a guy between jobs, supported by a hardworking wife. And as for your larger househusband movement, Robin,

I'm too busy folding laundry to join. The upside is I have more time to spend with Belle."

"He's great with her," Wren said.

"Oh, yes, Belle's wild about Lance," added Julia, who observed the simmering tension while stripping a label off a wine bottle with a ringed thumb.

Lance looked over at the babysitter, unable to interpret her tone and its implications. He recalled Max driving his Big Wheel hell-bent for leather while she came on to him in the van. He should tell Wren, but he didn't know where to start that particular conversation. He regarded Julia, sitting provocatively with her Maori tattoo and purple toenails: she wasn't someone he'd leave with his kid. She looked like she'd eat her own young. She caught his gaze and stared back, almost daring him to drop the visual connection.

"Julia, isn't it time to put Max down?" Wren asked.

"Yes, mistress," Julia said, staying put.

"Now, please," Wren said, even more quietly, and looked to Alec for support. He shrugged. Julia clunked down the wine bottle. She strolled upstairs to kiddy exile, where she would continue fertilizing the seeds of Belle's public rebellion.

Following Julia's exit, Dave asked, "How old is Belle?"

"Eleven tomorrow," said Darlene.

"That's why we're celebrating at Darlene's Diner," Alec said. "Her party launches the restaurant."

"Is she excited about tomorrow?" Dave asked.

"Thrilled," Darlene said, smiling.

Alec added, "Who wouldn't be excited about the biggest birthday in her life?"

"Lance?" Dave asked. "Is that your read on the situation?"

"Belle's petrified," Lance said quietly, looking away from Darlene.

"Did Belle tell you that?" Darlene asked, leaning forward, her chest dangerously close to a moussaka puddle.

"She doesn't have to," Lance said, leaning away from Darlene. "It's the opposite. She's been very quiet about tomorrow. She's a new kid in a new town—she's afraid of all those strangers, all those kids she doesn't know, or the ones she does who remind her she's on the bottom of the food chain, when she used to be on top."

"What can you expect?" Darlene asked. "We just moved."

"It's not what I expect," Lance said. "I'm an adult."

"Who spends ninety percent of the time in short pants," said John Juan.

"Hey, I'm just a guy who puts my shorts on one leg at a time," Lance continued, "but we're talking about how Belle feels. It's not like she has experience and can measure her current sadness against it. Belle would prefer a backyard barbecue; hold the clowns and the piñata. And, after the guests split, she'd love some serious mommy-daddy slug time on the couch, watching *Hannah Montana* reruns until the sugar rush wears off and she crashes in her clothes between us. For Belle, the worst part of tomorrow is that for kids, a birthday is their day, the one day a year that they are the center of the universe. As much as we tell her tomorrow's festivities are for her, she's aware, but can't articulate, that we're fibbing. We've co-opted the one day of the year that should be hers."

"It is for her," Darlene said, but hearing her own words, she could only admit they were false. It hadn't been an intentional lie. She hadn't set out to deceive her daughter. She had projected her own desires, for current success, for past adoration, for girlie center-of-the-world excess. (Darlene's mother had never believed in fussy birthday parties or sugary cakes; no streamers, no balloons, God forbid clowns or ponies. Presents were chemistry sets, or books, or trips to the Air & Space Museum.) Darlene said, with less conviction, "I wanted it to be for her."

"Of course you did, Darlene," Lance replied. "And maybe this party is what you would have wanted at Belle's age. That's natural, babe. But this isn't about you. Dave wants to know what Belle wants, and I guess he'd have to ask Belle directly."

"Would she tell me?" Dave asked.

"How easy is it to say what you really want, even for you?" Lance asked. "Maybe it's easier telling a stranger, maybe not. Often, what we want is a jumble of other people's expectations, their voices in our heads. Kids are no different. Belle is as desperate to please as the next kid, and what's tough is that what pleases her mother and what pleases me are different. What pleases her peers, her teacher, her scout leader, the boy she crushes on, the bully she fears: all different."

"How do you plot the course to help Belle get what she wants—and needs?"

"It's always changing, Dave. The funny thing about parenting is sometimes the direct questions work, but I learn more sitting on the bench in Encinitas Park with the other mommies."

"The other mommies?" John Juan scoffed.

"You know what he means," said Coco. "Listen for a change."

"I'm not offended," Lance said with a weary smile. "I guess I'm resigned. The upside of unemployment is that I'm the present father. I sit on a sunny bench and listen to sleep-deprived mothers bitch about their absentee husbands—and, don't kid yourselves, that's Topic A, ahead of breast-feeding, potty training, and serial biting. Resentment runs high. Sure, more husbands are doing diapers now, but they expect their wives to bow down every time they do."

"I never changed a diaper in my life," Alec said.

"Here! Here!" said John Juan, raising his glass.

"It's nothing to brag about, amigo," Coco said.

"Face facts: a huge amount of child care is grunt work—'women's work'—slinging one meal on the table after the other," Lance said. "Who wouldn't want to skip out on doing the laundry, picking up the toys, bathing the little suckers, and catch that last wave? Most working women I talk to confess returning to work is a relief. At least when they're at the office, they can use the bathroom by themselves."

"Do you see yourself as the mother, Lance?" Dave asked reportorially.

"Not me," Lance swiftly answered. "Darlene's the mom: I know which end of the sperm is mine. And this househusband label makes me queasy—try calling Coco a housewife."

"Don't even go there, neighbor," said Coco, pointing her manicured forefinger in warning.

"And I'm uncomfortable not paying my way."

"Lance's problem is ubiquitous," said Robin, like a professor turning away from an example on the chalkboard and facing the class. "When I interviewed couples for *Househusbands*, many wives felt guilty that they weren't attending PTA meetings and manning the bake sale. On the other side of the bed, many husbands tried to justify leaving their jobs, and abdicating control of the finances, without sounding like they were slackers. That creates a lot of marital tension, and kids sense that tension. These couples weren't radicals embracing home-schooling, they were ordinary people who had sidestepped the mainstream. Frankly, the resistance to their reshuffling of gender roles surprised them. And, for the men, not getting outside reinforcement was rough."

Weary of the discussion, Wren rose from the table and glided to the stereo, where she cued a Brazilian CD, hoping to take Lance off the grill. John Juan said to Coco, "Let's bossa nova, *hijita*."

"Have a dance, babe?" Lance asked Darlene as he got to his feet.

"I'd better check on Belle, if she's so freaked out," Darlene said tensely.

"I don't hear screaming," Alec said. "Chalk one up for the babysitter."

"There's nothing wrong with babysitters," Lance said, feeling conspicuously defensive (Big Wheel keeps on turning . . .). "They're just not parent substitutes."

Darlene sniffed and then retreated upstairs, her shoulders stiff and set. Lance shoved his hands in his pockets and tried not to sway to the beat of the music. He felt rebuked. How had the thread that bound him and Darlene gotten so twisted and frayed that even the simplest communication became loaded?

Dave shifted his gaze away from Lance's pained look to the dancers, thankful John Juan had finally shut up. He recognized the music—Arto Lindsay's "Crossed Paths"—and noted the familiar feeling: his story was about to shift focus but he was unsure where it would land. He had to observe carefully to follow the thread, while paying obeisance to the author who had brought him into the house. Peripherally, he watched Wren approach Lance. She dropped her hand lightly on Lance's right shoulder and grazed her fingertips across the ridge to his left, like a child trailing her hand along a hedge as she walked.

The lovers were hiding in plain sight.

Lance followed Wren out to the deck. Dave watched Lance's broad-shouldered back under the crisp cotton dress shirt. There was definitely something attractive in his lack of attitude, the welcome absence of a captain-of-industry swagger. Dave read the older man's walk: the surfer, barefoot treading sand, heavy-heeled stroll; the comfort in one's own skin earned by spending six months a year in nothing more than board shorts; the athletic grace from a sport that was all about balance in swirling waters. Dave's eyes flicked up; the bedroom doors were shut. When he looked down again, Lance had disappeared. He heard the oiled glide of the glass door to the deck sliding closed.

The music played outside via external speakers. The rhythm tumbled against the syncopated sound of the neighbor's German shepherd, who was barking at two teens sneaking a joint in a third neighbor's yard. Wren stood sheltered at the far corner of the deck. She could smell the kids' pot, mixed with the acrid stench of the not-so-distant fires. It reminded her of beach party bonfires, and sneaking off to the edge of the water to watch the luminescence and neck. Above and behind her, eucalyptus tree-tops waved violently on the hillside from the excessive Santa Ana winds, winds that were gusting up to eighty-five miles per hour farther north and east. Wren's arms formed an open V as she held the rustic wooden railing on either side of her narrow hips. Her eyes were in shadow, but her mouth had a different smile on it, one that Lance hadn't seen before, her lips parted slightly, the adjacent lines relaxed so there was just a faint suggestion of the counterbalancing frown line to come.

Wren had always been someone who said "I can't" and sought men who told her she could; she now knew she didn't need anyone to confirm she was capable. In the semidarkness, she had abandoned controlling her expression; her features neither reflected Lance's mood nor concealed hers. He neared her but they didn't kiss. He put his arms around her waist, his left hand resting lightly on her butt. She leaned in to him, smelling of flowers and, vaguely, of lamb and coriander, and rested her cheek on his crisp cotton chest, the crown of her head locked securely under his chin. She unwrapped her blouse, so that she was nearly naked from the waist up, but covered to anyone who would wander out. He felt the heat through his shirt. They swayed in place, her weight against his chest. They had never taken this kind of risk before, so near their spouses. It was like a cry for help, an unspoken desire to be discovered and end the tension of possible discovery.

"I can't survive one more of these dinners," Lance said.

"It was dismal, wasn't it?" she asked.

"The lamb was tasty," Lance conceded, "but there's no chance John Juan will ever offer me a job now."

"How can John Juan help you?" Wren asked, confused.

"He can hire me as a weekend weatherman."

"How's your Spanish?"

"Nonexistent," Lance said. "Why?"

"John Juan heads the local Telemundo station, Lance."

"I had no idea." Lance sighed. "I feel like such a dick."

"You shouldn't feel that way. John Juan should."

"He makes Alec look mild in comparison."

"There's something else you don't know."

"What?"

"I'm pregnant," she said.

Lance pulled Wren closer, feeling her warmth against his chest, brushing his lips on the crown of her head. He breathed her in. Inhale. Exhale. Inhale. He tried to wrap his head around the question *Mine or his?*—and send the potent words out to Wren on a soft exhalation—as they rocked in the agitated wind, surrounded by the scent of San Diego barbecuing. The sound of the eucalyptus trees shredding the air as they beat back and forth, and snatches of the neighbor boys singing "Bohemian Rhapsody," momentarily drowned out that of Dave banging on the sliding glass door, as much a warning as an attempt to get the couple's attention. The reporter opened the door and stepped out, using his body to keep anyone from following him. "Lance," he said, "Belle's throwing up. She's calling for you."

part III

saturday

chapter 15

The morning of the birthday extravaganza arrived following a rugged night of Belle basting the backseat of Darlene's Saab with the remains of her dinner, and a few encores into the bucket placed on the side of her parents' bed. Lance, Darlene, and Belle shared the king-sized bed, managing to sleep in despite a lawn mower's growl outside. Darlene awoke first, her sticky eyelashes slowly parting above raccoon mascara smears. She saw Belle's feet beside her on the pillow and smiled, an easy, closed-mouth slide that topped any toothy grin she'd ever produced for the camera. She leaned over and pecked her daughter's soles. She found adult feet repulsive, but would have kissed Belle's even if they were stinky and sweaty.

Still wearing her slip from the previous night, Darlene slid out of bed. She wobbled briefly, her hand rising to her head, and then collected the bucket from the bedside, peered in, gagged, and entered the bathroom. The toilet flushed. The shower ran, and ran, and ran. This awakened Belle. She looked up at Lance, happy to be sharing her parents' bed, smiling a sleepy but self-satisfied cat-got-the-canary grin. She righted herself, placed her head in the crook of Lance's arm, and wiped her mouth on his T-shirt. His eyes opened slowly and the first thing he saw was Belle's eyes staring into his.

"How're ya feeling, princess?" Lance asked.

"Better," she mumbled.

"Good," he said, ruffling Belle's curls.

"It must have been the hot dogs," Belle said.

"Sure was chunky," said Lance. "Nothing to do with jitters about today?"

"What's happening today?" she asked disingenuously, raising one eyebrow.

"You are cruising for the big tickle," Lance said, pulling out his hands and wiggling them with a maniacal Dr. Frankenstein laugh.

"You do that, and I'll ralph all over you."

"Been there, done that."

"Sorry, Dad," she said.

"No regrets, Coyote." Lance smiled. "I didn't like that suit anyway."

"I did," Belle said.

Lance sang, "Happy birthday, birthday, baby."

"Pancakes?" Belle asked.

"You got an itch?"

"Why?"

"Because I'm making them from scratch."

"Happy birthday, baby," Darlene said as she entered from the dressing room, conspicuous in a trench coat and bare feet. She walked over to the bed, bent over, and planted a big smooch on Belle's forehead. Her daughter wiggled away.

"Pancakes?" Lance asked.

"No can do," said Darlene. "It's nearly nine. I've got to hit the diner pronto."

"*No problema*," Lance said.

"More for us," Belle said, happy to have her father all to herself.

"What's on your post-breakfast agenda?" asked Darlene.

"*Nada mucho*—maybe kick a ball over at the park," Lance said.

"Are you sure you should play outside?" asked Darlene, concerned.

"Why not?" Belle asked.

"The air quality?" Darlene suggested. "The heat?"

"We're from Barstow," said Belle. "This is spring weather."

"If it's not in the three digits, it's not hot," Lance agreed.

"In Barstow, we'd be wearing sweaters. Don't worry, Mom."

"I'm not worried," Darlene said.

"Right," said Belle. "That would explain those creases on your forehead."

"How nervous are you about today, Darlene?" Lance asked.

"Me? Nervous?" Darlene asked. "It's only our financial future at stake."

"And I thought it was just my birthday party," Belle said.

"Of course it is, birthday baby," Darlene said from the door, her voice softening. She walked back into the room and sat on the edge of the bed. "It's all about you, birthday Belle. Eleven years old: you're a monster."

"Yes," said Belle, "but I'm your monster."

"True. You've got my scaly green skin," Darlene said, and wondered if she wasn't being the monster that morning. She sighed and resisted the urge to remove her coat and return to bed for a group cuddle. "Jesus, guys, part of me thinks we should cancel the party due to the fires."

"What part of you doesn't?" asked Lance.

"The part that knows Alec would have thrown a party on the last day of Pompeii," Darlene said as she pushed herself off the bed and reluctantly left the bedroom.

An hour later, Lance and Belle worked off their pancakes in Encinitas Park, kicking the soccer ball, trying to maintain the rhythm for as long as they could, back and forth, to the side, to the side, going long. The air quality was crap, and their throats were raw. There was a swath of blue above the ocean, but overhead, smudge-gray smoke clouds filled the sky like dirty insulation. Belle wore her retired Barstow soccer uniform: nylon goldenrod shorts and T-shirt gray from washing. GO RATTLERS! Intent on maintaining the rally, the pair didn't notice a silver Volvo SUV scraping the curb and disgorging Sam. The wet-haired boy flew flat-out toward them. He entered the game with a smooth steal, amping up the energy level. Lance fell back like a player tagged by his replacement and strolled toward the car. "Need help?" he called, watching Wren struggle with the car seat as she tried to unbuckle the sleeping Max.

"Damn," Wren whispered. With her back to Lance, she felt for the release lever that was beneath the car seat and between Max's legs. She crouched awkwardly while she tried to release the unseen mechanism without jarring the toddler, then she carefully raised the shoulder straps over Max's sleeping head. She lifted the sleeping baby giant, cradling his head and finding the right spot for it on her shoulder as she backed out of the SUV. Wren rose and turned, with Max heavy but reassuring against her chest, his eyelashes tickling her neck. She protected him— and he protected her; for Max, she could be stronger than she ever was alone.

"Need help?" Lance whispered.

No, she mouthed. In faded red yoga pants and a turquoise hoodie, her head angled to compensate for Max's weight, her smile content and mysterious, she was a beach bum Madonna. They walked to a nearby bench with a view over Rancho Amigo and the commuter railway station. They watched Sam and Belle circle each other, kicking the ball with a ferocity that had been absent earlier. A black Lab broke the circle, running from one set of scabby knees to the other, butting his head against their sweaty hands for pets they would gladly have given anyway. A yappy Chihuahua entered the fray, nipping at the larger dog's ankles and chasing him into the nearby bushes. Sam and Belle resumed their game. On the bench, Lance reached his hand over and rested it on Max's back, where it lay heavy and secure.

"You were so articulate last night," Wren said.

"That's what all the girls say," Lance said.

"Don't deflect." Wren fumbled to recapture their intimacy on the deck beneath the bougainvillea, unsure of her next step. Max stirred. "Really, Lance, you said what I couldn't—at least not without whining. You put into words that what you do, what I do, what we do, watching kids, not just keeping house but keeping the household going, is vital. It's as if, in this society, until a man says it, until a man stays home and receives no dollar compensation, the words lack weight."

"The words still don't have much weight."

"You're wrong," Wren said.

The pair looked up at the dismal, apocalyptic sky. Lance coughed. Max wiggled off Wren's lap, not fully awake. He ran on stocky but efficient legs in a serpentine pattern to join the bigger kids. Belle and Sam screamed, "Stinky diaper person on the loose," and ran from the little monster, holding their noses. Max chased Belle, then Sam, and then Belle. She shrieked with hands raised over her head, then did an elaborate trip and sprawl. Max pounced, pulling her ringlets like a horse's reins. Sam leapt on top, arms outstretched in flying-squirrel mode, a WWF-approved move that left the other two groaning and giggling.

"You could almost believe they're already a family," Wren said.

"You could almost believe we already are," Lance said.

"Could we just do it?" Wren asked, pulling her feet into the lotus position on the bench and clasping her hands behind her back.

"Do what?" Lance asked.

"Red light," Belle called from one hundred feet away. The boys froze. "Green light," she yelled. The boys raced.

"Just reconfigure the families," Wren mused. "Shift the kids into the same house. Have this baby together. Maybe have another, fast, our own, before it's too late."

"Wow," Lance said to mark a beat and give himself time to assimilate the idea. Was Wren's sudden breathlessness from her yoga position or her suggestion?

"Wow what?" she asked, reversing her arms.

"The idea blows my mind."

"Don't tell me you haven't considered it, sitting here watching the kids."

"Sure, Wren, I've fantasized about it. Here. Now. Every time we cook together in your kitchen; every time we're loaded in the minivan, just the five of us."

"Every time we close the door to your bedroom and spread the orange quilt."

"Then, too," Lance said. "But consider the collateral damage."

"Like what?" Wren asked.

"Divorce."

"Remarriage?"

"Recriminations."

"What if there's collateral damage anyway, Lance, even if we don't do this?"

"What if we don't get custody of the kids?" he asked.

"How could we not?" Wren asked. "We're the caretakers."

"Darlene is Belle's mother," Lance said. "And she needs me."

"I need you," Wren said, rubbing her belly absentmindedly. "Who do you need?"

"Isn't the question what the kids need?" Lance asked.

"Of course it is—if you don't hide behind that question as an excuse not to act."

"Have you told Alec?"

"About us?"

"No. That would be pure kamikaze."

"Self-immolation."

"Have you told him that you're pregnant?"

"I will, Lance."

"You have to, Wren."

"You tell him."

"Are you kidding?"

"Yes."

"Good," he said. "Because for a minute there I thought you were hormonal."

"I am hormonal," she said.

"Yes. But in a good way."

"Thanks. That's the kindest thing anybody's ever said to me—"

"And not wanted to get into your yoga pants."

"You're already in my yoga pants."

"Why don't I just casually walk up to him this afternoon and say, *Hey, Alec, wanna know what I do all day? Your wife and I sit around sipping lattes and waiting for her Clear Blue Easy results.*"

"Not going to cut it, right?" Wren smiled. "I want to have another few hours just to be pregnant and centered. To appreciate the miracle rather than the cynical, any-sixteen-year-old-can-get-knocked-up thing. I want to enjoy the idea that another being is sloshing around inside me, swimming in the yolk, having sense-memory dreams of shores she's yet to see. The little hands waving out from the sonogram, promising the future comfort of holding my hand. The limbs, the kidneys, the spleen, the heart, the wet lungs, are unfolding like time-lapse photography, even now, while I sit here in the sun, with the sound of the waves inaudible but there, to the west, I know it. I want to feel the connection clearly, without interpersonal static. What I'm saying is I want to share this moment with you."

Lance reached over and patted Wren's thigh. She winced, resisting her anticipation of his subsequent withdrawal, and her own. She sensed he might be incapable of making the break she required of him, but hoped to move him by indirect persuasion.

"Did I ever tell you about my father?" Lance asked.

"No," Wren said.

"He and my mother were best friends with the neighbors, the Jacobses. We were in their house. They were in our house. We shared one big perfect Slip 'N Slide lawn and every holiday except Hanukkah. But things got weird one Halloween. Mrs. Jacobs was pregnant with her third kid. She dressed like Mia Farrow in *Rosemary's Baby* and Dad was the devil. Nobody in the Jersey neighborhood got the joke—they just didn't let their kids trick-or-treat at the two houses. My mother understood. She was quiet, not stupid. By Thanksgiving, Dad was living next door. No real explanation, just a hearty laugh and a pat on the head, and a *mi casa es su casa*, nothing's-really-changed chat. Nothing changed except Mom was sobbing regularly and only left the house through the garage."

"What about the neighbor's husband?"

"Mr. Jacobs moved in with Mom and me—where else would he go? For months he would walk next door to get his laundry. Then Mrs. Jacobs had the baby. They named her Corinne, after my father's mother. It drove Mom and Mr. Jacobs crazy. They both just pooled their misery, looking out the kitchen window at the lights next door, drinking vodka in tall tumblers on ice, trying to pass it off as water."

"What did you do?" Wren asked.

"I played a lot of soccer. I kicked a lot of balls. I grew. Jacobs had a temper. I tried to stay under the radar. They pretended to do the right thing: Dad married Mrs. Jacobs; Mr. Jacobs married Mom. After a while, Mom and Mr. Jacobs couldn't stand the sight of each other. They weren't in love and Jacobs had no use for me."

"Were they happy?

"Does that sound happy to you, Wren?"

"Your father and Mrs. Jacobs: were they happy?"

"Completely. Extravagantly. Obnoxiously. Dad bought her a new car on Valentine's Day—it sat on their driveway with a big red bow for three days. Finally, Mr. Jacobs had it towed. It was impossible to be next door to them, much less in the same room. They glowed. They existed for each other. They doted and pet-named and pecked. It's easy to be cynical, but they were right: it was true love."

"Did it last?"

"I don't know. Mom bailed. She didn't tell anyone; she picked me up on the last day of school and drove west. I haven't heard from Dad since fifth grade."

"Fuck me," said Wren, stunned. She rocked back and forth on the bench.

Lance put his hand on Wren's belly, knowing it was too early to feel a kick. "That's a load, huh?" he asked.

"Everyone has baggage," Wren demurred.

"That's not baggage," Lance said. "That's a U-Haul truck."

Belle snuck behind Lance and tapped his head. "Tag, you're it," she said. He jumped from the bench, running before he was walking, chasing Sam flat-out across the field while Max waddled behind. Sam was out of easy reach, so Lance turned and chased Max, who circled Lance's feet, his short arms extended like a sleepwalker as he giggled in terror. Lance reached down, grabbed Max by his belt, and flipped him so that his fishy T-shirt fell over his serious upside-down face, exposing his round freckled tummy. Belle ran up and stuck her nose in Max's navel, shaking her head from side to side, her curls glistening like wet worms on the sidewalk, until Max laughed in short delicious giggles. She stopped and he said, "More, more," and she went back to set him off again, planting a full raspberry on his belly.

"I'll save you, Max," Sam said, knowing his brother didn't want rescuing. He grabbed Belle from behind and raised her off the ground even though she was taller than he was. She broke his grip, planted her feet, and cried, "Heeyah." Sam responded with a flying kick that fell six inches short. Belle returned with a jump front kick. Sam moved to grab Belle's shoulders and she used his weight against him, tipping him to the grass, where she proceeded to sit on his chest, her mouth pressing his cheek. For a moment Sam went soft, ceasing to struggle, blissed out. Max, released from Lance's grip, ran to sit on his brother's head, certain in his allegiance to Belle.

Wren observed from the sidelines, trying to live in the moment, to suck in the ether of the kids playing and Max keeping his teeth to himself, to recover from Lance's revelation. She had long wanted him to open up to her, but this was beyond her expectation. It cast a shadow on her fantasy: her family with Lance where they downsized and she opened a yoga studio and Lance ran the on-site day-care center. She wiped her eye, mindlessly removing an eyelash, or what could have been a speck of ash. She rose to herd the boys, her posse, back into the car, belatedly getting the children out of the harsh particle-filled air. She allowed thoughts of telling Alec about her pregnancy gradually to cross her mind like hot wind. She tried to envision a positive outcome of that discussion, to imagine Alec's reaction without seeing his angry face, his arrogant eyebrows, without flinching. Maybe, this time, she was pregnant with a girl.

Lance left the kids playing and approached Wren, wiping away a smudge from her left eye. She reflexively raised her hand to stop the intimacy.

"It's his," she said. "The baby's his."

"I figured," Lance said, although he hadn't been sure.

"I was always careful with you."

"Care full."

"Full of care."

"Full."

"Let's pack up the kids," Wren said.

"Let's party," said Lance.

chapter 16

By eleven A.M., ash occasionally dusted the coast. The cinders were pale specks of strangers' homes, their hidden love letters, so full of undamped passion, the writing careful or careless, cramped or calligraphic. All burnt toast, scraped and binned. Alec didn't pause to consider the strange phenomenon. He had driven to the Encinitas Starbucks to pick up coffees for him and Darlene. Carrying two lattes, he left the café and crossed the lot to his car, garrulous and confident. He never even considered canceling today's party despite the fine soot that intermittently fell from the overcast sky.

He was halfway to his next project, and that always gave him perspective on the current one. As he waited to pull out onto the Pacific Coast Highway, a city bus plodded past. He saw the ad for Mayor Hackett with two kids and a baby beneath the banner

YOU *CAN* HAVE IT ALL—IN SAN DIEGO. And printed below Her Honor's sensible shoes: SHE CAN HACKETT. He pulled out behind the bus into lazy Saturday brunch traffic.

After a twenty-five-minute drive, Alec slowed down and pulled in at Darlene's Diner, the first of many franchises. Even in this smoky dreck, the diner's facade had a shiny retro Jetsons look, with its silver aluminum siding and angular aqua-and-pink neon sign in the shape of an upended bass guitar. It was a flashy false front tooth at the center front of an outlet strip anchored by a Levi's, a Big Dog, and a KB Toys. The restaurant screamed fun. No motorists could miss it as they drove past on Balboa Boulevard, even in an unexpected ash storm.

What differentiated the restaurant from others were the internal features: the high-tech kiddy concert stage, the indoor playground (complete with hygienic industrial sand), and the laser-tag area. It was topped by a labyrinth of tubes, platforms, slides, and wobbly bridges that hugged the ceiling above the dining area. But what really made Darlene's Diner stand out from Chuck E. Cheese's was the adult comfort zone: club chairs set in conversational arcs nearby, a full bar, a rocking sound system, and—the pièce de résistance—a staff of bonded babysitters to ensure that the kids were safely entertained while the parents relaxed enough to open their wallets.

Inside, Darlene paced and squeezed a plastic ball from the play pit. Workers circled around her, preparing, and vying for dominance. Her hand skimmed the pink-and-aqua Formica bar that curved at the edge of the dance floor. She was barefoot, with white tissue separating her newly painted hot-pink toenails. She still hadn't removed her trench coat. The restaurant struck her as too theme park, so "it's a small world after all." If a kid heaved (was Belle really okay after last night?), or dropped a chili cheese dog, his mother would be mortified. The old Darlene's was funky enough that no single cheese dog had any impact.

"Hey, pretty lady," Alec said upon seeing Darlene. She brightened.

"Coffee? For me?"

"Just the way you like it—grande breve latte."

"Thanks," she said, taking the cup with a shaking hand. "Does my face look blotchy? Did you see the ash? Should we cancel? I think we should cancel, shouldn't we? Is it right to bring people out in this?"

"It's just a little ash," said Alec with a wave of his hand. "Don't worry, Darlene, this isn't Mount St. Helens."

"It drives me crazy when people tell me not to worry."

"Short trip. . . ."

"Do you think that's funny, Alec? Today has gotten way out of hand."

"Are you going to blame me for the fire now?"

"I had this great idea," said Darlene, looking up at Alec with his bright morning face and eyes that rarely betrayed any doubt. "I had an idea that I know turned you on. I dreamed of a family place that catered to modern moms who could unstrap their god-awful Baby Björns, rest their swollen ankles, and sit a spell. This morning, I look around and I see Bride of Denny's. How'd this happen?"

"I should have gotten you a decaf," Alec said.

"I need the full caf. Belle was up barfing half the night," said Darlene. She turned away from Alec and walked toward the kitchen.

"Wren was a little nauseous this morning, too," said Alec, trailing Darlene. "It was that lamb."

"No," Darlene said as they entered the kitchen single file. "Belle skipped the lamb. It wasn't something she ate. She was just freaked out to the bottom of her belly."

"She'll be fine once she sees all those presents. Target sent a gift basket; they're angling for a tie-in."

"You don't think she'll feel like the bearded lady?"

"What on earth are you talking about, Darlene?"

"That's Belle's fear. That she won't be the birthday girl. She'll be the biggest freak at the circus: the bearded lady."

"It's a fear," Alec said, in his confidential, calming-a-friend-off-a-bad-acid-trip voice. "You're the parent. Redirect that emotion: she's the trapeze artist in pink tights holding the spotlight above the crowd. Your mission, little lady, is to allay her fears, not absorb them." Alec approached the walk-in refrigerator, opened the heavy door, and lifted his eyebrows, saying, "Step into my office."

Once inside, Alec boosted Darlene onto a stack of ground-beef cartons as immovable as bricks and looked straight into her worried green eyes. "You know we're doing the right thing," Alec said. "We've been planning this project for eighteen months. This is Darlene's Diner—and you're Darlene."

"So that's who I am!" Darlene was so near Alec that she

inhaled his coffee breath. She flashed back to last night, and their fight in his kitchen, and realized here she was again, too close. She felt more vulnerable now without her righteous anger, a drawer full of knives, and Lance in the next room. She had thought she came out on top that round, but the memory of the studied blankness in Wren's dark eyes haunted her.

"What's with the trench coat?" Alec asked.

Darlene fumbled with the trench's top button. Alec brushed her hands away, taking over. He opened the coat to reveal Darlene in a fitted pink acrylic waitress uniform with white collar and cuffs.

"Ta-da," said Darlene, with an awkward shimmy, still trying to please despite her unease. "What do you think?"

"Sexy. You'd put a French maid to shame," Alec said, his hands resting too long on the ribbed pink fabric covering her thighs. "I know what you need."

"What's that?" Darlene asked as Alec's mouth covered hers. He leaned into the kiss, a forceful laying-claim to her mouth. This was more than she had expected and it took her by surprise in a way that made her breathless. Part of her—the remote part at the back of her brain that wasn't struggling with the physical situation up front—wondered if she'd asked for it. Had her playful flirting opened the door to his chapped lips sliding on her lip gloss?

Darlene sensed Alec's detachment in that same kiss. It lacked tenderness. It wasn't playful like their verbal exchanges. The smooch was openmouthed, as if Alec were gobbling fried chicken in front of the game. That shocked her as much as the act itself: The total impersonality of it. How it reduced her to the hamburger meat beneath her butt. It robbed her of her Darlenitude.

But it was just a kiss, after all, she thought. An embarrassing moment, nothing she had to tell Lance about, not really infidelity. But she underestimated the rapidity of Alec's follow-through. He unbuttoned her uniform and spread it with the delicacy of the Jaws of Life parting a rib cage. He pulled down the acrylic shoulders over her upper arms, and buried his face in her cleavage. She looked down and saw the embryo of a bald spot. She didn't know how to pull back without making it seem like a bigger deal than she expected it was. She had demanded attention, but had not bargained for this. She felt sacked, like the quarterback of a weaker team.

And yet, Darlene was aroused. After all that predictable marital sex (add the fabric softener, lick the left nipple), at least Alec's lust lunge was spontaneous. Or so she thought at that moment, to the extent that she was capable of independent thought. She shuffled off her worries and let go, guilty and thrilled. She was so weary of being responsible. Right then, she wasn't wife or mother, entrepreneur or hunter-gatherer. So this was sex as it had been in college, irresponsible, without rules, occasionally dirty, and temporarily empowering.

Alec lifted her farther on the boxes, his arms around the back of her thighs. Her head banged back. This was definitely risky, she thought, and wrong, as she looked upside down at ice-cream tubs and cases of cheese. A page ripped out of the smart-women, stupid-choices handbook. What if one of the chefs walked in now? But she didn't stop Alec; her desire to please him collided with an urgent rush on her part to surrender to the moment. Alec delivered the rough, on-the-counter, ripping-off-her-top sex she had wanted from Lance on Tuesday in their designer kitchen. But the reality didn't live up to the fantasy. The penetration was quick, as rhythmic as a metronome atop a beginner's piano. It was total frat-boy sex. After nearly eighteen months of flirting, that was all there was—a sucking sound as he withdrew.

Alec stood back to admire his work and returned his guy to his pants with a smile (another customer served). Darlene raised herself on her elbows. Her pink acrylic uniform was alarmingly unwrinkled; so the fabric's durability was truth in advertising.

"I have a surprise for you," Alec said.

"That wasn't enough of a surprise?" Darlene asked, flush-faced and annoyed. They hadn't even used protection.

"Different." Alec smiled. "The mayor is announcing her candidacy at our party."

"Huh?"

"Will she go for another term: yes or no? The mom mayor tells all live from Darlene's. It'll bring in the local TV news cameras and the papers, too. It's dream coverage."

"No way," Darlene said.

"This will put us over the top and raise our profile sky-high."

"Jesus, Alec, I hate surprises—especially when my underwear is around my ankles. Today is already a total zoo. . . ."

"Well, this is San Diego." Alec chuckled.

"Did anyone ever say you were funny?"

"Never accused of that. . . ."

"I'm not going into what you have been accused of, because that direction is a mudslide," said Darlene, her voice rising. "But Belle already suspects this birthday party is not for her. I spent last night trying to convince her otherwise and, fuck it, she was right all along. It's not about her. And I was total bullshit, shining her on."

"She's a kid," said Alec, feathering his hair back into place. "She'll get over it."

"Aren't we partners? I'm having serious second thoughts. Look around: this place is Denny's with lip gloss."

"Curb your neuroses, Darlene," Alec said sternly. "This is business. You're just cranked up about the opening and you're letting your anxiety bleed into your judgment."

"No," Darlene said. "I'm not. And I don't need your cheap psychoanalysis. What I do know is that as a partner, you're not forthcoming. You've been working this mayor angle and you didn't consult me. My gut said we should slow down, work out the kinks, and make sure Darlene's actually replicates the original diner. That's what's going to make it unique, and branding that is what's going to sell. You can't brand bullshit."

"Says who? Suddenly you're the expert. We're not slowing down; we're speeding up. This project has spent more than enough time in development."

"I disagree."

"It's not your call. You've been as active in this launch as I've let you be, but the business doesn't need you anymore. Face it, sweetheart. You signed away your name back in Barstow when you were so desperate to escape; now it's time to sit by the seashore, collect your checks, and leave the driving to me."

"Screw you," Darlene sputtered with rage.

"Been there," Alec said, checking his zipper, "done that."

"What was that, then?" she asked, but she knew the answer. She had completely misplayed her hand in their business partnership. Alec had pushed her to a point of weakness and swooped.

"I gave you what you wanted," he said.

"I didn't realize I wanted a quickie on a stack of ground round, hold the orgasm," she said, lashing out and hoping to hit a target. "There are high school juniors that wield their dicks with more finesse in the backseats of their mothers' cars."

"Pull yourself up by your panties and straighten out," Alec said, taking his keys out of his front pocket. "We have a restaurant to open."

"I see why you're always trying to brand other people," Darlene spat, hoping a suitable follow-up would materialize from her mouth. "There's no market for aging womanizers." Zing.

"I'm running errands," Alec said, reflecting that he was really running away—toward Wren. He needed her comfort again, her midwestern sense of balance. He tried to conjure up that hot afternoon on the Chelsea tar beach when he carried her to the roof's edge and she cleaved to him, those large brown eyes full of trust and hope in the future. She'd needed him, and he needed her to need him. Alec said, "I'll grab Wren and the boys on my way back."

"Ah, the happy family."

"At least Wren isn't dogging me."

"You're sure?" Darlene asked.

"Fuck you."

"Been there," Darlene said, buttoning her uniform, "done that."

In the silence that followed Alec out the door, Darlene removed a rubber band from her wrist and pulled her mane into a high ponytail, as if clearing her hair out of her face would yield clarity of thought. Surprisingly, she realized, it did. She now understood that vacuum in Wren's eyes. It was the steely, glazed anger of a wife trying to keep up appearances while her husband continued to misbehave; his cheating didn't only betray his wife, it came to shape who she was—and that compounded the betrayal. It took more than meditation to cope with that level of mind-fuck. Darlene assumed that if she were ever in that position, she'd simply walk. But then again, she'd never been in that position.

How had she gotten so off course? Sure, she'd wanted to leave Barstow, but not end up here, beached on the shore of someone else's bloated dream. She couldn't entirely blame Alec. Sure, he was a dick, but she was a big girl. He'd swept her up in his insatiable appetite and, for a while, she had confused it with her own. For eighteen months, she had ridden the tide of Alec's vision, ignoring Lance's warnings. And there it was, proof positive: Alec had laid claim to what he had already assumed was his for the grabbing. But it was no random act, Darlene realized. He knew he could cross the line from flirtation to action, because now that they'd launched, he no longer needed her. The sex was all about power, and their intimate exchange had shifted the balance even more from her to him. The realization stung. Was it too late to make today work for her? She'd striven too hard. She wasn't about to run away with her tail between her legs now.

Forty-five minutes later, Darlene delivered her Gipper speech to her new waitressing staff while standing atop a vinyl dinette chair in the dining room. She gazed over the mismatched vintage tables and chairs—red, yellow, pink, and orange. She'd spent a lot of currency with Alec convincing him that the funky look was viable. She'd argued it was economical. She was thinking bottom line. He countered it could be copied for less from a restaurant supply chain; buying in bulk would create an economy of scale and could be incorporated by far-flung franchises. Old tables had history, she argued; yeah, he said, history of mom and dad arguing over money and dry pot roast. At least you had pot roast, Darlene said, and won that battle—but which ones had she lost?

Now she stood atop the orange vinyl chair in the same fuzzy pink bedroom slippers she used to wear in Barstow. Her customers had called her the Abominable Big Bird when she wore them. They were women who had watched their share of Sesame Street as adults. Now she stood before and above two dozen young women who had learned the alphabet watching the PBS kids' show. In general, they were happy girls, happy to beat out their friends and get waitress jobs with the promise of tips, rather than folding jeans at the Gap for a flat rate and a 20 percent discount.

The irresistible onion-loaf aroma wafted into the dining room as Darlene talked briskly about this historic day at the restaurant in a town that couldn't have cared less about history. Assembled before her, the staff, in identical pink minidresses and pink platform Keds, reminded her of Pepto-Bismol bottles. Their tan bodies and wasp waists would alienate any mother arriving with a screaming whelp in tow and an insatiable craving for a hot fudge chocolate chip ice-cream sundae to stop the buzzing in her head. The servers even intimidated Darlene. They were so peppy-cheer-squad in their response to her bland exhortations she feared they might suddenly jump up and make a human tower.

When the young women returned to filling sugar bowls and jostling to see who would become alpha waitress, Darlene went to straddle a lilac pony in the middle of the indoor sandbox to collect her thoughts. She rocked to and fro, her elbow resting between its pink ears and her chin in her hand, then realized she was starting to tingle. She caught the Aryan-blue eye of one of the three professional babysitters she had hired from a pool of early childhood development majors from San Diego State University. He watched her with a smirk in his white sweater vest and pink seersucker slacks.

Okay, she had blundered. Sex with Alec did nada for her, literally and strategically. She didn't love him. She didn't want him. Hey, he wasn't leaving Wren, anyway. Not that that had ever been her goal. As if she had a clear goal. That would have meant having a coherent plan, and Darlene realized she had never really had one. Alec, however, had a strategy. And she had played right into it. She had just sacrificed her previous advantage: he had wanted her, and she was unavailable. As long as there was that sexual tension, she got away with more. That was over. In Alec's book, she was yesterday's half-eaten sandwich. And it got worse: he was still her business partner—and now he had something on her.

Darlene was more vulnerable now than she had been before. Sure, Alec had knocked her sideways, but she had to exploit her limited remaining advantage. The diner still bore her name. Lance was still her husband, her secret weapon. She could really have used him then to talk her down, but she couldn't turn to him now, not with this pathetic act of infidelity. It was so cheap, such total grab-ass, and yet such a complete betrayal of what she and Lance were as people.

She realized, right then, that she was the farthest she'd ever been from Lance emotionally, and she felt the physical pit-of-her-stomach pain that Belle must have been feeling all along. The pit of her stomach was a lonely place, and one that any fool could have seen Alec was incapable of filling. Lance was the person she ran to when she was bruised or sad, or ecstatic. When she had some small triumph or defeat in her day, he was the one she told. And Belle felt the same way, the same connection to Lance. Maybe a key to finding peace with Belle was not in competing for Lance's attention, but in sharing his emotional generosity. There was more than enough to go around; his love wasn't some zero-sum game.

Lance had been reaching out to Darlene, just last night in the bathroom while they were getting ready to go to Alec and Wren's. And she had rejected him. At the dinner party she had looked to Alec and ignored her own husband. Now, with the opening only minutes away, the diner seemed less important, not more. Her relationship with Lance and Belle was more pressing, not less. The opening would come and go, but she had to reconnect with her family.

An hour later, when Lance pulled into the parking lot with Belle, the party was in full swing and Darlene was ready to start calling local hospitals to see if they'd had an accident. Of course, her husband had gotten lost finding the restaurant, even though he had driven the route twice the previous week to get a fix on it. It wasn't his fault. Because of emergency vehicles on I-5, he got redirected from his planned route and had to take surface streets, mistakenly heading east toward the fires and barricades and increasing smoke and confusion. When he left Encinitas, he could still see patches of blue above him, but as he drove, the sky turned orangey and close.

Under a sun that had become a small round angry Godzilla eye, Lance had sped through a bleak area of half-empty industrial parks, the debris of failed dot-coms. The farther east he drove, the more he encountered drivers with video cameras out documenting the wildfires, perhaps in hopes of fleeting YouTube fame.

Because Belle sensed they were lost, the shriek of passing emergency vehicles and Lance's increasing nervousness magnified her fear about the bogus birthday party. By the time he turned the minivan around and headed southwest, he and Belle were totally silent, and the Neil Young CD was playing the fifth track for a third time.

"I hate Neil Young," Belle said.

"He always speaks highly of you," Lance replied shakily.

"Right, Dad," Belle said. "I don't think so. I'm nobody."

"Maybe," Lance said, "but you're my nobody."

Lance killed Neil Young mid-warble, switching to news radio. A ten-year-old boy was admitting he had started one of the wildfires playing with matches in the canyon behind his house.

"That's dumb," Belle said.

State troopers had shot and slain a man deliberately setting fires behind the house his ex-wife shared with her new boyfriend. Belle switched back to Neil Young, and they didn't hear the announcement that Encinitas had been added to the voluntary evacuation list.

"What a freak show," Belle said when they finally drove past the entrance to Darlene's Diner. It was a hub of activity. Eyewitness news vans were jockeying for position. Techies rolled out cable and positioned satellite feeds. A hearty man in Carhartt carpenter shorts bowed his shoulders in response to the weekend producer's barked orders via cell phone. Two preteen boys with spiky bleached hair perched on stingray bikes, curious about the activity. Maybe they'd see a celebrity, or at least a familiar TV reporter. Neither of them had the guts to ask the adults what was happening.

"I'm going to find a parking space," said Lance. "You find your mom."

"I'd rather find a parking space."

"Me, too," Lance said, "but I have the license."

"Five more years and I will, too."

Lance shuddered at the idea. Belle behind the wheel; Belle driving home in the dark; Belle drinking Southern Comfort in the backseat parked below the Mission San Diego de Alcala (so, maybe that was just his experience). It was hard enough to accept how much she had matured, how she wasn't some toddler like Max who needed a parent hovering over her at every moment. How much she was her own little person. He knew he had to let go—and stay close simultaneously. It seemed like such a tall order. When he was her age, he and Ethel had left New Jersey and he had grown up overnight, had become his mother's primary source of support. He would hate to repeat that pattern, but he knew that he and Belle were each other's favorite person, their bond was the tightest.

"Oh, God, there are Jade's parents," Belle said, and pointed. Lance slapped down her hand. They watched John Juan help Coco climb out of their Mercedes SUV. Next to her husband, Coco resembled a small, angry child, her body stiffened against some perceived slight. Then Jade stepped out of the backseat. In short-shorts and platform thongs, she displayed an impossible stretch of tan legs that seemed the exclusive domain of young girls who didn't fully realize their impact on adults. Belle said, "Like I would invite *her* to my party."

"Okay," said Lance, "I'm doing one lap around the parking lot so you don't have to go in with them. Then I'm dropping you off."

"You owe me," Belle said.

"Big," said Lance.

"Triple big," said Belle. They circled around the parking lot, then Lance stopped the car and Belle jumped from the van onto her black Converse All Stars. She was back to wearing her Barstow rags: ripped boy jeans, faded blue T-shirt, her curls crunched under a minor-league baseball cap. An oncoming Ford Bronco honked three times to move her out of traffic, its driver ignorant of the fact that she was the birthday girl. Overwhelmed, she didn't pause to notice that the Bronco was actually leaving the area, shuttling its jaded crew over to Qualcomm Stadium, home of the Fighting Aztecs. That was where the mayor was squatting with Governor Arnold Schwarzenegger, having pulled out of the party at the last minute, instructing her husband to keep their kids inside and out of the toxic air. Across town, at that very minute, the politicians were in flat-out state-of-emergency mode, making a joint request for the president to declare the county a disaster area.

Belle lamented that the wildfires buoyed on hundred-mile-per-hour winds hadn't caused a cancellation of Darlene's opening. The situation on the ground resembled the Depression run on banks she'd viewed on the History Channel. She saw families with kids she didn't recognize running for the entrance to get inside and away from the smoke. To reach the glass double doors herself, Belle needed to cross the gauntlet of cables and wires, the red-suited women with microphones and shellacked hair competing for stand-up space, the burly shorts-wearing men squawking into headsets.

And then, more chaos, as the news passed from producer to producer that Mother Mayor was no longer expected at Darlene's Diner. Pull out! She was with the Governator at Qualcomm. Darlene's Diner had been a human interest story on a slow news day, carrying the possibility of the mayor announcing her candidacy onstage and becoming a lead—but now it had become Nero fiddling while Rome burned. The mayor had state and national photo ops, the kind that made her candidacy an action demanded by grateful voters, a Rudy Giuliani–style shoo-in—if she didn't screw up. So the news-machine unplugged, untangled, and headed to Qualcomm—that is, those staffers who didn't live in Poway or points east, who were standing on their roofs spraying garden hoses against the oncoming blaze.

Darlene frantically ran out of the building. She was wild-eyed in her fuzzy slippers and the pink synthetic waitress uniform whose buttons looked about to burst. "Belle, where have you been?" she cried.

"In the car," Belle said. "Dad got lost."

"But it's a straight shot down Highway 5. He practiced."

"We got rerouted because of the fire."

"I should have brought you with me this morning," Darlene

said, chastising herself. She should have anticipated this possibility and taken over the driving. If only she had brought Belle and Lance with her, Darlene thought. If only she'd canceled the party because of the fires. She bit her lip, trying to hold on to her best intentions, trying not to project her anxiety onto Lance and Belle. How could she ever face Lance? How dare she get so furious at him for simply getting lost after what she'd done? "Fuck me," she said.

"You owe me a quarter," Belle said somberly.

"What?"

"You said a bad word. You owe me a quarter."

"I have justification. I was worried sick," Darlene said as she took Belle by the right hand. "Where's Dad?"

"He's parking the van." Belle gestured back over her shoulder with her left thumb.

"Why aren't you wearing the dress I laid out for you?"

"That pink thingy? I'm too old for mother-daughter dressing."

"You're eleven."

"You remembered!" Belle said sarcastically.

"Of course I remembered. What do you think all this is?" Darlene asked, dropping Belle's hand and raising her arms as if advertising the diner behind her.

"Total insanity? It's my birthday, Mom, not Halloween. I'm not going to be the only person wearing a costume at my own party. And I'm not going as a waitress." Belle flashed a defiant look.

"I don't have time for this shit," Darlene groaned, rubbing her forehead.

"You owe me another quarter," said Belle, stretching out her empty palm.

"Here's a buck. I'm buying myself a few more cuss words. Now let's go inside."

"I don't want to," Belle said, immobile on the sidewalk in front of the diner.

"Oh, great," said Darlene, taking a big breath and then biting her lip again.

"You're pissed off, aren't you?"

"Don't say pissed off."

"Pissed off."

"Am not."

"Okay. You're angry."

"Maybe."

"Are, too. Whenever you bite your lip, I know things are about to fly."

"They are not." Darlene looked into Belle's eyes, eyes like Lance's, dark brown and impenetrable. Yes, Darlene was angry. She was screaming freaked. There was some stupid man's goo running down her inner thigh and a city full of strangers in her restaurant. And then there was a beautiful child who looked nothing like her and everything like the man she had betrayed— and the girl was absolutely right.

Darlene didn't allow herself the luxury of reacting. She stepped over her own anger like sneakers discarded in the middle of the

TV room, and reached out to Belle. She took her daughter's hand again, wondering how it was that children's hands always fit as neatly as Cinderella's glass slipper into their mothers' hands. The thought, and the snug feeling of Belle's sweaty hand in hers, began to calm her down. She tripped over a cable just as she was turning to Belle to say, "Watch out for the cables." They both laughed.

"Hey, Mom, doesn't it seem like the reporters are leaving?"

"I can't tell if I'm coming or going; I'm not worrying about the camera crews," Darlene said as she led Belle to the side of the entrance and knelt down on the concrete walkway. She faced Belle, who also knelt, ruining the effect. "Here's the deal, baby Belle," Darlene said, tucking Belle's curls into her baseball cap. Belle flinched and replaced the fringe. "I've got a lot riding on this restaurant being a success today. I know we used to have fun at Darlene's in Barstow, and we pulled that restaurant out of the dust and made it ours. But this restaurant here is a whole new ball game, and I feel way out of my league. I feel like the new kid in town walking around with the back of my skirt tucked into my underwear and no friends around to tell me that my butt's to the breeze."

"What about Daddy?"

"What about Daddy?"

"Could you not answer a question with a question?"

"Could you not be so grown-up?"

"Don't worry, Mom. I'm not," Belle said. "It's just that Dad's so freaked. You should have seen him in the car. He couldn't have found the Starbucks by himself, he was so turned around. I just wanna know where he fits into all this."

"Right there in the middle, baby. Right there with you and me. Don't worry about Dad. That's my job. And this restaurant, if it takes off, will be good for all of us. It's already made it possible for us to move out of that crummy desert apartment, and live by the beach, and for you to have a pool, and a Barbie Dream House, and a turtle—"

"And a puppy?" Belle asked eagerly, sensing her opportunity.

"What's wrong with Boxy?" Darlene demanded.

"He doesn't bark," said Belle.

"You drive a hard bargain, sister," said Darlene. "Okay, we could do the puppy thing. If it's small. And short-haired."

"A beagle?"

"Sure," Darlene conceded. Despite what she had said, she would have bribed Belle with a slobbering Saint Bernard if it had gotten her daughter into the restaurant right then. "And we'll take it over to Encinitas Park and watch it run around and Daddy and I will hold hands and, I don't know, maybe we'll make you a little brother or sister. Would you like that?"

"Daddy would," Belle said.

"What about you?" Darlene asked. She made herself wait for the answer, though every atom in her body wanted to get up and go inside.

Belle shrugged. "Yeah, sure." She was in no hurry to move now that she had her mother's full attention. "A baby would be okay, if I could still have my puppy."

"The two aren't mutually exclusive," Darlene said. "Now let's go inside and flash some big birthday grins and get this thing the hell over with."

"Mom, did you just say all that to talk me into going inside?"

"You got me," Darlene said. Her daughter had called her on her bullshit. Good for Belle, even if it stung. Being a mom had changed her, Darlene realized, but maybe that wasn't such a negative. Maybe it was a sign of growth. Belle changed every day, and was still Belle. And that was a good thing.

As for motherhood, it wasn't some one-size-fits-all spandex outfit that a woman wiggled into; Darlene was constructing it one piece at a time in collaboration with Belle, and Lance. She liked this piece, where she and her daughter communicated intimately, eye to eye, even if they disagreed. Maybe, just maybe, she wasn't so incompetent at this mothering thing after all.

"So, did my evil scheme succeed?" Darlene asked, feeling more connected to Belle than she had in a long time. "Are you ready to party?"

"Yeah, Mom, take my hand," Belle said, extending her arm. "Let's make this look good. Let's do it for the dog."

"Here, help your old mother up," Darlene said, her right knee cracking as she rose. "Is my skirt tucked into my underwear?"

"No, Ma. You look great."

"Thank you. You, too. What a pair of babes."

"Except . . ."

"What?"

"You didn't button your dress right."

"That I can fix," Darlene said, mortified.

chapter 17

When Darlene and Belle entered the diner, San Diego's premier kiddy cover band—Barry Beige and His Scary Monsters—were playing "Yellow Submarine." Barry, still bobbing his white-blond shag and as thin as he had been at fourteen, could claim to have been at both Altamont and Woodstock. (Okay, he claimed it, but there were no living witnesses.) There was a chain-saw hum when the group slid into the chorus and the crowd chanted along, "We all live in a yellow submarine, yellow submarine, yellow submarine."

Belle squeezed Darlene's hand. It was unclear who was holding whose hand, who was leading, who was following in this mass multigenerational mosh pit. They both hated crowds; they'd love to turn on their heels and run. Their eyes adjusted to the darkness of the black light as they watched three fluorescent girls flit by, long blond hair streaming behind like contrails. Anonymous kids wove through the crowd in paper-plate masks—a ferocious tiger, a monarch butterfly, a pink Power Ranger. Two mullet-headed boys with glow-in-the-dark white T-shirts chased each other, one crying, "Kamikaze," while the other tripped over plastic balls that had escaped from the ball pit and sacked a toddler.

Darlene took a deep breath and hunkered down, guiding Belle toward the sound of the band—which had segued into "Octopus's Garden" in their Beatles medley. Meanwhile, from the opposite side of the room, Wren's sister, Robin, and Dave, the *Newsweek* reporter, threaded their way through the hyper crowd, heading toward the stage. Robin wore a blue-rhinestone-studded stretch denim pantsuit with a red neckerchief and red sling-back stilettos. "*I'd like to be under the sea,*" Robin sang as she two-stepped behind Dave. She clung to his hips as if he were leading a conga line in his starched jeans and crisp blue-striped oxford shirt.

Dave would have liked Robin to be under the sea, too, he reflected. Having this harpy clinging to his butt like a G-string was getting way too close to this story. But then, she was no longer the story. This was no longer a 750-word author profile with mediocre placement. He smelled the smoke behind the fire: he was on site at a breaking national news story. His editors were manically texting him and he was ready to fly. He would knock out a human-interest sidebar culled from his personal petri dish of locals, and then jump into the fire himself, find the hottest part of the story, and be on it like an eyewitness at Hurricane Katrina.

Dave scanned the room for Lance, but couldn't find him. Instead, he towed Robin toward the stage, where Alec was climbing up next to the band.

Alec now stood beside Barry, cramping the front man's swagger as he swung into the last verse, his bangs bopping to the music. The intrusion annoyed Barry, but he bluffed it, singing directly to Alec, *"We would be so happy you and me,"* and letting Alec do the Rex Harrison talk-sing to *"No one there to tell us what to do."*

Barry and Alec joined together at the microphone to sing the chorus. And the crowd, full of pint-sized Scary Monsters fans and their adoring parents, joined in for a raucous finale. The moment was psychedelic in a way John, Paul, George, and Ringo had never intended, Dave concluded.

"Right on, man," Alec said. "Rad. Let's hear it for Barry and the Scaries. The Monsters will be taking a little break . . . to drink some blood—heh, heh—and then they'll return for another set. In the meantime, I hope you'll let me tell you what's so special about today for me besides free ice cream."

Alec stood center stage and paused dramatically, smiling out at the crowd, a handsome benevolent king treating his happy villagers to a harvest blowout. "This is a big day," he said in a quiet husky whisper that commanded the audience to simmer down. "This is a big day," he repeated, his rich voice rising, "not just for us gathered here grooving to the music. Naturally, our hearts go out to those in the path of the fire, and our brother firemen braving the blaze. God love and protect them all. But let's not allow the smoke to blind us to a great day in the life of San Diego, a day of gains as well as losses, hope as well as grief.

And that's not just because it's Belle Ramsay's birthday," he said, gesturing, with a generous warmhearted smile, into the crowd where he assumed she stood, "although Belle's eleventh birthday would certainly give us reason to shake the maracas.

"No, today's a big day in the life of this city, America's finest. We have often been in the shadow of Los Angeles, happy to follow, not lead. But that's changing. San Diego is ready to lead, not follow. And Darlene's Diner is one of the reasons.

"Let me tell you why." Alec's voice got low and gravelly again, filtered by emotion. "One night when I was driving home from Vegas, I stopped for coffee. I was feeling kinda low. I'd been trying to make things happen in San Diego, trying to lead, not follow, and, well, I was coming up empty. And you can ask my wife, Wren, I'm not that kind of guy. So I stopped for coffee at some tin-walled trailer because the pink-and-blue neon caught my eye. Five hours later, I knew I had my dream.

"I stepped through that creaky door and I drank the best coffee I'd ever tasted. One A.M. and it was fresh-brewed. The place was packed and people were connecting. Then I got my sign from God—I met Darlene herself. That pretty lady in pink is Darlene's Diner, your happy home away from home, kids and parents alike. She came over and poured me a refill. And that little lady—she's out there now among you—raise an arm, Darlene," Alec said, to modest applause, without allowing time for Darlene to cut through the crowd and join him onstage.

"That lady with the sweet smile that warmed the coffee was a San Diegan. She just glowed like a beacon. She wanted to come back home, but she wasn't leaving without her diner. We talked all night, facing each other across the table, spilling our hopes and dreams for the future. We shared pictures of our kids—Sam, Max, and the birthday girl, Belle. At dawn, when Darlene was walking me to my car, I bet she thought she'd never see Alexander Graham Marker again. But I knew differently. If she wanted to come home, I was gonna help her. Darn if we didn't bring the whole thing down here."

Loud applause followed.

"We're the real deal, right, Darlene?" Alec smiled and paused briefly again to survey the crowd. "We're not just another Denny's. No way! We'll never be a plastic chain with plastic food. Although don't be surprised if we start spreading out over California." Alec laughed again, a big, hearty, inclusive you're-in-on-the-ground-floor-with-us laugh. "Next stop, Orange County!

"Did I get that right, Darlene? Look around you. This is Darlene's dream. I couldn't be more grateful that she shared it with me. But that's not all she shared." He paused long enough for Darlene to consider how much she'd shared that day. "Darlene gave me an insight into what it is to be a mother. And when she did that, she gave me back my family. I was so busy out in the world, doing what fathers do—making money—that I lost touch with what's important, what's real. I'd like my wife, Wren, and sons, Max and Sam, to come up and join me up here.

"C'mon, sweetheart," Alec said to thunderous applause. He stretched his hand into the audience and lifted Wren onstage, encircling her waist. Hidden hands passed Max and Sam up behind their mother. Alec picked up Max and swung him onto his shoulders, then wrapped an arm around Wren. She squinted into the audience, shielding her eyes from the light—it was impossible to distinguish whether she was embarrassed or ashamed. They made a handsome family—Alec big and preppie, she delicate and freckled, their boys with her beautiful features and their father's athleticism. They were as perfectly formed as the little families waiting at the station on a model railway display.

"Isn't she lovely?" Alec smiled as, behind the family, the band stealthily returned to their spots, picking up drumsticks, strapping on instruments, kicking aside the playlists in Alec's block-printed handwriting. "I'd like to introduce you to my family: my lovebird Wren; our two sons, Sam," Alec said, sweeping the boy's brush cut as the kid stood at Boy Scout attention and tried not to flinch, "and Max. Wait. Where's Max?"

"Here, Daddy, here!" Max said, from above Alec's shoulders.

"Sam, have you seen Max? You didn't leave him in the car, did you, Wren?"

"I'm happy to go check," Wren said, sidling stage right.

Alec pulled Wren back toward him with a long arm, while Max squealed, "Look, Daddy, look. Here I am." Max pounded Alec's skull like a bongo. Alec swung him off and said, "Boys, I've got a surprise for you."

"A newt, Daddy, is it a newt?" Max asked. Sam was old enough to be quiet and wary—surprises were rarely a good thing with their father—and so he let his dad have his say before he reacted.

"No, son, it's not a newt. Not even close. This morning, your mother told me something special. I'm going to be a father again. And, Belle, I hope that it will be a daughter like you, and we'll all be together celebrating her eleventh birthday right here at Darlene's Diner."

"I want a newt," Max said. "Newty! Newty! Newt!"

Behind them, the Scary Monsters began to play Wren's favorite Crosby, Stills, Nash & Young tune, "Our House." They began quietly, just Barry singing, "I'll light the fire."

Wren tightened her slim arms around Sam's shoulders; her freckled hands clasped together on his small, square chest. She hugged her little man close for comfort. Wren caught Lance standing in the audience stage right, his eyes on her face. She was too myopic to lock eyes from this distance, and Lance read her refusal to connect as a shove away. He dropped his head as if facing a sudden chill wind. Wren blinked.

Was it pain Wren saw in Lance's brown eyes? Was it betrayal and confusion? Was he asking the question that was so obvious to her: Lance would have expected this display from Alec; but why was she going along? But then, her vision was blurry and she could be projecting her own thoughts. Why was she going along? Why hadn't she resisted Alec when he returned home to pick up her and the boys, obviously chastened by some recent defeat, so clearly needy as he climbed the steps to their big expensive hollow house in his rumpled khakis?

Wren had been watching for him, waiting in her window spot, while the boys watched *Power Rangers*. She had been awaiting another Alec, the arrogant, strutting executive. She had been waiting to tell him she was pregnant and hear him roar and say sarcastically that her timing was impeccable (although it was he who had jumped her late one night before she loaded her diaphragm), or patronize her and say if that was what she needed, she could have the thing. She never expected to see the chastened, humbled Alec, the boyish Alec with the broken wing. He walked in, sweaty and red-faced, and said, "Give me some sugar," in a low voice.

Anything else, anything but Alec needing Wren so desperately, and she would have had the strength to leave. She tested him right then. "I'm pregnant," she said, forcing herself to look him in the eyes.

"We're pregnant?" Alec had asked in his cracked, rumbly voice. And then he cried. Alec swept her up, lifted her like he had on that Chelsea tar beach so many summers ago, and held her close. And he had tears on his cheeks. Real tears! She was almost sure of it.

Anything else and Wren would have had the strength to leave Alec. Not that day, maybe, with all the public static, but that night. Or soon. Very soon. Right after the school year ended. But that wasn't going to happen anymore. Not that year. Not the next.

Behind Wren, Barry Beige and His Scary Monsters kicked into gear and Lance realized his moment had passed like a just-missed freeway off-ramp. His happiness had been within reach, just today, on the park bench, while the kids played red light, green light. If only he had committed. If Wren had just flat-out said she'd leave Alec. Was she just waiting for Lance? Was he waiting for her? Was that why they'd ended up with people like Darlene and Alec, people who couldn't sit still, people who had to act, to swim or die? Lance chided himself: If he had just moved in, put his arm around Wren's shoulder, taken possession. If only he'd said right then that he'd leave Darlene. Wren had opened like a flower. She was there. Hadn't she told him she was pregnant even before she told Alec? How much clearer could she have been?

But no, Lance had waffled. Always waiting to see which way the wind blew, Santa Ana or Pacific breeze. He was never as decisive with people as he was in the water, bodysurfing, taking waves as they came without expectations. He had confided his past as if it were an excuse not to leap into Wren's arms, but that wasn't what he had intended. He had opened up too late, trying to explain his mistrust of domestic happiness, his firsthand knowledge of its consequences. It had been his invitation to Wren to lead him out of the confusion.

Lance had missed the wave. That moment in Encinitas Park was the moment. Wipeout. Barry, center stage, crooned "Come to me now," as Alec mimed the song's actions, pulling Wren closer, leaning her head against his chest, and stroking her forehead. Two tears slipped down Wren's cheeks. Alec leaned down to kiss them away, then joined in lustily with the final verse, singing to Wren, "Our house," while Lance saw his dream receding in the distance—gone—because he hadn't committed.

Only for you. Lance mouthed the words, but Wren couldn't read them on his lips. She watched Darlene sidle up to him. The younger woman raised her chin and whispered into Lance's ear.

From Wren's vantage point, the gesture looked intimate, romantic.

"What a load of crap," Darlene said.

"Bring in the wheelbarrows," Lance agreed.

"This whole thing is so over-the-top," Darlene said.

"No argument here," Lance replied with a dour stoicism to which his wife was unaccustomed. He was supposed to be jollying *her*. This was *her* big day. Where was the support? She was irritable to the point of bursting like an overbaked potato; she hated the crowd, the noise, the band's manipulative rehash of that syrupy CSNY tune. Two cats in the yard—really.

On top of that, where was Belle? She could be skulking in some tube in the maze above Darlene's head. Those tube things made Darlene claustrophobic. She couldn't handle searching for Belle up there, crawling along like Alice in Wonderland after she took the pill that made her larger. Darlene fingered her buttons, even though she'd already set them right. She was nervous about being so near Lance, in case he could smell Alec on her. She didn't need to worry; the aroma of the onion loaf smothered everything else.

"I can't believe Alec stole the whole opening out from under me."

"What's not to believe?"

"Asshole," she said.

"Tool," he said.

"You were right," she conceded.

"That's a big comfort." Lance turned to his wife, noticing, but not commenting on, her peculiar pink polyester outfit.

"But if Alec's the Big Kahuna of assholiness, why do you constantly want me to be more like him?"

"I don't," she insisted.

"Sure you do, Darlene. You've been saddled up and on my back for months. I can't do enough. I'm the slacker's slacker." He looked down and realized he had her attention. "I know I'm not the Second Coming, Darlene, but I've picked up behind you on this wild ride. While you've been out in the world, finding your bliss—"

"And making money," Darlene said.

"Yes, and making money. Agreed: swimming pool, double shower, three-car garage. . . . Big support! Rah! I've got your back. But while you've been focused outward, I've been fighting the fires on the home front. I'm not complaining. I like what I do. Screw me—I enjoy the day-to-day of my current life. The more time I spend with Belle, the better."

"That's a good thing," said Darlene, uncertain where he was going with this in the middle of the mad crush. "Right?"

"That's a very good thing," Lance said. He led Darlene through the crowd, feeling her hand tense in his. The first three years they had been together, they always held hands, and rarely did any more. There was no room here that was private, so he ducked into an old-fashioned photo booth along the wall stage right. They shared the tiny bench, their hands clasped and resting on his left thigh and her right. He closed the curtain with a loud scrape that nobody heard but them, thanks to the band.

"What I was getting at last night, Darlene, is that I don't resent what you do. If being Darlene of the Diner makes you happy enough, and makes us enough money, terrific. But someone has to look after Belle's welfare. It's a big job, too, even if it isn't a career. And when you tell me today's overdone, I don't know what you expected. You spent day after day with Alec: how come you didn't see this train wreck coming?"

"What would you have done differently?" asked Darlene, with a look of concentration on her face.

"First, kept Belle and her birthday out of it, simply by giving her a chance to say no at the beginning. Not asking her if she wanted a big party and bribing her into what you wanted, but asking her what she wanted and giving her the time to work it out. To get what's important to Belle, you have to listen to her, and read her reactions—you have to find the still moments," Lance said.

"It's in those moments without static," he continued, "doing nothing much, that I chisel Belle's feelings out of her. I listen really hard, and ask questions to understand where Belle really lives emotionally. The idea of childhood being a happy time because you don't have economic responsibilities is bogus. Kids have very little control over their daily lives, and they feel that intensely. You can't protect kids from their emotions, and you can't bullshit them about what they feel."

"I didn't think I was bullshitting her," Darlene said, recalling her chat with Belle outside the diner and realizing her mistake even as she protested.

"Then, Darlene, you were bullshitting yourself. Today's

party oozes with Disneyland syndrome. It's like this: if you take Belle to Disneyland, and scream louder than she does on the Matterhorn and buy her every pizza-popcorn-pretzel she requests, every souvenir that will fall forgotten under the car seat by the time we reach home, she'll remember that as her childhood."

"I'm not that bad, am I?" she asked, her forehead corrugated once again. "Look around: this is a place for parents and kids."

"I am looking around, Darlene. And so are you. That's why you're in such a sweat. I'm not criticizing you for it; that's a healthy reaction. This is not you. This is not where we began."

"I tried to tell Alec—"

"Listen, Darlene, this isn't about Alec and the diner. It's about raising Belle, and her individuality, putting her needs first," Lance said, picking his words carefully. "And, honestly, I'm not sure we have a home here yet, and that's part of the problem, particularly for Belle."

"We have a great home," Darlene protested.

"We have a great house here, Darlene," Lance said. "In Barstow, we had a home."

"I'm not going back," Darlene said, snatching her hand away from his.

"No one asked you to, Darlene. That's not going to happen, so stop being paranoid. But you want to know about Belle's feelings and I'm trying to clue you in. Today freaks her silly. I'm trying to bring you back to her, and her birthday, and us, the three of us, and maybe even, who knows, the two of us."

"*Two of us, riding nowhere,*" Darlene said with a sigh, remembering the two of them sharing Lance's bathtub when they first got together, surrounded by bubbles, listening to scratchy early Beatles, singing along. Then, they were living in the moment, magical times. It seemed so long ago, as if it had happened to two different people, as if she'd watched it in a movie.

"*We're on our way home,*" Lance sang. "And you know how bad I am at navigating, but here's where I'm coming from: it's so easy for parents to forget, and lately what I'm so present about is that big memories are likely to come from little moments. It's in moments like standing side by side in the kitchen, scrambling eggs, when I'm flooded with Belle and what a great kid she is."

"She is a great kid, isn't she?" Darlene asked.

"The tops," Lance said. "I don't have a problem with Belle. But the disconnect between you and me has left her stranded. We need to come together again like we were in Barstow, and it's not something that you can delegate to me to fix. Belle needs to grow up in the sunshine of our love, as much as any plant needs light to grow. And we've been short on that lately. Today's a total wake-up call: it's easy to fall in love, Darlene, but harder to juggle laundry and lovemaking. I need you to help me set the course, so I can carry it out. And, please, don't crush my balls just because I'm raising a good kid and running Girl Scout cookies."

"I'm such an asshole," Darlene said, smacking her forehead.

"That doesn't help me," Lance said, shaking his head. "We both have our asshole tendencies, but analyzing them is just a black hole."

"What would happen if we just split?" Darlene suggested.

"Split up?" Lance responded.

"Where did that come from?" Darlene asked. "No, just leave. Leave here."

"Right now, Darlene?"

"Why not, Lance? We could try that baby-making thing."

"Aren't you forgetting something?"

"Alec won't miss us," Darlene said. "He's in an adoring crowd when he's in a room by himself."

"Not Alec. Belle," Lance replied.

"I'd love to see Alec's face when he finally introduces Belle and she's gone."

"Let's not make stuff any more traumatic than it already is," said Lance solemnly.

"Sorry I bummed you out, babe," Darlene apologized.

"I was prebummed," Lance said.

Darlene didn't pause to ask what he meant. "Okay, Lance, let's just get Belle through the monster cake."

The pair emerged from behind the photo-booth curtain, with Lance leading. Barry Beige and His Scary Monsters had wrapped their Crosby, Stills, Nash & Young medley. Many mothers were openly weeping, divided between their crushes on David, Stephen, Graham, and Neil, and the gap between those dream lovers and their current domestic lives.

Lance looked straight ahead, hugged the wall with his left shoulder, and reached back with his right hand to lead Darlene toward the stage. (There were things he'd do for her—like getting her onstage where she belonged—that he'd never do for himself alone. If this were a rock concert, he'd make for the last row of the balcony.) At center right, flooded in light, Wren appeared wan and awkward, holding a wiggling Max in her arms while Sam stood close to her hip, trying to avoid his brother's kicks. To Wren's left, Alec said in his confident emcee voice that could butter popcorn, "This day just gets better and better. I couldn't be more pleased, honestly, to introduce Mayor Hackett, an old and dear friend of the family. . . ."

There were urgent whispers from the front of the stage. Alec stepped forward, steadying himself on the stage edge with his free hand. He bent to hear a man with a press credential who whispered insistently. Alec whispered back, listened with an ear turned to the audience. In the anxious pause, Barry picked up the slack and looped the band into their zydeco version of "Under the Sea" from The Little Mermaid. The whispers continued, harsher and louder, and then Alec backed up, trying to bury his irritation and reshuffle his game plan.

"All righty," he said. He dismissed outright the warning from a second-string San Diego Union-Tribune reporter that his Encinitas neighborhood had been called for voluntary evacuation in the wake of the uncontrolled wildfires. It was an exaggeration. Alec lived with a view of the Pacific Ocean; his neighborhood would never burn. What irked him was that he'd also learned that Mayor Hackett was a no-show. The TV newshounds had received the word twenty minutes before and had already pulled out. With all he'd done for Hackett, she'd stood him up at the altar. Sure, the fire was big, and she should be down at Qualcomm with the governor, but where was his heads-up? She could have had her husband make the courtesy call.

"Mayor Hackett . . . ," Alec began, his face reddening. He was ready to skyrocket, but he had to stuff his angry face down into his neck like a used parachute. He continued, "Sends her . . . regrets."

The remaining press—holding out for a last-minute appearance by the mayor with a statement on the wildfires—made a mad retreat. As they went, they groaned, grumbled, pulled their microphones, shuttered their cameras, and elbowed children with paper-plate masks out of the way. Nervous mothers grabbed for their children's wrists as the children twisted away, wanting to follow the Pied Piper pull of the cameras to see whatever was happening. Fathers lifted kids onto their shoulders, balancing them by their ankles and hoping the ice cream they were eating wouldn't drip onto their own heads.

"I couldn't be more proud of her," Alec said in the wake of the press's flight, although neither his face nor his voice expressed pride. But he was slowly turning himself around, finding his rap, so he said, "Our mayor is a gal of action, and a wife and mother, and if anyone can get things straightened out at Qualcomm Stadium with Arnold, it's her. This is a challenging time for San Diego and Southern California, and we appreciate all of you who braved the poor air quality to come down and celebrate with Belle, despite the smoke. The mayor has repeatedly told me how proud she is to see another homegrown business in our backyard by the sea, here in America's finest city. In her honor we're naming her favorite sloppy hash brown potatoes Hackett Hash."

Alec threw a look over his shoulder at Wren, who was still wrestling the baby octopus Max. All she wanted to do was escape offstage and bribe the boy with sugar until his rush broke and he collapsed into car-seat sleep. She knew it wasn't the holistic approach, with the benediction of the *Tofu Times,* but it worked. Alec had a *Help me* look in his eyes, but Wren was unsure how to move things along. She wasn't privy to the program, or to Alec's secret deal with Mayor Hackett that she would announce her intent to seek a second term from the stage that afternoon. It would have been a political coup for him and a media splash for the diner—but it was all arranged before the Santa Ana winds swooped in. Wren shrugged, looked at Alec with a widening of her dark eyes that corrugated her freckled forehead, and then began to inch off the stage.

Beyond Wren, Alec spied Darlene. Lance had led her to the edge of the stage, where she was feeling more secure. When Alec caught her eye, she raised her hands in apparent helplessness, shot him a smile as sweet as a Hostess Sno Ball, and winked. The band kicked in with "*But that is a big mistake*" from "Under the Sea." Now Barry was just screwing with Alec's head. Alec turned his back to the audience, which was continuing to mill about uneasily. That was when Sam slid away from his mother toward his father and sang in the same rhythm, "*and that is a very big cake.*"

"Cakey! Cakey! Cakey!" Max cried.

Uproarious applause was followed by kids chanting, "Cake!"

The parents added rhythmic clapping, relieved that the awkward moment had crumbled into confection—something the kids got, and that also signaled the beginning of the party's end. After the cake-cutting, exits could be politely made.

"And now," said Alec, closer to solid ground, a man with a plan who had come very close to teaching all the kids in the audience how to really throw a mega-tantrum, "let's drag that humongous cake down here. Dim the lights, please."

The lights lowered. And then three perky waitresses wheeled the cake through the crowd. The Barbie-shaped confection—large enough to harbor a stripper—wore a frothy white Cinderella ball gown. The blonde's plastic head and shoulders were separated from the original life-sized doll with a circular saw. Frosting curlicues made the gown's fluttery cap sleeves and modest sweetheart neckline. Graduated layers of angel food cake buried in butter cream frosting fanned out to form the skirt. A candied green parakeet put the finishing touches of turquoise icing ribbon on Barbie's left shoulder; a twin bird cinched a pink flower corsage to her waist.

The waitresses rolled the cake up the wheelchair ramp stage right, and the crowd gasped as Barbie tipped sideways, threatening the culmination of 123 man-hours by a local boutique bakery (run by the mayor's former volleyball sweetheart). "Disneyland," Darlene whispered to Lance in the wings.

"Upstaged by a cake," Lance agreed. He laced his fingers in Darlene's and followed the cake onto the stage at a safe distance. At least she got his point; his wife was listening. It was a start. Wren shot him a sad, longing smile, but Lance missed it; he was looking across the stage to the opposite wing. A small figure in boy-cut jeans, a faded blue T-shirt, and a reversed baseball hat hung back, her eyes ducking to her Converse high-tops.

"Dad," Sam stage-whispered, with a jerk of his head, "Belle."

Alec (with Max back on his shoulders like a second head in a horror movie) motioned Belle to enter the light. She approached when Alec launched himself toward her with the microphone, Max's adoring eyes a miner's beacon above his father's forehead. The birthday girl entered with the martyred shuffle of Joan of Arc in Act III, burn cycle.

Alec gave Belle the microphone, which was heavy and awkward in her small hands. She was afraid she'd drop it and embarrass herself in front of the rowdy crowd, so she cradled it in her left palm as if it were an armed nuclear device that might go off at any moment as she gently tapped the bulb. It emitted a squawk of sound. She stepped backward. It was on, all right.

When Belle raised her courage enough to lift her gaze to the audience, she saw Julia standing at the lip of the stage staring up at her with blue Viking eyes. The babysitter pumped her right fist. Belle looked away. She spied her parents hovering behind the monster cake. Whoever picked that cake did not know who Belle was, and she suspected her mother had made the choice. Belle was so over Barbie. She was ready to donate her precious pink Dream House to the Rancho Coastal Humane Society Thrift. Lately, she hated big efforts, false dramas, and excessive gushiness. She was into plain.

When Belle realized Darlene and Lance were holding hands, she felt suddenly sturdier. Her parents joined were her safety net. Until that moment, she had lugged around the fall-out from their marital discord like a brown-bag lunch filled with unsavory items. Like most kids, she still believed in the myth of her parents. It existed on a higher plane. Marriages were predetermined, the connection of soul mates. Their partnership was the foundation of her world. She did not want to look behind the curtain and see the relationship guts.

"Speech," Sam yelled from where he stood stage right with Wren.

"Speech," Jade cried, anticipating the new girl's total meltdown.

The kids in the audience chanted, "Speech, speech."

Belle looked to Julia, who stood three yards from her feet. The babysitter raised her right fist again and mouthed, *We're pissed off.* . . .

Smiling shyly, her right bicuspid snagging her bottom lip, Belle tugged her baseball cap lower on her forehead like a commando and said, "Hi. My name is Belle. And today I'm eleven." The crowd roared.

"Whoa," said Belle, holding up a hand to quell the crowd and retreating.

"Happy Birthday, Belle," Sam yelled.

"Thanks, Sam." Belle stopped. She smiled at Sam. He pounded his heart with his fist and then left his hand on his chest as if pledging allegiance. He wasn't invisible to Belle anymore. They were in this together. She realized belatedly that maybe she did have an Encinitas friend, even if he was a boy. "Happy birthday to me," she said.

Alec took that as a cue and started to sing "Happy Birthday." The band kicked in. But Belle yelled, "Wait!" a little too fervently. The drums crashed to a halt.

"I just don't feel like this is a party for me, Mr. Marker," Belle said, her voice catching. She turned toward her mother and continued slowly, "Mom, I'm sorry. Really I am. It's just that today is my birthday, my party. I don't want to mess up your big day. I'm just, well . . ." Belle paused and whispered, "Scared."

Belle didn't want to cry, and she couldn't wrap words around what really upset her: that she was just a prop, as disposable as the ridiculous cake. And how angry that made her feel, and small, and betrayed. She couldn't say things like that ordinarily, much less standing on a stage in front of strangers holding a stupid microphone. She didn't want to be a lamb-to-the-slaughter daughter, but she didn't feel much like a lioness, either.

"I'm freaked out . . . ," Belle said when the pause between words became unbearable. Not talking was almost worse than talking. She flashed on driving over to the diner that day beneath the orangey sky; and how panicked her father was, and the anxious sound of sirens passing as he pulled over to the curb to let fire trucks and ambulances pass. She continued, "About the fires. How can we party while the Witch Creek Fire burns?"

The audience hushed. The crowd was listening. Belle touched her cap and continued, her heart fluttering, "Embers are flying on the wind from roof to roof in Poway and Ramona and Rancho Bernardo, and the people who live in those houses are afraid. They're watching everything they own catch fire and disappear. I'm worried about their kids, too, kids like us."

"I'm worried, too," Darlene said, stepping forward on pink fuzzy slippers.

"We're worried, too," said Wren, joining Darlene.

"And I'm worried about the animals," said Belle, vaguely aware that she had avoided the sand pit and had reached safer ground. Her voice grew stronger. "What's happening at the Wild Animal Park? Is that big lion I saw napping on the roof of a Jeep there okay? And how are all the dogs and cats and turtles? Let's pay attention to them."

"You go, girl," Julia called from the audience. Once a rebellion began, you couldn't control its path, any more than you could predict a wildfire. But judging by the color of Alec's neck, Belle had scored a direct hit.

"It's cheesy to sing some old song about 'Our House' when our homes are safe but so many folks may be homeless." Belle turned from the audience and started to walk away. She saw her mother, smiling with shiny wet eyes, and stopped. Belle wasn't finished yet. She suddenly had momentum. She felt the adrenaline; in this chaotic moment, she had control over how the party unfolded—or unraveled. Belle turned to face the audience again, and spoke clearly into the microphone: "Let's stop singing and pitch in. There's tons of food here. Let's open up the diner for folks who need our help."

"Belle, that's a terrific idea," Darlene said as she approached her daughter, pulling Lance in her wake. "Let's turn Darlene's

Diner into an evacuee center. We'll open our doors to neighbors in need. Let's not wait another hour. Let's start collecting blankets, food, and bottled water. And who's taking care of those animals?"

"We are," Belle said.

"How are we going to do this?" Alec asked, incredulous, his brow furrowed.

"We'll figure it out as we go along," Darlene said. "We always have."

"This is Darlene," Belle told the crowd as Darlene wrapped an arm around her daughter's waist. "She's my mom."

"We'd never be able to help today without Lance, my husband," Darlene said.

"Dad," Belle said, weaving her free arm around Lance's waist, tucking him close.

"Right on, sister," said Sam, joining the center-stage crunch. It was Belle's day, but they were in it together. Alec stepped forward to resume control, but Wren grabbed his elbow and shook her head no.

"I wanna get down," Max cried, squirming on his father's shoulders. Alec raised a hand to quiet his son. Max pulled it to his mouth and chomped.

"Fuck," Alec cried, angrily setting Max on the floor and going for a forehand swat that didn't land. "Get back here."

Max skipped to Belle at center stage and took her left hand, leading her to the edge of the stage. She said, "We've got a lot of work to do."

"So let's get started and kick some ash," Darlene said, supporting Belle but not invading her spotlight. The girl basked in her mother's approval. They shared the same side at last, fought the same fight. "Alec, can you raise your pal the mayor and tell her we're here to help?"

"Done deal." Alec shrugged, with a little push from Wren, as the pair joined Darlene and Lance at center stage. Sam stepped forward and put his arm on Belle's shoulder. She let him rest it there, moved into it, in fact. He smiled a broad, toothy grin, Wren's smile. It wasn't lost on Wren or Lance that the pair, arm in arm, presented a reverse image of themselves.

Lance was seeing Belle in a different, public light. She was standing tall and stubborn, her own person. He felt the pride of a father who had taught his child how to ride a bike and watched her glide away down the street, knowing she would fall, but also that she would be able to pick herself up.

And it wasn't lost on Lance that Belle didn't make center stage solo. Even if he'd never have the sand to stand up in public like that, the fact that she could reflected on him. Belle's ability to speak her mind in a way that he would never do was a testament to his success as a parent. He had found the father he was looking for in himself. He wasn't going to walk away from that, however big the sacrifice. He felt proud—not the stingy sin of pride but the justifiable bounty of delight in accomplishment. He had given Belle the gift of empathy; Darlene had given the child the power to act on her convictions.

Belle was a combination of roads chosen and rejected, he reflected, quiet moments and cataclysms, a toss of DNA. He couldn't protect her from her particular Big Wheel rides into oncoming traffic. He couldn't protect her from the slamming injustice of a world crammed with Jades and Julias and teachers like Mr. Baumgart. But he could work to ensure that his daughter didn't become a Jade herself, a destroyer rather than a builder-up. And he wouldn't become a parent who lacked the guts to make hard choices.

Lance considered his own father, the man's cavalier assurance, "You'll understand someday," after he'd moved in with Mrs. Jacobs. Lance understood the impulse once Wren drove into his life in her mom-sized SUV. But he couldn't forgive his father's choice. On one level, Lance got that it was never his fault that his dad had left, despite the rejection he still felt. And yet, it was a lie for his father to claim it had nothing to do with Lance. His father's selfish actions exiled him from his own childhood. And he had been wandering in that desert, reacting, not acting—until now. As his mother had said, "Follow the path of least resistance, Lance, and sooner or later you will face a mountain you can't climb." He had reached that mountain. Now he would scale it.

He could envision a parallel life with Wren, a cozy one-true-love world surrounded by children unscarred by divorce, not the scarred angry kids Sam and Max might become, the potential divided loyalties of Belle. He saw another parallel world where his own parents remained together. In that version, he and his best friend shared endless nights in the garden, swapping secrets from their own adolescence, not uncovering their parents' indiscretion. In that parallel world, Lance grew up in Princeton Junction, attended college, and lived at the center of his own life, not dragged like an old muffler behind a dinged Dodge Dart.

And then there was this world, right here, right now. He had a lovely house at 1212 Pacific Breeze that needed to be filled, not with furniture, but with living: Scrabble games and ice-cream binges. He had a best-in-the-world daughter, a more-than-good-enough wife. He would have to reweave the frayed cord that linked him and Darlene, but that wasn't up to him alone.

Sensing Lance's gaze, Darlene looked up and noticed, as if for the first time, how he was aging. His dark brown eyes seemed to recede a bit, his face a little more leathery from all that California sun. And yet, she liked what she saw, the random indents of his smile, the benign look of kindness, an openness she didn't recognize in many other men. He would be one of those men who were boyish until, suddenly, one day, he became old.

And Lance had been good to Darlene, cleared her path and patched her wounds. If, as a working woman, she was bull-dozing old sex roles, the male would naturally change along with the female. She had to be as accepting of Lance as she wanted him to be of her. He had supported her through this ridiculous diner adventure, taken the risk alongside her, taken better care of Belle than she could have herself. She had a man who made her daughter's lunch, who poached salmon, who was neither jealous of her success nor afraid of her failure. She had a man who wanted to have more babies with her. She had a man she could trust; and, from now on, he would be able to trust her.

"You're my rock, Lance."

"You're my roll," he said.

part IV

sunday

chapter 18

On Sunday afternoon, Wren and Alec stood side by side on the street in front of their house on Obsidian Lane, their throats raw. Theirs had been the only structure on their hill to burn down, a victim of the quirks of flash-overs and spot fires, the last victim of the Witch Creek Fire. Fire trucks blocked the road, but there wasn't much left to do. The neighbors stayed out in force, in medical masks and shorts, pajamas and slippers, faces covered in soot, wielding garden hoses, defending their roofs from errant embers. Women she had never talked to approached Wren, touched her shoulder, and voiced their concern and sorrow. She was bedraggled but dry-eyed as she regarded the charred remains and curling smoke. The fireplace rose like a tombstone marking the grave of the massive house at the center of this community wake.

Wren heard the *clack clack clack* scrape of a skateboarder sla-loming down the hill behind her, followed by his mother's screeched and ignored admonishments. She put on sunglasses, trying to cover her odd elation. The house had always dwarfed her; the neighbor wives were strangers still. She looked up at Alec, and saw that he was crying real tears, twice in two days. She reflexively raised her hand to comfort him. But she felt free of the house, that awful monstrosity, rejecting the Barbie sleepwalking through someone else's dream house of her for-mer life. She would start afresh with Alec in a bungalow that hugged the shore, with a new baby, a tighter bond, on a street where she knew her neighbors, where she would put down roots.

Tonight the Markers would bunk at the Ramsays' house. The boys were already there, now that the evacuation had been lifted, watching TV and chewing through the Girl Scout cookie supply one box at a time, Thin Mints, Do-Si-Dos, and Tagalongs. Lance, Darlene, and Belle sprawled near Sam and Max on the big overstuffed couch. Darlene rested her head on Lance's shoul-der. His bare feet were on the coffee table. Belle had her head in her mom's lap and watched TV sideways. SpongeBob served another crabby patty. Darlene had her hand up to the knuckles in Belle's dark curls as she slowly scratched the girl's scalp, soothing her like a cat, so there wasn't a bit of tension in her young body.

Darlene felt the urge to get up; there must be something that needed doing, a bill crying out to be paid. She began to push away from the couch, but she hesitated. She didn't want to startle Belle away, so she sank back into the sofa. Sure, Darlene was restless; that wouldn't change overnight. She made lists in her head; maybe she could take up knitting. She was so not a knitter. But she reminded herself that there wasn't anything more important than this. Who cared who cooked, or who microwaved; who worked or stayed home; whole grain or white? Not children. Food, although essential, could be prepared by anyone. But unconditional love was the most nourishing meal a mother could serve her children; a steady diet of bullshit and deceit was more dangerous than Lucky Charms and Coke.

In the laundry room, the dryer buzzed. Lance put his feet on the floor. "Leave it, Lance," Darlene said, softly touching his thigh. He returned his feet to the coffee table. Belle had polished her dad's toenails, alternating between electric-orange and midnight-blue. The Ramsays sat united in the clarity of disaster averted.

On that bright October afternoon, the coastal temperature was sixty-nine degrees and all the windows were open to the ocean breezes. Outside in the backyard, the automatic pool cleaner doodled on the deep end's chlorinated surface; in the front, birds-of-paradise ruffled in the soft wind while bougainvillea released brilliant fuchsia petals on the patio. All along Pacific Breeze, lawn mowers growled, and the sounds of unseen children cavorting in backyard pools rose up, high-pitched and hilarious. At Rancho Amigo, the sprinklers wafted lazily while a lone Mexican man in khaki coveralls and elbow-length black rubber gloves scrubbed graffiti from the school's sign.

Traffic was stop-and-start beneath the arching green Encinitas banner on the Pacific Coast Highway. Just north, at the year-round flea market, tourists sifted through used clothing on outdoor racks, looking for the vintage Hawaiian shirts they'd never wear back home, and then crossed the highway to buy some Swirly Goodness at the Pinkberry frozen yogurt franchise.

Within the walled gardens of the Self-Realization Fellowship ashram farther south, forty weekend visitors in neat lines of eight practiced a wildlife sanctuary of positions—cobra, crane, and eagle—before a wizened yogi. A knee creaked; a bee buzzed its own ohm. On Swami's Beach below, a tan teen addressed the rugged surf. Surrounded by foam, he dove deep into the chilly water, shooting under the waves until he reached a moment of calm beyond the biggest breakers. There, he treaded water, with the Pacific Ocean laid out in front of him to the west, endless and comforting, and then he turned toward shore, where the sun sparkled off the ashram's gilded onion dome. He squinted in the brightness of reflected light, treaded, treaded, and then headed back into the thick of the waves, weightless, losing himself in the lightness of perfect day unfolding into perfect day.

The hot winds had passed as suddenly as they had appeared. Tomorrow, the coastal high might rise to seventy-two degrees, or dip to sixty-seven. And today, under the achingly ideal blue sky, fire and wind, ashes and soot, seemed like weather conditions that only happened elsewhere. Until the next Santa Ana arrived.